The

MINUSCULE

MANSION

of

MYRA

MALONE

MINUSCULE

MANSION

of

MYRA

MALONE

Audrey Burges

Berkley
New York

BERKLEY
An imprint of Penguin Random House LLC
penguinrandomhouse.com

Copyright © 2023 by Audrey Burges
Readers Guide copyright © 2023 by Audrey Burges
Excerpt from *A House Like an Accordion* copyright © 2023 by Audrey Burges
Penguin Random House supports copyright. Copyright fuels creativity, encourages
diverse voices, promotes free speech, and creates a vibrant culture. Thank you for buying
an authorized edition of this book and for complying with copyright laws by not reproducing,
scanning, or distributing any part of it in any form without permission. You are supporting
writers and allowing Penguin Random House to continue to publish books for every reader.

BERKLEY and the BERKLEY & B colophon are registered trademarks of
Penguin Random House LLC.

Library of Congress Cataloging-in-Publication Data

Names: Burges, Audrey, author.
Title: The minuscule mansion of Myra Malone / Audrey Burges.
Description: First edition. | New York : Berkley, 2023.
Identifiers: LCCN 2022010973 (print) | LCCN 2022010974 (ebook) |
ISBN 9780593546475 (trade paperback) | ISBN 9780593546482 (ebook)
Subjects: LCGFT: Magic realist fiction. | Romance fiction. | Novels.
Classification: LCC PS3602.U74198 M56 2023 (print) |
LCC PS3602.U74198 (ebook) | DDC 813/.6—dc23/eng/20220318
LC record available at https://lccn.loc.gov/2022010973
LC ebook record available at https://lccn.loc.gov/2022010974

First Edition: January 2023

Printed in the United States of America
1st Printing

Title page art: Dollhouse © BNP Design Studio / Shutterstock
Book design by Alison Cnockaert

For my parents, Dennis and Jená: my first yarn-spinners,
my first readers, my first editors, my first love story

And for Nina: our Trixie, whom we'll never stop missing

The

MINUSCULE

MANSION

of

MYRA

MALONE

An Unpredictable Place to Start

(From *The Minuscule Mansion of Myra Malone*, 2015)

ONCE UPON A TIME, THERE WAS A HOUSE.

Now, before you read any further, stop a moment. Take a deep breath, if you're into that sort of thing, and think. I want you to visit the place that popped into your head when you read those words, because they opened almost every story I ever heard as a child, and if you're going to spend some time here with the Minuscule Mansion, those words are as good a place as any to get started. *Once upon a time, there was a house.*

What kind of a house do you see when you close your eyes? How many rooms are in it, and what's inside them? If you could live there, where would you sleep, what color would your guest towels be, and how would you take your tea? What music would echo against the walls? Is it coming from a fancy stereo, or an old Victrola?

If you're a fairy-tale kind of person, maybe you've conjured up a stone cottage with a narrow, arched front door—you'd have to duck down so you wouldn't hit your head on the wooden frame, and if you look carefully, maybe you'll see a gentle depression at the top of the curved timber where countless visitors have done just that. Maybe that's why there's a friendly, tufted ottoman right by the entry, so you can plop right down and rub your noggin for a bit while you look around.

Or maybe fairy tales aren't your thing. That's fine. My friend Gwen isn't a sparkles-and-gingerbread kind of person, either, and the house in her head is a glass beachfront affair, all sleek surfaces and light, like Superman's Fortress of Solitude with considerably more Prada and pool boys. Also, she has a pet dolphin for some reason? Just go with it. Everyone gets to imagine their own walls, and the wonders they hold, without having to think about how well dolphin poop dry-cleans out of Italian leather. (No, I don't know why she lets the dolphin on the couch, either, but I'm not here to judge.)

Anyway. Whatever your house is—wherever you'd dream of spending your own once-upon-a-time—it's yours because you make it that way. You get to pick out the furniture and the artwork, the cans stacked in the cabinets, the knobs you use to open them, because it's your imagination, and that's your only limit.

It's mine, too, except I get to do something else: I get to make mine real.

I suppose some people have that ability, too—endless money and time to make their dreams take shape—but I don't have that. What I do have is a minuscule house that is also very, very large. A mansion, in fact. *The* Mansion. (It gets irate when I don't capitalize.) And the Mansion is a canvas for a very particular kind of art. It's a gallery of tiny dreams—some my own, some inherited, some generously shared with me by friends and family and people like you. And I get to use those dreams to populate an entire world. I can make a little bathroom with a seafoam claw-foot tub, or a bedroom with itty-bitty roses sprigged on every surface. If I can't find the right china cabinet for the dining room, I can make what I want to see, because the ones who taught me—my grampa Lou and his wife, Trixie—handed down every bit of their skill in woodworking, painting, sculpting, and sewing, and what they didn't teach, I've taught myself. I know what gemstones look like water and what pen can draw the most convincing chain stitch on a washcloth that's too small to sew. I can be eclectic or traditional, modern or romantic, and the Mansion absorbs those dreams into its walls.

I wasn't sure whether, or how, to share them with anyone else. But I'm willing to give it a try.

· 2 ·

PARKHURST, ARIZONA, 2015

This teapot wants to be part of the room, but it can never really belong.

Myra stopped typing and watched the cursor blinking back at her, waiting for her next insight. Every word was curated and every letter was hot pink. When she closed her eyes, she could see faces staring back at thousands of screens, longing to set foot into the tiny room. She stepped away from her desk and crouched in front of the Minuscule Mansion on its wide platform in the cabin's attic, peering into the diminutive library at the rear of the house. She reached tentative fingers toward the teapot with its painted porcelain daisies and pushed a silver tray underneath it, trying to make it seem less incongruous with the library's fireplace. She set two rocking chairs on either side of the painted flames.

It was wrong. It was all wrong. Worse, it was far beneath her standards.

"This one doesn't work." She rocked back on her knees and stared at the room. "I'll give it a minute, but I don't think I'm going to change my mind."

Gwen looked up from her own laptop without missing a keystroke, her face studiously neutral. Myra could tell she was trying not to roll her eyes. "You've been working on the library for how many weeks now? How long do you think you're going to be able to enthrall them with *Nancy Drew and the Case of Where the Hell Should I Put this Teapot?*"

"You said I need to use it. This was your idea, not mine." Myra's work on the library was, like all things in the Mansion, entirely for herself. But her stories, her photographs, and her intricate curation of the house absorbed the attention of her followers—first hundreds, then thousands, then (how?) hundreds of thousands—who anxiously awaited each new posting from *The Minuscule Mansion of Myra Malone*. The site had been Gwen's idea, and when the miniatures started showing up on Myra's doorstep a few weeks after it went live, Myra's shock had given way to discomfort. The Mansion belonged to her. She had not invited visitors. But Gwen checked the packages each weekend, gleefully updating the Mansion's social media accounts with effusive thank-yous for whatever tiny porcelain clown or small set of matching brass andirons had arrived unbidden in that week's mail.

"I said you needed to try to use *something* someone sends you," Gwen said. "As an experiment. You don't need to use everything—you shouldn't, actually, because the more exclusive you are, the more they'll try to get in. It'll increase traffic."

"I'm going to put things back the way they were. This isn't going to work."

Gwen plopped her laptop down on the attic's wide floorboards. "Far be it from me to second-guess the great Myra Malone, but let me check something." She stood, strode to Myra's side, and snatched the teapot from the Mansion, scrutinizing its delicate porcelain in her palm.

"Really?" Myra looked up with relief. It was rare for Gwen to grasp the seriousness of these decisions.

"Yep. It's just a goddamn teapot, not an ancient Mayan talisman you've got to place just right or be crushed by a giant stone boulder. It's a shame. You've been pushing it around for twenty minutes, so it kinda got my hopes up that it might be something important."

"No one's making you stay here, you know. You could head on back to your office, Gwen, and leave me to work."

"I love you, too, Myra." Gwen stuck out her tongue and was instantly seven years old again and teasing her childhood friend, despite the fact they were both thirty-four. "And it's Saturday. Saturday is always our site-updating day. Don't forget *The Minuscule Mansion* is an investment for me, too—I'm still counting on it being something big. Pun absolutely intended." She scooped up a tiny rocking horse from its corner of the library, releasing it to sway back and forth on the palm of her hand in time to the pensive motion of her head. The chipped paint of its red saddle caught the light as Gwen weighed and rejected ideas without ever speaking aloud. Watching Gwen think was like watching a spectator of a tennis game that no one else could see. "You could auction space, you know. Sell spots in the Mansion. Whole rooms that people could decorate." She gasped. "An essay contest!"

"No." Myra didn't feel the need to elaborate. She took the rocking horse from Gwen's hand and put it back in its corner of the library.

"Please be careful," she said. "I made that horse with Trixie and Grampa."

Gwen scowled, more at the rejection of her brilliant idea than the rocking horse reprimand. She was a planner. No small idea was safe from her efforts to expand it; vast multimedia empires structured themselves in her head. Myra wished, sometimes, that she'd never even shown Gwen the Mansion. But that would have meant going back decades, back when they were both seven and Gwen shoved her way into Myra's attic after she moved into the neighborhood and announced they were going to be best friends forever.

At the time, Myra hadn't left her house in close to eighteen months. When the hospital finally discharged her, she was five and a half years old. She had spent half a year clinging to life, and when she clawed her way back into the waking world, she discovered its every detail dwarfed and terrified her. It was too big. Only the cabin felt safe. It was safe because her grandfather, Grampa Lou, had slotted its beams and walls together himself long before she was born, imbuing the structure with the sense of calm he always inspired. It was safe because its attic sheltered the Mansion, which had belonged to Trixie—Grampa's wife—before the accident that killed her and nearly killed Myra. It was safe because the Mansion sheltered Myra's soul in ways she couldn't explain, giving her new worlds to explore—on a more manageable scale—and then whisking those worlds away, a secret between Myra and the house.

Myra defined the boundaries of her life by the walls around it. She remained as closed off as the Mansion itself, hinged shut within her own body. Her only friendship existed because Gwen created it with sheer force of will—and a lack of other available options—as she barreled up the attic stairs from grade school, then college, and then graduate school to find Myra exactly where she'd left her: indoors, upstairs, decorating rooms no one else saw. Until finally, six months ago, Gwen stamped her foot and insisted the Mansion was too beautiful not to share with the outside world, tossing Myra's latest printout of a story into the air with frustration and yelling that it was time to let the hundreds of pages of prose live somewhere people could see them. *If you won't share yourself, then at least share your work. Share the stories about your work. Let the world come to you.*

It was too late now to rescind the invitation—Gwen's, certainly, to say nothing of the legions of virtual visitors she'd attracted. Now Myra had this teapot—hundreds of teapots, in fact, in different sizes and designs. Boxes and bags overflowing with teapots, coffeepots, chocolate pots, even a couple of itsy-bitsy brass samovars. All vying for a spot in the Mansion. Myra absently grasped the stone acorn charm around her neck, moving it back and forth on its chain as she gazed at the library again. Volumes of Plath and Baudelaire sat on its stained cherry shelves, waiting for high tea to be laid before the marble fireplace with its cheerful painted flames.

This teapot wants to be part of the room, but it can never really belong.

Myra knew exactly how the teapot felt.

She tucked it back in its packaging and brushed her hands down the front of her slacks, removing the last traces of the outside world from her skin. Below her, in parts of the cabin she avoided, precarious stacks of unopened boxes and crates leaned against every wall, narrowing hallways and shrinking rooms. And below that, hidden underneath the boxes, were envelopes of increasingly garish shades, their yellows and oranges and reds meant to convey the same urgent warnings as a venomous animal. *Danger. Danger. Ignore me at your peril.*

Time is running out.

PARKHURST, ARIZONA, 1987

"DO I HAVE ANY LITTLE GIRLS LOOKING FOR PRESENTS? Anyone? I guess I've gotta drive this boat on back to the present store, then." Grampa Lou held his hands atop his forehead like a visor, turning his head from side to side, a periscope blind to the small pair of yellow pigtails bouncing just underneath its line of sight.

Myra knew that he could see her. She knew that he was teasing. But her grandfather had a particular way of teasing that could veer from lighthearted to oblivious, taking too much time to recognize that his six-year-old granddaughter was not enjoying the joke.

When she realized her jumping wasn't enough to get his attention, Myra shouted, "Grampa, you have me! You have me. I'm looking for presents!"

"You? Oh, no. You're not a little girl. You're old enough to drive now, surely?"

"Grampa! No. I'm only six."

"I'm pretty sure that's old enough, my little acorn." He scooped Myra up in his arms and brushed his rough fingers against her necklace, which she'd never taken off since Trixie clasped it on her neck for her fifth birthday. "Little acorn" was Trixie's nickname for her, one that stuck for the whole family after Lou married Trixie when Myra was two. "Trixie'd be so happy to see how careful you are with that necklace, Myra."

Myra gathered the acorn in her hand, its warmth and heaviness always a surprise. "It reminds me of her. Should that make me sad?"

"Remembering the people we love is always a little sad when they're gone. But a little happy, too. Now, let's start some driving lessons." Lou started walking Myra toward the car, opening the driver's-side door of his enormous Lincoln sedan, so out of place in this mountain suburb perched on the edge of the Mogollon Rim with its dirt roads, its typical traffic only trucks and SUVs. He plopped her behind the wheel and put her hands on the wide circle of leather-wrapped metal, the surface cold as ice but covered in skin. Myra heard a shout behind them.

"Dad? What do you think you're doing?" Myra's mother, curlers still in her hair, a lit cigarette dangling from her perfectly painted mouth, ran up the gravel drive toward them. The screen door on the cabin's entry hissed and slammed shut behind her. "Get her out of there."

"I'm not doing a thing, Diane. Just pretending to give the girl some driving lessons."

"Driving's not a legal pastime for six-year-olds last I checked, Dad."

"Who's to say she's not a natural? I've got a few phone books right inside to pop under her butt, and I can slam on the brakes if I need to."

Myra glanced from one grown-up to the other, waiting for the joke to play itself out as it always did. Lou had always loved teasing, but his ability to pick up on others' reactions to his jokes had diminished since the accident. Trixie had been a moderating influence, a puzzle piece that brought the family into harmony, and since her death, their relationships had fallen out of tune.

"What are you doing here, Dad?"

Myra sighed with relief. A side attack—a change of subject—would sometimes get Grampa off track, distract him into another conversation. And sure enough, he stepped aside from the car door, far enough for Myra to scramble out from behind the steering wheel. She raced to her mother's side and tugged on her hand. "Grampa says he's got some presents, and he needs someone to give them to so he doesn't have to take them back to the present store."

"Presents, huh?" Diane pointed to the trunk of the sedan. "Whatcha got in there this time?"

Lou rubbed his hands together in a gesture that looked less like glee and more like an effort to warm his palms. His breath escaped from his lips in a slow whistle that expanded into a cloud of steam in the cold November air, a stiff breeze from the north blowing the cloud away and carrying it south, off the cold edge of the Arizona mountains, back down toward the desert he'd return to later. "Well, let's just take a look now, why don't we?" He walked slowly to the car's trunk like a game show host and held out his keys to Myra. "Go on ahead, little acorn."

Myra took a deep breath before shoving the solid key into the lock and turning. The trunk sprang open with a *boing* that surprised her every time, more a jack-in-the-box than a car, given that its contents were always unpredictable.

This time was no different.

Lou chuckled, a low rumble radiating from his tall and narrow frame as he ran his thumbs under his suspenders like Santa Claus. "I heard you say how much you liked them the last time you visited," he said. "When Trixie made that casserole, remember?"

Myra didn't remember, and even if she had the kind of memory for casseroles that one wouldn't ordinarily associate with a six-year-old—a category of human not known for intense casserole appreciation—the trunk's contents still would have made little sense. Piled high between the wheel wells were at least six flat crates packed full of squat blue cans, and every can bore the same image.

"Are those . . . are those Vienna sausages?" Diane's confusion came out in a whisper that Lou, still chuckling, seemed to interpret as wonder.

"Sure is! Too good a price to pass up, especially since Myra gobbled up that sausage potpie. She couldn't get enough of it, remember?"

"Dad." Diane shook her head. "I barely remember myself. That was . . . what, New Year's? Two, three years ago?"

"Well, I remember it perfectly. Myra went through that stuff like a pig with a gravy trough, no matter what you say. Trixie used to talk about it all the time, isn't that right?" Lou directed the question over Diane's shoulder, as if her stepmother were standing there behind her instead of buried in a corner plot beneath a river birch at Saint Mark's, an hour's drive away. As if she'd put her parchment paper hand on one hip and nod, say, *Right as rain, Lou*, and help unload a trunk's worth of Vienna sausages for the perplexed recipients of Lou's largesse. And, really, Vienna sausages would have made as much sense as anything else about Trixie, who entered their world as strangely and suddenly as she left it.

"Okay. That's . . . very nice. Myra, can you say thank you to your grandfather?"

Myra stared at the little blue cans and knew with thudding certainty that her mother and father would stack them dutifully in the laundry room. They would open one every day, finding new recipes and casseroles and dishes to serve them in until every wet, rubbery cylinder was consumed. They would plate those sausages on her Rainbow Brite tray, next to another of the floppy dill pickles still stuffing the pantry in tall gallon-sized jars procured during Grampa's last visit to a warehouse store. The next time she ate in front of Grampa, Myra was determined to keep her mouth turned down into a continual frown of disgust. If she didn't, who knew what jack-in-the-trunk might be waiting for her?

She reached for a blue can and held it in her hand the way she might hold a wet, dead leaf, or a particularly slimy worm. "Thank you, Grampa."

"You're welcome, honey. You enjoy those, you hear me?"

"Yes, Grampa."

"You want some right now?"

"No, thank you."

"Are you staying with us tonight, Dad?" Diane talked over Myra's head, peering into the car to see if Lou's battered hold-all was in the front seat. Her father was a frequent unannounced guest at the cabin since Trixie died, showing up around dinnertime to sit next to his son-in-law in the back bedroom, where the two would play games until one or the other fell asleep like children at a slumber party. Dave was as silent as Lou was gregarious, and the two complemented each other in a way that left Diane feeling like the third wheel in her own marriage—

but at least he provided the benefit of another person to talk to, which was a benefit that Dave and Myra didn't often provide, withdrawn as they were into their own heads.

"No, not tonight. This was just a quick day trip to pick up some pantry goods. I ought to be heading back before the roads get dark. But before I do, Myra may want to check the back seat."

Myra, still staring with disgust at her can of Vienna sausages, looked up at Diane with alarm and saw the same alarm play across her mother's face. "We're really full up on food. If you give us anything else, we're going to have to add on to the house—"

"It's not food." Lou reached for Myra's hand, which she reluctantly gave him, putting the can of sausages on the ground where—with any luck at all—Grampa might back over it with the Lincoln. "Let's just get this back door open, shall we, darlin'?"

Myra hated the doors on her grandfather's car. They were heavy, swinging of their own accord, and had caught her fingers more than once. She hung back and shook her head. "Can I go watch TV?" she asked her mother.

"Myra. Don't be rude."

"It's okay, Diane. She's probably still overwhelmed by the sausages. Here, Myra. Let me open it for you." He gripped the chrome handle and swung open the door, wide as a barn's gate, then swept his arm before him with a magician's flourish. "It's all yours, honey."

Myra released Lou's hand and took a tentative step forward, then two, and then climbed completely onto the cold leather back seat.

It was too big for her eyes to take in all the details at once, even though so many of them were familiar. She saw the Mansion's swoops and scrolls of white gingerbread trim arched across the tiny eaves, their reflection shining out from real glass windows. She ran her hands along the wide, pointed roof with its hundreds of tiny shingles, a circular turret curving gently around one front corner. The house was enormous, perched on a platform of plywood that was poking depressions into the front bench seat, bordered with a diminutive fence of wrought iron. A lantern hung from a hook along a front walk, painted to look like flagstones.

Myra heard Grampa chuckling behind her. "We may never get her out of that car, Diane." He stuck his head into the car. "And she may have to stay there anyhow. It was near impossible to get in there, and it'll take all of us to get it out."

Diane poked her head into the car next to her father's and gasped. "Dad, it's huge." She reached a tentative finger toward the iron fence. "Did you—did you make this?"

"A few details here and there. Bits and bobs. It used to be a little smaller because it didn't have this." He ran an affectionate hand over the platform. "But the house itself belonged to Trixie. She had it when she moved in, and we moved it straight to the attic, it was so big. She and Myra went up there and played with it sometimes. I think she always planned to give it to Myra someday."

Myra had never told her mother about the Mansion. While Trixie had never outright told her the tiny house was a secret between them, Myra tucked it away like a jewel in her pocket, a special place that existed only in the attic of her grandfather's A-frame house on its bend of the river, suspended in a bubble of magic that existed nowhere else. When Trixie died, and when Myra finally emerged from the depths of gauze and pain that enveloped her in the hospital, her first thoughts had been about Trixie and the Mansion, followed by overwhelming sadness at the thought that she would never see either one again.

Diane gripped her father's elbow. "Dad, if this belonged to Trixie, don't you think you ought to—"

"What, keep it? Wait for her people, whoever they are, to come try and grub their greasy hands all over something she loved? The family that didn't even come to see her when—" Lou pulled a handkerchief out from his jeans pocket and ran it over his face as if wiping off sweat, despite the November chill. "When we lost her? No. I don't think I should keep it. I think Myra should have it."

Myra let out a sigh of relief, a tiny breath that only she could hear and she hadn't known she was holding. She was so certain that he might keep it, alone and unloved, too big to move. She was afraid that her mother would say no and that she would have to watch Grampa back out of the driveway, the house huddled in the Lincoln's back seat, leaving Myra before she could even open the Mansion up or take an inventory of the wonders she knew were tucked inside.

"It's hinged, by the way." Lou pointed to brass buckles on the house's backside, shut tight. Myra already knew. "It opens up like a clam on its side, and there are little rooms on hinges inside, too—it kind of unfurls. Damnedest thing I've ever seen. I've only got it clamped to the platform so she can still move everything around. And there's a whole hatbox full of other little things Trixie used with it—that's in the front seat. Good thing I'm not staying the night. I didn't have room for a toothbrush left over!" He walked to the passenger's side and pulled out a round hatbox covered in tattered silk the color of dead roses. "I've got no idea what all's in here. Furniture and stuff. Lots of fun."

"Where do you think we can even put something like this, Dad? I mean, it's very nice, and Myra will love it, but it doesn't seem like a toy. It seems like a museum piece. Do you think—"

"It belonged to Trixie, Diane." The roughness in his voice froze them both, and Myra watched as he dragged a gnarled hand over his eyes. "It belonged to Trixie. And now it belongs to Myra. You can keep it in the attic and she can play with it there. That's what she always did with Trixie. It won't take any room."

Myra calculated whether begging would be well-timed, whether it might tip the scales to a yes or make a no more certain. She decided to risk it. "I love it so much, Mom," she said with a reverence usually reserved for candy. "So much. And I will take such good care of it, I promise." She turned her wide blue eyes to Lou. "Granny Trixie would be so proud of me, Grampa. I'll be so careful."

Lou nodded. "I know you will, little acorn." He gazed at his daughter and arched one eyebrow. "How can you say no to a face like that?"

Hours later—after Grampa and Mom and Dad wrestled the house and its platform out of the car, up the front walk, and up the narrow stairs to the attic, and Grampa helped her unbuckle the house and swing it open on its heavy hinges—Myra gazed into the mirror set above the house's wide fireplace, wondering what about her face made it so hard to say no, and saw one blue eye wink back at her.

It happened so fast that she must have imagined it.

She didn't know how to wink.

· 4 ·

PARKHURST, ARIZONA, 2015

BY THE TIME MYRA STARTED FINDING THE COLORED EN-
velopes, their increasingly urgent shades of yellow, orange, and red
scattered in unexpected places like autumn leaves, it was almost too
late. Diane had always kept secrets from Myra, working to protect her
daughter from reality and the outside world as if she were still a child
and not a fairly self-sufficient woman in her thirties, albeit one who
never went outside.

In the end, it was Gwen who broke the news, her sleek BMW
crunching up the gravel driveway to the cabin, its sturdy logs unchanged in the decades since Grampa Lou built it. Myra didn't go to
the door, knowing that Gwen would do what she always did: stride
through the front entry and straight up to the attic, just as she had
when they were children. She was still out of breath when she reached
the top of the stairs.

"Did you know about this?" Gwen crossed the attic in two steps and dropped a newspaper in front of the Mansion, a red circle around a classified ad.

Myra picked it up. "Why would I know about a property auction?"

"Because the property being auctioned is your house."

Myra squinted at the tiny newsprint, having only noticed the address of the local courthouse where the auction would take place, and not that her address—her cabin, the Mansion's cabin, her entire life—was the property on offer. "How—how is this possible?" Myra looked at Gwen with alarm. "Did you see my mom downstairs?"

"She's in the backyard, digging."

"Of course she is." Diane never stopped attempting to turn their high-desert backyard into a lush and productive garden, and the fact that they'd only ever gotten a few dozen tomatoes over the decades—and even those only using cold frames—never deterred her. Her latest obsession was roses, planted in profusion along the southern side of the house, and replaced as they inevitably succumbed to cold and insufficient light, dwarfed beneath the ponderosas.

"How long does she stay out there?"

"Hours."

"Want me to wait with you?"

"I'm not going to wait." Myra stood up and looked around the attic for her battered pair of clogs, the only shoes she ever wore, when she wore shoes. "I'm going to go talk to her."

Gwen's eyes widened. "Well, good. No time like the present. I'll come with you."

"No. You stay here." Myra pointed at the pantry. "Stack those cans."

"But they're the size of thimbles . . ."

"It'll take a while. Do it anyway. I'll be right back." Myra walked down the stairs and picked her way through towering boxes and headed to the backyard, stopping on the way to retrieve the colored envelopes she'd been finding, and then banged through the rear screen door.

Diane's mouth opened in surprise. "Myra? What are you doing out here?"

"Well, Mom, it seems like I'm going to have to spend a lot of time outside if the house gets sold from under us, so I figured I ought to come out here and ask if you have any plans you might want to share with me. About the house. That's getting sold out from under us. In six weeks."

Diane set her mouth in a grim line. "I didn't think it'd happen so fast."

"That's not much of a plan, Mom."

"I thought they'd give me more time."

"Still not hearing a plan, Mom."

"I need to call John and ask if we could stay—"

"Mom! What the hell is the plan here? Why didn't you tell me you were having money trouble? I thought the house was paid off!"

"It was."

"I'm not liking that past tense. What changed?"

"She took out a reverse mortgage," Gwen said, emerging from the back door. "The bank's in the auction announcement."

"What on earth do you need a reverse mortgage for, Mom?"

Diane stared back and forth between Myra and Gwen, her shoulders slumped. "This and that."

Gwen stepped forward and put her hand on Myra's shoulder. "The boxes, Myra." She pointed into the cabin with its stacks and stacks of

corrugated containers arrayed against the walls and narrowing hallways. Myra's bedroom on the second story, and the attic itself, had
been the only two rooms in the house not filled. To the extent that
Myra noticed the boxes at all, she often noticed they were unopened,
or opened only once, their contents still inside. She ran into the cabin
and picked a box at random, a large one just next to the kitchen door.

"Mom?" Myra pulled out a rose-pink handbag, its supple leather
untouched in its tissue paper wrapping. A paper fluttered out from
beneath the purse, a receipt showing a sale price of $797.99. "Why do
you have an $800 purse in a box?"

Gwen opened another box, and a long, low whistle escaped from
her lips. "Frye boots. Oh, these are beautiful. They still have the paper
inside—"

"I didn't want to spoil them." Diane stood silhouetted in the light
from the back door. "I thought they'd be lovely, but I never had the
right moment to wear them."

"Does—does this box say Valentino?" Gwen opened another box,
releasing a silk gown, pouring out of its tissue like rich cream.

"Mom, what is all this stuff?" Myra's eyes, for the first time, took in
the narrowness of the rooms, the few remaining paths for walking, the
precarious stacks of parcels and boxes and unopened mail. She spent
so little time downstairs, so little time with her mother, the clutter
barely registered. Her mother and father had separated more than ten
years before, when Myra was enrolled in her distance undergraduate
program, completing assignments on a series of increasingly powerful
laptops perched on an old oak desk in the attic. There was an argument in the cabin's kitchen—Myra heard it, but barely registered it
until he was gone, and then she felt as if Dave had been gone a long

time. He had tried, for a while—for years—to convince Diane, and Myra herself, that it was time to try to rejoin the world outside. For Myra to go to a regular school, for the family to eat out in actual restaurants, take trips to places beyond the wide ponderosa forest around the cabin. Myra shook her head with a vehemence that shook her whole body, and Diane would yell that Dave was upsetting Myra. Until he stopped trying to upset anything else—the boat they sat in, the one Diane wouldn't rock. He simply disembarked.

He came to visit rarely, living in a sleek condo near the ski resort with his girlfriend, whom Myra had never met, sending occasional rambling emails that read more like monologues than an invitation to write back.

The boxes and bags stacked up over time, and given the volume of packages that arrived for Myra in a given week—tinier packages than Diane's, to be sure, but still—Myra had never questioned whether the boxes filling the house were a symptom of a different kind of emptiness.

"I didn't want you to worry." Diane crossed the room to an aqua-colored box with a white ribbon, handing it to Myra. "I got you so many beautiful things, but it was never the right time. I thought that maybe we could give ourselves little treats whenever we left the house, and try to find some way back out . . ." Diane gestured toward the wide mountains behind the cabin. "There's a whole world out there I left behind, Myra."

"Are you saying you did this on purpose?"

"No." Diane started walking toward her bedroom behind the stairs, picking her way through the narrow passages. "I'm just so tired, Myra. I'm going to close my eyes for a little while." She shut the door behind her before Myra could say another word.

Myra looked at Gwen. "What—what can we even do?" She sat down heavily on a teal velvet armchair, still partially encased in foam wrapping. "How does this even work?"

Gwen sat down on the floor. "I'm not sure. It'll be easy enough to find out how much she owes, and there will be penalties and other stuff like that. I think it all has to be paid off. I don't know if it's got to be done on the courthouse steps, or if you can call the bank, or what. But I can find out."

"Why would she do this?" Myra gestured hopelessly at the boxes. "She doesn't need any of this stuff!"

"She needed other things, I think." Gwen sighed. "I should have said something earlier. I noticed, and I knew you didn't notice, because it's not the kind of thing you'd pay attention to."

"What's that supposed to mean?"

"Exactly what I said. You don't pay much attention to other people. Even when they're right in front of you. It takes a lot to jump over your walls, and I think your mom got tired of trying. She's been lonely a long time. Some days, when I come to work on the site, I just sit downstairs and drink tea and let her monologue for a while. It's like a word typhoon. But she's always here, alone, all the time. And she has been for as long as—"

"Don't you say it."

"I won't say it. You didn't ask for it. And you would have been fine if she left, for sure. I just think she forgot how."

Myra remembered a birthday—some long-ago milestone, sixteen or eighteen—and a cake her mother baked in the shape of a car, the hopeful look on her face while she lit the candles. *There are places we can go*, Diane had said.

Myra hadn't even taken a bite. She hated cake. She was furious that her mother had forgotten. Another drop in a deep bucket of misunderstandings that had led to this moment, this realization that Diane had forced a new reality: *There are places we can go, because we can't stay here.*

Myra shook her head. "No. We can fix this. I have money." She calculated sums in her head, the growing nest egg she never touched. "I put away most of what I get from writing."

"I get you the best jobs I can, and our clients love you, but, Myra, I'm not optimistic that freelance copywriting money is pay-off-a-bank money. And even if it was, you can't spend everything you've got and not leave yourself any cushion. There has to be another way."

"I'm all ears."

"Come back upstairs. We'll think of something." Gwen beckoned Myra back into the cabin, a strange reversal of her usual efforts to pull her outside it. Myra followed her into the house, and the two of them walked slowly through the maze of boxes, retreating back to the attic.

Myra sat down next to the Mansion and buried her face in her hands. "I don't even know where we can start."

"Somewhere. You don't have a choice. Just—let me think for a minute." Gwen approached the growing stack of miniatures and gifts in the corner of the attic, all sent by hopeful readers vying for a space in the Mansion. She picked up an ornate box no bigger than a pack of cards, still wrapped in its cellophane, the tiny porcelain doll inside nearly obscured by a mass of blond curls. "In the meantime, I wish you'd let me convince you to use a prettier doll. You've been sent so many!"

"I never wanted to use dolls at all. Remember?" Myra reached into the Mansion's kitchen, trying again to balance the wooden clothespin in front of the blue enamel stove. The stovetop held a diminutive Le Creuset Dutch oven, its harvest-gold color richer and more convincing than the frizzed yellow yarn atop the clothespin's round head. Myra rather liked the contrast, because the doll felt like an interloper, and it was better for her to look out of place.

Gwen reached into the kitchen and grabbed the clothespin, holding the doll next to her face and matching its frown. "Hi, I'm Myra. My super-awesome, social media–genius BFF says that people want to see me living in the Minuscule Mansion, and I went all passive-aggressive and made this clothespin doll that looks like a prop from *Little House on the Prairie: The Sad Years*. I can't even wear cute shoes, because I don't have feet! My outfit is an old handkerchief, probably used. No wonder I'm so pouty! I'm the loneliest thirty-four-year-old clothespin in the whole, wide world!"

Myra snatched the clothespin back from Gwen. "I'm not lonely. I said I didn't want to use dolls at all, and this isn't a doll. It was sewing practice. That handkerchief was my granny Trixie's. I made this back when she was teaching me how to sew—I have a couple others over in the hatbox. But I gave this one my hair." She ran her fingers through the yellow frizz on her head, never tamed into a style that looked anything other than shockingly angular, like a geometry problem no hair product could solve. "The Minuscule Mansion isn't about people. It's about stuff. Tiny stuff. It's about tiny rooms you want to walk into but can't, not really. It's like all those home-staging shows. You make something that someone can see themselves in. They can't see themselves if it's full of other people." She held the doll next to her face and matched its sad face the same way Gwen had. "But you want a doll, so fine. I added a doll. I don't have to like it."

Gwen sighed and shook her head. "Myra, this is what I keep trying to explain. For you, it's about the stuff. But you've created something that's bigger than just you. People might have started reading because of the tiny stuff, and the stories you wrote about the stuff. But that's not why they stayed. They stayed because of all the little pieces of you that wind up inside the stories—all those little glimpses of a person they want to know. A person they want to join for tea in that library with the teapot they brought as a gift. A person they want to be happy. That's what brings them back."

"I didn't ask for any of that."

"But you've still got it. And, really, don't you feel like you owe them just a little? I know you don't step out much in all of . . . all of that." Gwen waved her hands in a chaotic, jerking motion toward the attic's dormer windows, gesturing to the world outside. "But I do, Myra, and I'm here to tell you that people need a little lightness. Truth be told, it's miserable out there a lot of the time. Let us have some happiness. Maybe even some romance!" She picked up another ornate box that held another porcelain doll, this one male, and wearing a tuxedo. She held the dolls together and made smooching sounds.

"I'm a private person, Gwen, not a recluse. I'm aware of 'all of that.'" She mimicked the herky-jerky motion toward the windows. "But I try to keep the Mansion the way Trixie kept it. I still have every piece of furniture she gave me, almost." Myra frowned, looking again like her clothespin doppelgänger. Lately, some pieces had gone missing or shown up in new places: the aqua-painted credenza with its broken hairpin leg and little record player, a mahogany chifforobe in the main upstairs bedroom. Two porcelain umbrella stands painted with elephants. "She didn't give me any dolls, and I never had any desire to get any. I had enough to keep me busy."

Myra watched Gwen bite the inside of her lips, holding back words. Some response to *not a recluse*, most likely. Myra could probably count the number of times she'd left the house in the last two decades without using all of her fingers and toes, but she refused to call herself a recluse. She had a whole world in her attic, and a whole world outside it that she could visit through screens without ever really setting foot there. And now the residents of that world wanted to invade hers. She was the opposite of lonely.

Gwen opened her mouth into a wide O. "I've got it. It just hit me. What about the contest?"

"What contest?"

"You never seem to remember all my great ideas. The essay contest. You have followers who are champing at the bit for a chance to put their stamp on the Mansion. All we need is to let them do it. They all read your stories. Give them an opportunity to write one of their own, and the winning essay's author gets to decorate a room in the house."

"We can't pay off a mortgage with essays."

"We can with entry fees. We'd need to figure out how much, and depending on how much we'd need, maybe we can auction off some other opportunities. Name the staircase! Get a bench in the garden! We can turn it into a whole little universe of branding." Gwen clapped her hands over her mouth. "Lunch with you! Top prize could be lunch with you and a one-on-one tour of the real Mansion. Up close and personal."

"There is no way that anyone is going to pay to have lunch with me." Myra paused, considering. "Please don't make me have lunch with someone."

"I'm just spitballing ideas at this stage, Myra, but you're going to have to step a little outside your bubble to fix this." Gwen spread her arms wide, encompassing the house and its village of unused retail goods. "Because your bubble is on the market."

Myra followed the arc of Gwen's gesture, taking in the rough-hewn logs her grandfather had hand-notched together long before she was born, the windows looking out on mountains rising in the distance. Everything that sheltered her. Everything she knew. "Point taken."

"Well, at least I've gotten through to you on something. Now—if we let a reader decorate a room—what room do you think they'd like best?"

Myra looked up with alarm. "You mean you'd really make me use what someone else picked out?"

"That's what 'decorating' means, last I checked. How many times have you redone the rooms in there over the years, anyway?"

"More times than I can count." Myra didn't mention that the house was never really finished, because she'd never really found all of it. New rooms would sometimes appear overnight, blank canvases in three dimensions, sometimes the size of a closet, sometimes a ballroom. She would spend days or weeks completing them and, the next morning, find them gone. Every handmade piece of furniture, every hand-sewn handkerchief or painted book or vase, every piece of floorboard, swallowed by the Mansion. Each such project honed her skills—design, and sewing, and woodworking—that she'd learned so many years before from Trixie and her grandfather. And letting all that work go, swept away to wherever the Mansion took things, still hurt sometimes.

The first time it happened, when she was eight, she cried for days, and her parents wouldn't let her near the attic, saying it was high time she spent some time outside because *nothing in the yard can hurt you, Myra, there's no one who can see you there.* But over the years, the disappearing rooms became less sinister. She felt in her bones that the rooms weren't gone. They were living somewhere else, and someone else could feel the love she had poured into them. She never took pictures of the new rooms before they disappeared, never wrote about them on her blog, never talked about them. But she remembered every single one with photographic clarity.

"If you redecorate all the time anyway, a reader-designed makeover shouldn't be a big deal. That probably won't even be the most popular prize, if we auction off the lunch tour with you."

Myra groaned. "Can't we please pretend you meant that as a joke?"

"I never, ever joke about business."

"The Minuscule Mansion isn't a business."

"Maybe not to you. But the sponsorship offers that keep popping up in my inbox tell a different story." Since Gwen handled all the business details for the Minuscule Mansion's site, the official email account for the site came directly to her. In a few short months, she'd established a post office box and a limited liability company in Myra's name, and she'd put everything together so seamlessly that Myra barely noticed. She knew there was an entity bigger than herself, surrounding her and the Mansion like a bubble, but it was so transparent that she forgot it was there most of the time. Gwen worked for the biggest marketing firm in Phoenix, and she was very, very good at her job.

"I don't want sponsors, Gwen."

"But sponsors want you. And you'll feel differently when we find the right one. The right ones, actually. Just like the book deal."

"I'm not going to write a book."

"You're already writing one!" Gwen held up her phone, the Minuscule Mansion's site glowing from its screen. "A little spit and polish from the right people, maybe a couple of new essays, and boom, front table at Barnes and Noble without breaking a sweat. Especially if we can attract a couple of celebrity endorsements."

Myra felt her breathing go shallow, her heart starting to race. "It's too much, Gwen."

"Myra, honey, I love you. I do. But you think everything is too much." Gwen grinned, a curve the polar opposite of Myra's crossing her face, and looked exactly the way she had when she showed up on the front stoop after moving into the neighborhood at seven, knocking on Myra's front door while wearing a tiara, four necklaces of Mardi Gras beads, and a plastic ring on each and every finger. *Hi! I'm Gwen and my dad said there's a little girl who lives here and she's going to be my best friend.*

That was the thing about Gwen: she was always right.

· 5 ·

PARKHURST, ARIZONA, 1988

MYRA BLINKED AT THE LITTLE GIRL STANDING ON HER
front stoop. She had never seen so many accessories in her life. She
didn't know where to rest her eyes.

"Myra, you need to say hello." Diane rested her hand on her seven-
year-old daughter's shoulder. Myra had never mastered greetings. Or
partings. Or talking to people generally.

"Hello," Myra whispered.

"Hi! I'm Gwen. I came over to play."

"I'm working. Goodbye, now." Myra turned on her heel and headed
back toward the stairs to the attic.

"Cool! My dad works at home, too. He's got a workshop, like Santa,
but instead of toys, he makes big metal monster computers. Sometimes
he lets me turn the screwdriver! Sometimes I hold the toolbox. Sometimes he lets me play computer games! I got one where I'm in the Olym-
pics. I'm really good at swimming. Not real swimming, but computer

swimming. I swim on the computer all the time. Do you ever swim? Are there swimming pools here? Dad says the mountains are too cold for swimming pools, but I bet he hasn't even looked. Do you know?"

Myra reached the top of the stairs with Gwen on her heels, and the sudden stop in noise made her pause and turn around. "Do I know what?"

"Do you know if there's swimming pools here?"

"Oh. I think maybe. At the college. It's really big and cold."

"Cool! Can we go swimming there?"

"You can probably go."

Gwen tilted her head to one side, one chestnut braid brushing her shoulder. The end of the braid had a zigzag pattern embossed into it, like someone had used a hot iron to press wrinkles instead of smoothing them over. The dark gloss of her hair reflected curled ribbons in pink, orange, and neon green. "We'll go together. What does your swimsuit look like? Mine's got pineapples on it."

Myra shook her head. "I don't have a swimsuit."

"Oh! That's okay. I'm not all unpacked yet but all my boxes have labels on them. Dad likes to know where everything goes before it gets there. I have a whole box with summer stuff because in Scottsdale I go swimming every day! I probably still will when I go to stay with Mom. But right now I stay with Dad and that's okay because my mom and dad both love me very, very much. I have a swimsuit with watermelons on it, too. Do you like watermelons? They're pink!"

Myra opened her mouth, but nothing came out. Her lips were parted in a perfect O, like her favorite goldfish in the fish tank downstairs, but she hadn't managed to find words before Gwen pushed past her into the attic.

"Ohmigod ohmigod ohmigod, you have a dollhouse! You have the biggest dollhouse ever! This is even bigger than the Barbie Dream House that Stephanie on the corner by my mom's house keeps in the room where her gramma stays at Christmas! She lets me play with it sometimes, but only when her mom makes her because I'm the guest." Gwen gasped and pointed at Myra. "Ohmigod, I'm the guest here, too! That means you have to let me play with it." She ran toward the doll-house and scooped up a Queen Anne dining table, holding it up to her face. "Is this real wood? Everything in Stephanie's house is plastic. This is so cool!"

"Stop!" The word forced itself out from the depths of Myra's lungs. "Put that down! Right this second!"

Gwen jerked upright and put the table back down. Myra sprinted over and restored it to its proper place.

"You sound like my dad when I mess with a CPU." Gwen grinned. "That's the big brain a computer uses. He says, 'The CPU is not a toy, Gwendolyn Christina Perkins.'"

"This isn't a toy, either. It's a mansion."

"I'm not dumb! I see it's a mansion. It's the biggest dollhouse I've ever seen!"

"It's not a dollhouse."

"It's not?"

"Do you see any dolls in it?"

Gwen glanced around the attic, then crouched to peer into the rooms. The house was hinged open because Myra had been working in one of the rear bedrooms, but she always buckled it tightly shut at night. "Where are the dolls?"

"I don't have any."

"What kind of girl doesn't have any dolls for a dollhouse?"

Myra shrugged. "Me, I suppose. And stop calling it a dollhouse."

"Has anyone ever told you you talk like that lady on *Murder, She Wrote*? I don't think I've ever heard anyone our age say 'suppose' before. You're seven, too, right?"

Myra nodded. She didn't know what her word limit per day was, but her chest felt unaccustomed to this much talking.

Gwen didn't seem to notice. "If you don't have any dolls, who lives in the mansion?"

"No one. I mean, the furniture does. And the plates and the cups and the candlesticks. All the stuff you see."

Gwen tilted her neon-accented head again, a confused look crossing her face. "I mean, I like stuff, too. Little stuff is cool, I guess. But it seems sad that no one uses it."

"I use it." Myra was a little surprised by the fury, the defensiveness, that came out with the words.

"Okay. Okay. Can I use it, too?"

Myra heard her mother bustling about downstairs. She could picture the little tray with violets painted on the corners, and the Fig Newtons that Diane would arrange in a delicate fan of rectangles above a few wedges of apple spread with peanut butter. Apple smiles. Myra always ate her snack alone. She worked on the Mansion alone. She knew her mother didn't like that she was always alone. She also knew her mother wouldn't let her send Gwen away.

"Only when you are supervised. Only when I supervise you." Myra balled her hands up into fists and set her jaw, anticipating a disagreement.

Gwen narrowed her eyes, then smiled. "You really do sound like that detective writer lady, but I kinda like it. Weird." She shrugged. "What are we doing?"

Myra was perplexed by the question. *We* was an unfamiliar word. "I'm working on the biggest bedroom."

"Ooh, fancy. Do you have one of those big beds with the pointy sticks and a canopy?"

"I don't know. I'll look." Myra walked to the corner and opened the dusty-rose hatbox, never entirely sure what she might find inside. Opening it, she plunged her hand into a disorganized pile of armchairs, teacups, and tiny green spider plants in Blue Willow pots, and emerged with her fingers wrapped around an oak headboard with sliding panels, a wide mattress with a counterpane of crushed blue velvet, and a brass elbow lamp. "I have this."

Gwen grimaced. "Not what I would pick, but okay. Bring it on over. Where'd you get all this stuff, anyway? My mom takes me to Toys 'R' Us all the time and I've never seen any little dollhouse stuff like this."

"My step-grandmother."

"Your step-grandmother? Is that like an evil stepmother?"

Myra shook her head so hard her ears rattled. "Not evil at all. She was so, so nice. She was a little strange, but so's my grampa Lou. I miss her."

"Where is she?"

"She died. On my fifth birthday."

"How? Was she real old? My great-grandma died, but she was real old."

Myra closed her eyes and heard shattering glass, screams that must have been metal on metal but still, even now, felt as if they tore themselves whole from her own chest, beneath her own crushed ribs. "No.

She wasn't old at all. It was a car crash." She took a deep breath, wondering for a moment if she could tell the story. She couldn't remember ever forming these words before, ever sharing it with anyone. Not even the nice police officer who held her hands, sheltering them from the biting snow hissing through the frigid December wind, telling her, *We've got help coming, sweetie, we've got help coming, don't you let me go, now.* The one whose brown-eyed gaze kept Myra's blue eyes focused so she wouldn't turn around, wouldn't look at what was left of the driver's side of the car. The one who said, *I don't mind, sweetie, I don't mind at all,* when Myra told her, *I'm sorry my hands are sticky.* Her birthday cake, once shaped like the number five, had been sitting in her lap when the car careened off the icy highway. Its pink icing and sparkling candy flowers—fashioned from gumdrops she'd helped Trixie flatten with a rolling pin that morning—were now smashed everywhere. Impossible to mend. Impossible to fix. And all her fault.

Myra felt the warm attic air plummet by degrees, cold enough to see her breath, but Gwen didn't seem to notice.

Gwen whistled. "That sucks. I'm not supposed to say that word, but it's so perfect."

Myra wrapped her hand around the acorn charm on its chain beneath her chin, remembering the way Trixie used to wrap her arms around her and kiss the top of her head five times. *Once for love, twice for life, thrice to keep you safe from strife, four the elements that bind us, five for all that intertwines us.* "It . . . does. It does suck. It's the suckiest."

Gwen laughed so hard she fell backward and almost hit the corner of the Mansion with her head. Her neon ribbons tangled with the wide branches of the oak tree. Myra rushed to help extricate her, leaning over and untangling the tendrils with intense focus.

Gwen held still and gazed up at her. "Were you in the car crash, too? Is that what happened to your face?"

Myra froze, her mouth opening and closing like the goldfish again. Wordless.

"I'm sorry, I'm sorry, I'm sorry. Dad always says I talk too much. Forget I said anything. I'm sorry, Myra." Gwen reached up and pulled her hair loose from the oak and from Myra's hand, sitting upright, and clasped both her hands around Myra's. "I'm so sorry. This is why I don't have a lot of friends. This is why I don't have any, not really. Please forgive me, Myra. Please don't make me go away."

Myra opened her mouth again, waiting for words. But she didn't want to make Gwen go away. For the first time, someone outside came in before she could say no, and now Myra felt a solid feeling expanding in her chest, and she realized it was spreading because of how empty she felt there. There could be room, maybe. Room for one person from outside, so inside, she wasn't quite so alone. "Yes," she murmured. "That's what happened to my face." And just for a moment, she felt the heat again, her skin too tight across the jaw that reset crooked, the spider's web of scars woven down the left side of her body beneath the turtleneck and long sleeves she always wore, no matter the weather. "You don't have to go."

The two girls sat a moment, holding each other's hands before pulling away.

"What was she like? Your step-grandmother?"

"She was like a fairy godmother."

"I've always wanted one of those!"

"I was the flower girl in their wedding." Myra ran to the closet in the back corner of the attic and retrieved the dress on its wooden hanger.

She had been only two years old when she was wrapped in its irides-cent folds, layer upon layer of watered silk taffeta ruffles the color of storm clouds, darkest midnight blue shot through with flashes of light. Tiny seed pearls were sewn into the scalloped neckline and on the edges of the sheer bell sleeves. It was a dress that anyone who had ever met a toddler would never dream of wrestling that toddler into. It wasn't even really a dress; it was a gown. The kind of garment a toddler might wear for her own coronation as queen of a pint-sized kingdom. But Granny Trixie laughed when Diane stared at the dress in horror and said it was impossible. *Myra can do impossible things. Myra's an old soul. She's got a soul that watched creation happen.*

Gwen whistled again. "That dress is amazing. I wish I had a dress like that."

"My granny Trixie made it." Diane had tried to make Myra donate it more than once, telling her she couldn't possibly remember wearing it enough to care. Myra always cried and Diane always relented until her next organizational purge, when donating the dress was always back on the table. *It doesn't even fit you, Myra!*

And it shouldn't. She had been only two when she wore it. She'd seen the photos enough times to recognize the difference in size.

But sometimes, late at night, when the Mansion was buckled and shut tight, Myra would sneak into the attic to check that everything was perfect, just as she left it. And sometimes it was perfect in a different way. A light might be shining from a lamp in an upstairs bedroom that had no wires. Flames might be leaping in the parlor fireplace, sending shadows in a ghostly waltz around the attic walls. The carved front door might swing open, and music might plink from inside, faint and beautiful and impossibly sad.

And on those nights, Myra could step into the gown and feel its neckline expand, its sleeves lengthen, its taffeta iridescence swirling into perfect folds cascading to the wide planks on the floor. She could feel its covered buttons slipping into place along the length of her back. She could plant her feet and feel herself grow taller, the windows of the Mansion twinkling farther beneath her line of sight than usual.

And she could hear a tiny whisper from inside: *Soon. But not quite yet.*

The Perfect and the Good Aren't Enemies
(From *The Minuscule Mansion of Myra Malone*, 2015)

SOMETIMES, THINGS JUST REFUSE TO TURN OUT THE WAY you mean them to. You may have been up all night refinishing a wobbly rolltop desk with every intention of fitting it under a still life painting of a bowl of peaches, and then you notice that the pink paint you used to make the desk quirky is exactly the wrong color, and it clashes with the fruit. So you move the painting, but the wall around it faded from the sun, and now you have to redo the wallpaper. And if you're going to do that, you might as well pick a scheme that matches the desk, except now that you're paying attention, the bed in the corner has an orangey patina on its scrolled wood headboard that clashes with the pink, too, and the rug on the floor was meant to pick up the blush of the peaches but now just looks dingy, and pretty soon it's wrong—every single element, all thrown into discord, all because you decided to try something new.

So, what do you do? Take out the desk, put back the peaches, call the whole thing off? Even though you know those faded walls have a hidden square of not-quite-right, and you can't unsee the way that tiny world is different than you thought?

Or do you start over, clear everything out, paint the walls, refinish the plank floors, and give yourself a clean slate? Decide whether the room wants to be an art studio, or an office, or a nursery?

This is a tough one! It happens to me all the time. I'll set out with the simplest plans, a minor tweak, and wind up with a choice between full-scale renovations and a shift of perspective. An attitude adjustment or a gut job. They both have their place, but in either situation, I've learned that nothing is ever a perfect fit. You can take a scene down to the studs and build it back up again, and you'll still miss that you cut the curtains a quarter inch too long. You can readjust what you already have—move pieces around, switch things out—and wait for that little voice in your head that says, *There you go. You're done.*

That voice never says those words to me. If it says them to you, congratulations. Mine tends to tell me I used the wrong shade of yellow on the baseboards, and what was I thinking, choosing yellow baseboards in the first place?

My mother always told me that "you can't let the perfect be the enemy of the good." When I was little, I thought of them as people— the Perfect, the Good—and pictured them sitting across a kitchen table from each other, pounding the butts of their forks and knives into the wood, calling each other names. I didn't like it. My parents fought like that, too, and I'd stuff quilt batting into my ears while I worked on the Mansion and tried to pretend it wasn't happening. I couldn't control what Mom and Dad were doing. But Perfect and Good? They were there in the attic with me, and I could do what my mother told me:

make them play nice. I couldn't let them fight, but I also couldn't let one win. There was room for both of them in the Mansion. I could help them find a way to coexist.

To do it, I have to convince Perfect that perfection is local—it doesn't have to be perfect everywhere. Perfect isn't eternal—how boring if it were, after all. It's transient. That's why it's special. The rolltop desk I worked to refinish all night was perfect in my hand when I decided it was done. But now, in the place I meant to put it, it isn't perfect anymore. That doesn't mean it isn't good. The Mansion gets to have its say, too, and the room hasn't decided what it wants to be yet.

So I have to listen, and let things rest, and work on something else. Maybe the peaches can hang next to the coatrack in the kitchen, near the pantry door. Maybe the wobbly pink desk really wants to be two pieces—the rolltop would make a pretty nifty bread box, and the legs can always be repurposed for other pieces, because pieces with matchstick-thin supports break sometimes. I can turn my attention to other rooms and other jobs. And after a while, I'll realize what that empty room is supposed to hold, and everything will fall into place. Until then, I can find comfort in everything else that's good. And really, that's pretty much perfect.

· 7 ·

LOCKHART, VIRGINIA, 2015

RUTHERFORD ALEXANDER RAKES III HAD NEVER HATED any job as much as he hated working front of house at Rakes and Son, pretending to care—and care intensely—whether the faux bamboo settee he was attempting to sell to the helmet-haired blond woman would appropriately flatter the southwest corner of her Florida room.

"It's a sunny corner, you see, but it's a dappled sort of sunlight—our neighbors absolutely refuse to cut back their overgrown privet hedge, it's disgraceful—and I worry that a print like this may make the corner too . . ." The woman trailed off and made a sort of jazz-handed gesture in the air before Alex's face. "Too busy. Too much movement. You understand?"

"Of course. We do offer a custom upholstery service, Mrs. Sherrill, and I'd be happy to give you some swatches to take home." He slid a thick binder full of cloth across the polished wood counter between them.

"Oh, goodness, if I come home with any more swatches, I think my husband may decide to turn the whole room into a man cave. He hates the whole idea of a Florida room—says if I want to feel tropical I can just move on down to Florida without him, can you imagine?"

Alex could imagine, could picture the beleaguered Mr. Sherrill sitting in a leather armchair while his wife attempted to get him to muster the interest that Alex's attention was a proxy for, hoping he might exclaim delight—or disgust, or any emotion at all, really—at a particularly lovely shade of cerise, or a repeating print of very small embroidered llamas, or a sedate chain-linked brocade. The bamboo settee was hideous, easily one of Alex's least favorite pieces in the entire block of linked riverside furniture showrooms. But it was a solid seller for Florida rooms, and every customer looked like Mrs. Sherrill. "He'll be so impressed with the final product, Joan. You have such exquisite taste."

Mrs. Sherrill's cheeks blossomed with rose-colored blotches that shone through the matte makeup caked thickly on her face. For a moment, she looked nineteen years old, blooming with the energy and passion Alex thought she must have had at that age, back before choosing a couch for a Florida room became the highlight of her day. "I do love it when you get a little too familiar, Mr. Rakes." Her voice dropped in register as she leaned across the polished wood, embracing the binder of swatches, lightly brushing his hand in the process. "Alex."

Alex smiled at her with a sincerity that bruised his heart, a mask to make a sale to a woman who needed something money couldn't buy. "Familiarity helps me know what customers want, Mrs. Sherrill. That settee is the last we have in stock, but if you purchase it today, I'd be happy to hold on to it for you—keep a close eye on it myself—until you decide about the upholstery."

"I'd be dealing with you for that, too, of course." Mrs. Sherrill reached a manicured hand into her Prada handbag, retrieving a credit card with shell-pink fingernails.

"Of course. The price today would be—" Alex looked down at the computer, shocked anew at the price the piece commanded. "Today it would be $2,799.99, or $2,925.95 with tax. Do you want me to go ahead and take care of that for you?"

"I do. Very much. Quality is worth the price." Joan Sherrill flashed a Cheshire cat grin. "And I'll look forward to paying for quality again soon, Mr. Rakes." She handed him the card nestled next to a creamy piece of cardstock, and Alex knew her name and address would be engraved into the paper's fibers at a price greater than many people would pay for a month's rent, and that a handwritten scrawl in fountain pen would tell him when and where he might find her. Alex had been handed many such cards. Sometimes he followed their instructions, and sometimes he didn't. But every piece of paper weighed a little heavier on his soul. Sometimes he'd find a bit of the blotchy-cheeked shy girl beneath the too-thick makeup and perfect manicure, and it would help him remember his own youth, the energy of his twenty-year-old self, trekking through China on the weekends he wasn't teaching English at a Beijing private school.

But most of the time, it just made him feel used, nearly used up, the weight of his decision to come home and help his father pinning him to Lockhart and everything he tried to leave behind. He ran Mrs. Sherrill's card through the scanner and handed it back to her with a receipt on which he wrote nothing at all, smiling with his teeth, his face nearly cracking with the effort. "Until next time, Mrs. Sherrill."

"Adieu for now, Mr. Rakes." She spun neatly on one red-soled heel and glided toward the frosted glass door in its reclaimed wood frame without a backward glance.

"Another of the bamboo settees?" Alex's father had approached as silently as a cat, his voice as deep and dour as the man who spoke with it. "I never expected them to be so successful. Put in an order for another twenty when you have a moment, won't you?"

Alex gritted his teeth. "Sure, Dad."

"Oh, now, don't start. I know they offend your delicate taste, but this is a business, Alex, not the kind of place that sells apothecary tables pieced together with, I don't know, old cigar boxes and barn door hinges." Rutherford Alexander Rakes Jr. paused to consider. "Actually, that would probably sell like hotcakes. See if you can find us something like that."

"Right. Barn door hinge cabinet. Finally, a project that will give my life meaning." Alex stood up from the rolling stool in its spot behind the iPad register and headed for the door.

"Where do you think you're going?"

"There's a pop-up thrift store in that old nightclub down the street. I want to check out if they've got any new stuff."

"Are you talking about that Velvet Cage place, or whatever it was called? That storefront is cursed. I've looked at it a few times for an accessories outlet, but I think I've decided I won't touch it with a ten-foot pole. It's killed at least ten businesses in the last four years, as I recall."

"It may kill this one before I can check it out again if you don't let me go."

"I know you view this . . . *occupation*—this finding mismatched bric-a-brac for pennies—a sort of hobby, Alex, but unless you're finding things you can put on the floor and sell, it's really a waste of time and money."

"You said you appreciated my eye for things."

Rutherford took a deep breath. "Fine. Take a lunch break. Go see what you can find. Then come back and sell some more settees."

Alex walked out of the gallery's front door and squinted at the bright sun sparkling off the canal outside. Rakes and Son occupied a series of refurbished warehouses in Lockhart. It had started out in a single storefront at the turn of the twentieth century, begun by Alex's great-grandfather, but the blue-blooded pedigree of the Rakes name—combined with Theodore "Teddy" Rakes's business savvy—had transformed it into a hub for decorators and aristocratic families up and down the Eastern Seaboard. Alex never intended to assume the Son portion of the business name. But his father was ill, and Alex had agreed to return and help for a short time that had already expanded into half a year, with no end in sight.

Lockhart was home only in the sense that Alex didn't have another place that met the definition. His father had sent him away to boarding school in the North Carolina mountains when Alex was five years old, hoping to instill the same military precision that Rutherford had gleaned from his own years there. It didn't take. And the strained relationship between the current Rakes and Son had never quite recovered from decades of estrangement and misunderstandings. Until six months ago, Alex was teaching English at a private school in China.

Returning to his genteel Southern roots was a sort of reverse culture shock, plunging him back into unspoken rules he'd all but forgotten: no white after Labor Day, no socks with loafers, pink polo shirts with khaki shorts acceptable on the golf course (and other places Alex tried not to set foot).

The riverfront charm of Lockhart had, at least, resulted in a kind of quirky renaissance, with cheerful eateries and funky thrift stores where Alex could wander when not tied to his father's business priorities. The one he'd found recently didn't even have a name, just a temporary vinyl sign hanging from ropes over the entrance, the word VINTAGE printed in purple letters. Maybe they'd heard the same thing as Rutherford about turnover in the space and assumed a more permanent sign wasn't worth the trouble.

A strange credenza in the front window immediately caught Alex's eye. Its flaking paint was mostly turquoise, but one of its front legs—a length of turned wood that looked as if it came from another piece of furniture—was bright pink. The rest of the credenza was supported on iron hairpin legs, and the cabinet had an empty cutout space on its right side, above sliding louvered doors. Alex approached the bored-looking college student lounging behind a glass counter filled with costume jewelry.

"Is that credenza for sale?"

The girl chewed her gum with a pop and readjusted the orange beret on her long blue hair. "If it's in here, it's for sale."

"Is it complete? It looks like it's missing a piece."

The girl craned her neck to look past Alex. "You mean the leg? Yeah, that's how we got it. But there's another part in back we were using ourselves. A record player. Comes with it, though, if you want it."

Alex considered. "Yeah, I think I do." The credenza had a lack of symmetry that he found charming, though he couldn't say why. "How much is it?"

The girl consulted a clipboard on top of the glass counter. "Seventy-five."

"Dollars?" Alex thought of the faux bamboo settees and their astronomical price tag.

"No, marbles. We sell everything for marbles here. We prefer Venetian glass." The girl's expression didn't change as she stared at Alex, seemingly waiting for him to admit what an idiot he was. When he didn't speak, she rolled her eyes. "Yes. Seventy-five dollars. And you can have the records that came with it for twenty-five, if you want them."

Alex nodded. Even if the music wasn't his taste, he could resell it. "Yes. I'll take them, too." He reached into his wallet and retrieved five twenty-dollar bills, handing them across the counter.

"I'm actually glad you're buying it so I won't," the girl said. "It's got a real Mansion feel, but I don't have a place to put it right now." She snapped her gum again, mouthing *Boyfriend trouble* with exaggerated zeal, as if expecting Alex to ask for details.

But Alex was caught on another thing she'd said. "What do you mean by 'mansion feel'?" The family home where Alex was currently staying was sometimes called a mansion, notwithstanding the place was so poorly maintained that the structure might collapse around his head while he slept. The credenza would fit with the rest of the motley pieces he'd pulled together from closets and rooms around the house—an old 1970s paneled headboard with a built-in bookcase, a brass elbow lamp that looked meant for a university library, and a blue crushed velvet bedspread that his father would probably burn as soon as look at.

"Just an expression." The girl tucked Alex's money in a white patent leather coin purse shaped like Hello Kitty's head. "You wouldn't understand."

8

Pantries and Perishables

(From *The Minuscule Mansion of Myra Malone*, 2015)

ANY WELL-APPOINTED MANSION MUST HAVE FOOD SUFFI-
cient for its occupants and, while you may have noticed the Mansion
has few occupants—okay, only one occupant, and only after Gwen
threatened to quit if I didn't add one—that occupant never goes hungry. The available food choices may not match everyone's taste, but
we're talking about a clothespin here, and since that clothespin is me,
I feed her what I was fed.

Which was, to wit, *whatever was on sale and available in bulk
quantities.*

So, let's talk about Vienna sausages.

Have you ever eaten a Vienna sausage? If the answer is yes, please
accept my sincerest condolences and suggestion that you browse the
Mansion archives for another article. Consider this a content warning.
I'm going to be talking about sausages in depth in a way that you might
find distressing. Thanks so much for reading! I'm sorry!

If you haven't ever eaten a Vienna sausage, congratulations! You've managed to escape the extruded clutches of a foodstuff that defined my childhood, along with crystallized Welch's grape jelly, pickles of questionable provenance, and generic juice Push Pops. While many of these items blend together in my memory into a congealed mass of sodium and fat, the Vienna sausages are distinct from their bulk-purchased brethren.

A Vienna sausage is a marvel of engineering. Gwen tells me they're like the meat sticks she used to eat with her cousins when they were younger, and that's the last thing she ever said about them, when we were seven, and she made me promise to never put them in front of her again. I don't go to grocery stores, so I'm not clear on whether a Vienna sausage is the kind of thing that a person could go to a deli and ask for. The only ones I know—the ones I ate, every single day, for years—come in cans, floating in water like rubbery, tubular apples you'd really rather not bob for.

My first cans of Vienna sausages—which is to say, the only cans I ever needed for the rest of my life—came from my grandfather. Grampa Lou grew up hungry. His early childhood in Oklahoma began in scarcity and ended in dust, choking the crops on his family's small farm and, soon after, choking his mother as well. He clasped one small hand in his older sister's, trudging behind her as she dragged them both west, away from their abusive father and the dust that threatened to bury them both. They landed, eventually, on an Arizona farm owned by a distant cousin, working through the day for a meager share of food that never fully fed all who washed up in that dry and land-locked harbor.

My grandfather never forgot hunger. When I was small, he spoke of

Hunger with an honorific capital letter, as if it were a person lurking in dark corners, always ready to pounce. I could not enter my grandfather's house without being immediately ushered to a table or a chair and having food put before me. The only weapon against Hunger was the shield of a loaded plate, and my grandfather found his most reliable source of ammunition in warehouse stores.

If a food was worth purchasing, Grampa believed, it was worth purchasing by the pallet. And filling his own pantry was not enough to forestall his fear. The greatest gift he could bestow was the absence of want: an endless supply of whatever food he heard one of us mention, in passing, as enjoyable. When I was a toddler, I reportedly demolished a plate while shoveling a Vienna sausage casserole into my tiny maw, and Grampa never forgot it. When I was six, he delivered an entire Cadillac's trunk of Vienna sausages to our cabin's door, chuckling and winking like Santa with a sleigh full of extruded meat. By then, I had learned a cautious mix of outward gratitude and measured enthusiasm: a gift was a gift and deserved thanks, and nothing broke my young heart more than a look of disappointment on my grandfather's face. But if I was too happy, my reaction could work against me later, becoming the foundation for a crate of some other bulk purchase.

By six, I had learned diplomacy, and I still believe that skill helped me earn the other gift Grampa brought me that day: this Mansion, this miniature world I share with all of you here. Grampa loaded it into his enormous sedan a year after we lost someone we both adored. The Mansion was hers, and we both felt that it carried her memory inside its brass-buckled frame. When Grampa married Trixie, my stepgrandmother, I was a toddler, but she never treated me like a child. She used the Mansion to teach me skills I still use to care for it today: sewing, and painting, and wielding tools. She and Grampa both taught me how to whittle and work with wood, and the three of us would spend hours with planers and glue and tiny pots of paint, building a refuge that we all needed.

Our focus on creating a world full of minute detail made the world outside seem more manageable. If I was observant enough, I could reduce something enormous or overwhelming into something small enough to be held in the palm of my hand, tucked into a small corner of a room, and buckled away for safekeeping. And that skill gave me power in a powerless time. When my world lost Trixie, I felt as if I could keep her spirit in the Mansion. Like she was never really lost at all.

In the end, it helped me keep my grandfather, too. The Mansion's pantry is never empty. I keep it stocked with bulk supplies of pasta and grape jelly, jars of ruby-red tomatoes, and cans and cans of Vienna sausages. If you look at the bottom of this post, I've included some pictures of the brushes I use to paint labels. Some of them are only the width of an eyelash, and I have to use a magnifying glass to create them. Some work I'm able to complete with Photoshop and a very high-resolution printer, but I like the hand-painted work best. With every stroke of color, I hear my grandparents. *Measure twice. Cut once. And here's another plate—eat, little acorn. Eat.*

9

ELLIOTT, ARIZONA, 1983

GRAMPA LOU'S HOUSE WAS SMALL BUT PRETTY, A MODI-fied A-frame rising out of the juniper near a narrow chute of the Verde River planted with river birches and cottonwoods. The acres of scrub brush had become more valuable in the decades since Lou purchased it for a song, and while the land spread through an undeveloped stretch of Arizona where most people only passed on their way somewhere else, as the boundaries of "somewhere else" continued to expand, the spaces in between became more desirable.

So when Lou called his family to tell them about his new lady friend, inviting them down off the rim to have a family dinner "because she'll be family soon," their first reaction was suspicion. Lou was cagey about how they'd met, but since he never had a setting between cagey and effusive, the lack of detail alone wasn't remarkable. What was re-markable was the openness of his words when he talked about how lonely he'd been—something he'd never admitted, even to himself—

and his calm tone when he talked about his travels, and the "wonderful woman" he'd met.

Lou traveled less than he used to back when he crisscrossed the country selling siding to big construction outfits. He didn't keep a suitcase full of samples anymore, but even once he retired, he never lost the urge to hit the road, to chat up strangers and figure out what motivated them, to use up his entire reserve of words and then return to his A-frame and scrub brush in silence and solitude. His wild swings between social and withdrawn were unpredictable, and had been ever since Diane's mother, his first wife, had died from cancer when Diane was small—small enough that she never registered her absence. She stayed with her aunt when Lou traveled for work, but otherwise was always with her father, helping him on building projects throughout her childhood, including the cabin where she lived with Myra and Dave.

As for Lou, when he slowed in his travels and started to talk about settling down into retirement, Diane and Dave would find him perched on the edges of the house in Elliott or climbing fences on the outskirts of his land, mending and improving and modifying as he always had. He didn't seem to long for any society beyond his own and his family's, so his announcement about Beatrix seemed a bolt out of dry, blue skies. All Lou would say was that he met her while traveling and knew, down to his bones, that she was meant to be part of his world.

Suspicion seemed appropriate.

But the first time they crunched down the long dirt road to the house and met Beatrix wearing an old pair of Hunter rain boots and up to her elbows in dirt and manure, she put them all immediately at ease. And none more so than Myra. Nearing two years old, she was a shy and withdrawn toddler who rarely spoke to strangers. But she immediately cooed over the flowers painted on the seed packets stacked next to Beatrix's wheelbarrow. The wheelbarrow was pink. She painted it herself. "This place needed some color," she said. Then she drew herself up to her full height—which was slight—and spread her arms wide with a gesture that seemed to welcome the world. "I'm so glad y'all are here. Lou's told me so much about all of you. I know it's odd to have some strange lady just show up in your daddy's house and say she feels like she's been waiting her whole life to meet you, but there it is."

The family looked at each other, and Diane—as usual—spoke up first. "You must be Beatrix?"

"I am. But please call me Trixie. I've got dinner all ready inside— I'm not going to invite you in because this place is yours and I'm just the new gal. But I hope maybe you'll let me earn my keep." Trixie winked at Myra, already holding her hand and gazing up at her in squint-eyed wonder, like someone might gaze at the golden edges of the sun before it bursts from behind a cloud.

Trixie had that effect on everyone. You didn't realize how cloudy the day had seemed before you felt her warmth on your face.

They followed her into Lou's cabin, which seemed very much the same since their last visit and yet subtly shifted, as if its front door opened into a parallel world where everyone was a little bit happier. Every corner that once held any bit of gloom was now transformed with something colorful—a sprig of juniper and daisies in a tiny vase, a peacock-colored silk scarf draped across an armchair. The scent of the air carried its own warmth and an undercurrent of flowers and spice. Lou's rough-edged table was laid with china that had never left a cabinet, and looked relieved, happy even, to be holding cornbread and soup and, on a dish that must have been intended for Myra, an enormous pile of macaroni and cheese with cut-up hot dogs. Myra started to head toward the table until her eyes were caught by a shimmering heap of deep-blue fabric near the sofa, and she toddled in its direction.

"Oops, that looks fancy, sweetie." Diane scooped her up before she could dive into the shimmering depths.

"Oh, she's welcome to explore it." Trixie laughed. "I haven't really gotten started, and it hasn't told me what it wants to be yet. I have to spend a little time listening to the fabric for a while before I know for sure. Maybe Myra can help me figure it out."

"She's a little young to sew," Diane said.

"Maybe so, but she'd be good company while I work on whatever it's meant to be." Beatrix picked up a round box next to the sofa, an old hatbox covered in dusty-rose silk. "I've got some little things in here she could play with, and maybe she can pick up a few little tricks along the way. Skills she can use when she's bigger." Trixie pointed to an incomplete blue quilt draped across the back of the sofa, its surface dotted with embroidered constellations across a pattern of broken stars. "You're never cold once you learn to sew."

"You've been talking about those business classes you want to take for years, Diane," said Lou, emerging from the kitchen. "Why don't you let the little acorn come spend some time with us every so often, give you and Dave some time to yourselves? You've been talking about that business degree, haven't you?"

Diane and Dave looked at each other and then at Lou, perplexed. They brought Myra down for periodic visits, but usually Lou would drive up the mountain and visit their cabin on his way to or from the nearest warehouse store. It was true that Elliott was close enough to the main road that Diane could stop on her way to Phoenix and could leave Myra there if she had errands to run that were easier without a toddler in tow. It was also true that she had discussed going back to school. But she hadn't yet discussed this possibility with her father.

"We can talk about it," Diane said. "It'd probably be several days a week, though, Dad. Are you sure?"

"We're sure." Lou draped an arm across Trixie's shoulders, and they both beamed.

They sat around Lou's unused dining room table as a family, flatware clinking against china in a sound that seemed at once utterly unfamiliar and completely welcome. Lou told the same stories he'd told a million times before, but each one was punctuated with Trixie's laughter in a way that made them seem new. Trixie perched her chin on her hand and asked Lou to tell stories she'd plainly already heard—*Talk about that man with the peacock at the airport*—with enthusiasm that resonated for Diane and Dave and Myra, all of whom loved Lou's exaggerated tales and who had never expected to find another person who loved hearing them quite as much.

After dinner, they sat companionably in the living room, and Trixie threaded a fat needle for Myra with a length of yarn and handed her a flat plastic grid shaped like a heart. "If we're going to sew together, it'll help if you start here, because learning how to move the thread in and out can be the hardest part at first." Myra beamed up at Trixie, then patted the soft ball of yarn in her lap. "Pink," she said.

"Your grampa said it was your favorite," Trixie said. "I hope you'll have a lot of time here to work with it."

Everything seemed out of the ordinary in a perfectly ordinary way.

· 10 ·

LOCKHART, VIRGINIA, 2015

ALEX RETURNED TO RAKES AND SON IN TIME TO SEE HIS
father approaching a severely fashionable couple circling a splintered
coffee table fashioned from an old ship door—or what some factory
believed an old ship door to look like. When Rutherford saw Alex, he
made a beeline for his son instead. "Well? Did you find anything
amazing?"

"Nothing you'd like. But I did pick up an interesting credenza–
record player thing. I was going to grab a hand truck and borrow
a trailer to get it over to the house." Alex started walking toward
the stockroom behind the gallery, but his father put a hand on his
shoulder.

"Not before you finish your chores." Rutherford gestured toward
the couple and the coffee table. "Help Boris and Natasha over there,
and then you can go pick up whatever mismatched monstrosity you
bought."

Alex straightened his posture and walked slowly toward the couple, who he soon realized were in the midst of a heated argument. He stood discreetly a few feet away as they alternately pointed at a smartphone's screen and at each other.

"It's not the right look," the girl hissed, her dark hair sliced in a point to her chin, a dark wing of midnight eyeliner swooped above each pale green eye, both of which she rolled at her beanie-wearing companion. "It's not Mansion aesthetic At. All. Jeremy." Her thudding emphasis on each word hung in the air with reproach.

"Mansion aesthetic is about finding what speaks to you, Kirstin. That's what Myra always says. And this piece here—" Jeremy rubbed a hand over the rough surface of the table, and Alex hoped he wouldn't stab his fingers with splinters. "This speaks to me."

Alex saw his moment and took it. "It speaks to a lot of people. And it's a rare find. Not a lot of pirate ships out and about on the high seas that we can source for coffee tables these days." He reached deep into his reserves for another smile and found one, despite thinking he'd used his last one up on Mrs. Sherrill. "It's a lovely piece."

Kirstin looked up from her phone. "Is this your best price?"

Alex kept his smile pasted to his face, unchanged. "It is. Everything in here is our best price." His father's words echoed in his head: *No discounts. Ever. For the kind of customers we attract, our prices are part of our mystique.* "But we do offer customization services at a very reasonable rate. This piece isn't upholstered, of course, but some strategic hand distressing might really set it off." *Hand distressing with a belt sander might make it less likely to cause a lawsuit. I need to talk to Dad about what he lets on the floor.*

Kirstin narrowed her eyes at Alex and glanced at the table. "Do you offer restaining? Less of a walnut, more of a maple? I'm trying to achieve a look like this." She held the phone screen a few inches in front of Alex's face, showing a midcentury-modern table that looked almost, but not quite, entirely unlike the table Jeremy wanted.

"Er . . . we do, but it's generally easier to go darker than it is to strip and refinish in a lighter stain. Particularly when a piece like this has such an established . . . patina. We do have some lovely midcentury pieces in the adjacent warehouse. Could I walk you over there?"

"We're just browsing for now." Kirstin snatched the phone back and scrolled farther down. "What about something like this? Where can we find bedroom furniture?" She handed Alex the phone again.

"Bedrooms are mostly in Warehouse Four, but a piece like this—" Alex froze. He zoomed in on the picture, certain the resemblance couldn't be as clear as it seemed at first glance, but the image was a perfect facsimile: a sleek headboard in polished cherry, a sliding panel that concealed a bookshelf. A brass elbow lamp perched on one corner, catching the sparkle of blue crushed velvet on the coverlet, all completely off trend and unstylish in a way that Alex adored. One of a kind, or so he thought, before seeing it reproduced in miniature.

"Do you, like, need a minute?" Kirstin asked, and Alex realized his mouth was open as he stared at the phone.

"Wha— No. No, it's just that this bed looks like—it looks a little like mine, actually."

Kirstin's face brightened. "Is it for sale?"

"Oh. No. I mean, there are some headboards that are a little like it in Warehouse Four—which, like I said, I can walk you over to." Alex resumed breathing, trying not to let confusion creep into his voice. "What site is this, by the way?"

Kirstin raised her dark and tailored eyebrows into twin arches of surprise. "You've never heard of *The Minuscule Mansion*?"

"No. Is it a store?"

Kirstin laughed with an exclusive trill that carried scorn, the pleasure of realizing someone was so very out of the loop, and that she would be the one to clue them in while making sure they knew how very, very foolish they should feel. "*The Minuscule Mansion of Myra Malone* is not a store. I wish it was! I'd buy anything in it. Myra is a genius, but I'm trying to learn how to match her eye. I've even sent her a few pieces, and a pair of silver candlesticks wound up on the library mantel for a few weeks, so I know I'm learning."

Alex steeled himself for the barrage of eye rolling he knew his next question would bring. "Who is Myra Malone?"

"She's a hermit. Lives in some back-of-beyond mountain place out west somewhere. Arizona, I think? But she has this amazing dollhouse. Calling it a dollhouse is insulting, actually. It's a real mansion. The kind of place you could live—really *live*, you know?—if you were the size of, like, a clothespin. But she writes about the rooms and the furniture and the Mansion in a way that just sweeps you up with her. It's gorgeous and perfect and I just want to curl up in a chair and talk to her over tea for a while." Kirstin held her phone up to Alex's face again. "I mean, just look at it."

For the second time, Alex was unable to close his mouth, and equally unable to make words come out of it. His stare homed in immediately on the carved front door, the wide front steps sprinkled with leaves from an unseen oak that he knew, without looking, loomed in the northwest corner of the yard. A yard he knew was surrounded with a wrought iron fence, a gate he walked through each morning on his way to his little blue Mini on the street—

"You said this is a dollhouse?"

"It is *not* a dollhouse. I told you that." Kirstin sighed with disappointment. "Unfortunately, it's the size of one, which is too bad. Wouldn't you just love to live there?"

Alex clapped his mouth shut before he could let the words out. *I do live there. I sleep in that bed every night. I sweep those oak leaves off the steps.*

What the hell is going on?

PARKHURST, ARIZONA, 2015

"I'M BEGINNING TO THINK I MADE MY SNEAK PREVIEW email for the contest a little too wide-open." Gwen clapped her laptop shut and grimaced with disgust. "I should have known that 'Describe what you'd do to the Mansion' would bring out some creeps."

Myra glanced up from the palm-sized settee she was embroidering with small French knots. "Do I want to know?"

"Probably not. Let's just say some people really, really love your house in a way that's not entirely appropriate for a family publication."

"Eww."

"Yeah. I'll put some filters in place. No biggie. Have you thought any more about what room you'd like to auction off?"

"You make it sound like I'm going to hack off part of the Mansion and give it away."

"No! Not at all." Gwen paused and tilted her head, thinking. "Although we could make a reproduction—something they could keep.

We'd have to make two of everything, but people would pay more for a chance to get something they can hold in their hands, especially if it's something you made."

"I'm not fast at making stuff, Gwen."

"No, because you're a perfectionist. But remember that they're going to win the chance to tell you how to decorate, so if it's too detailed, the wait would be on them. We could say that up front and set some other limits, too. And we'd have the entry fees in the meantime, and that's the important thing."

"That's the thing we have to do quickest. The bank's not going to take my word for money that may come in. I've got to have it in hand."

Gwen put on a serious face—what Myra had come to think of as her "business face"—and leaned forward. "I'm going to help however I can, Myra, but this is the part where I have to be realistic with you, just like I'd be with any client. This is a total long shot. Your mom has this place in hock to the tune of six figures in prime mountain vacation territory. We've got to pull out all the stops, and this still may not work."

"We have to try. Besides, you keep beating me over the head with reminders that I need to engage-engage-engage, so I thought you'd be all in."

"I am! As your manager and your marketer, I'm all in. As your occasional boss and an investor in a business that'll have an even better year if the Mansion really takes off, I'm all in."

"But?"

"But. As your best friend, I'm worried. I don't want you to get your heart broken." Gwen leaned back and looked around at the attic's exposed beams, the light shining in through the windows. "I wish your heart wasn't quite so tied to a dusty old attic, but I care about it all the same."

"I know." Myra stood next to her best friend and put her hand on her shoulder. "And thank you."

"So, when are we pulling the trigger on this contest?"

"Already done." Myra walked across the attic to her desk, picking up her laptop and handing it to Gwen. "I posted information this morning, along with pictures of the room."

"Why didn't you tell me?"

Myra shrugged. "It came together pretty quickly."

Gwen opened the laptop and scanned over the latest post on *The Minuscule Mansion*, scrolling to the photos at the bottom. "That upstairs bedroom, in the turret? I remember that one." She walked to the Mansion and crouched in front of it. "This was the first one we ever played with together." She picked up the bed near the center of the room, rubbing the crushed-velvet coverlet and opening the sliding door on the headboard. "I think this is even the same bed we used."

"It is. I haven't worked much on that room. There's so much glass from the windows that there isn't a whole lot to do on the walls. I kept meaning to add a closet or something, but it's mostly the room where I keep pieces that need work, or that I haven't found another home for yet."

"It's a good idea for the contest, then—not a lot they can mess up, I suppose. There aren't even a lot of walls to paint."

"Right. Unless someone's really into something like hand-painted terra-cotta tiles or collecting tiny succulents or teacups or something like that. Redecorating it won't take long."

"Redecorating won't, probably. But the other part might take more time. You buried the info about the grand prize."

"I don't know what you're talking about. It's there."

"Yes, I see that. The pale lavender eight-point font makes it a little hard to read, wouldn't you agree? It's going to be difficult for people to bid for lunch and a tour of the Mansion with Myra Malone herself if they don't even know that prize is available."

"They'll know. They'll just have to look hard for it." Myra released an exasperated sigh when she saw Gwen's business face again. "Look, these are people who are big fans of miniature things, right? Small fonts shouldn't be an issue."

"Myra."

"And lavender isn't the normal font color. It sticks out like a sore thumb. I might as well have highlighted it."

"Myra."

"Fine. Okay. I'm joking."

"How many times do I have to tell you not to joke about business?"

"I still don't know how you think this is going to work. What do you expect me to do? Have someone come here and step over all the boxes downstairs? Meet somewhere with the Mansion, unpack it on the table of a restaurant or some conference room, something like that? And who's going to pretend to be me—my mom? You?"

"No one is going to pretend to be you. You are going to be you."

Myra's hand, its spider's tracing of scars, flew unconsciously to her face and crooked jaw. "I don't see people."

"I know."

"I can't see people, Gwen."

"That's something I *don't* know. Or at least I don't agree with it. I think you've spent so many decades convincing yourself that you just made it true. But it isn't true, Myra. People see you every day on that blog. More of you than you realize, I think, because it's not like the ad campaigns and the ghostwriting and the words you write for other people. You write those words for yourself, but they paint a very clear picture of who you are, and that's who people care about. It's who I care about, too. I know that person better than anyone, and it's high time I stopped being the only one." Gwen grasped Myra's hands. "It's time to let yourself have more than this attic, Myra."

Myra glared at her. "I have everything I need."

"I think you've convinced yourself of that, but it isn't true. It's like your mom said—there's a whole world out there you both turned your back on, and she filled the hole that world left with stuff she never used. You filled it with stuff, too—just on a much smaller scale. If this whole experience you're going through means anything at all, Myra, let it mean that you take down some walls."

"That's a funny speech from someone who wants me to show those walls to people who want to pay to get inside them."

"Well, we're all full of contradictions. We contain multitudes."

A series of pings from Myra's computer drew their attention to the screen. "Sounds like we've got people sending in entries already," Myra said.

"Whee! Let's see who wants to play!" Gwen grabbed the laptop, her face lighting up. "I thought fifty dollars might be a little steep to fill a creepy dollhouse room with tiny pieces of furniture—stop looking at me like that, I'm kidding, lighten up—but we've already got twenty entries just for the room decorating alone, and you just put up the post a few hours ago!" She clicked around a bit more, opening her mouth in shock. "And we've got two two-hundred-dollar entries so far for the lunch!"

Myra shook her head. "I can't imagine who in the world would have any interest in that."

"Well, let's open one up and see!" Gwen clicked on one of the emails and started speaking in a deep and booming voice, like an orator in a Roman forum. *"Good morning, Ms. Malone. My name is Alex Rakes. I live in Lockhart, Virginia. My house is, and I mean this quite literally, the Minuscule Mansion. Or, to be more accurate, a mansion that is not at all minuscule, but is very much full-sized, and it looks exactly like the one on your site. The bedroom you're decorating is the one I sleep in."* Gwen paused and cast a puzzled glance at Myra, then continued reading. *"If that's not enough to win whatever crazy game you're playing here, then I don't know what is."*

· 12 ·

ELLIOTT, ARIZONA, 1985

"ONCE UPON A TIME, THERE WAS A HOUSE." TRIXIE REACHED across her lap to grab Myra's small hand, adjusting the tiny thimble on her index finger so she could push the stitch through the layers of fabric on the quilt square. The incomplete quilt draped over the sofa was a broken star pattern pieced together in deep shades of lapis and turquoise, shot through with silver thread.

Myra pushed the needle with intense focus, looking for it on the other side so she could try to direct it back through again. Sewing time with Granny Trixie was one of her favorite things, an activity they could do together while her mother attended classes in Phoenix. Trixie always told her stories over squares of colorful fabric. "Can it be a mansion?"

"It can. It can be whatever the people around it need it to be. It wasn't always a house, but it was always a shelter. A refuge."

"Who lives there?"

"A lady."

"All by herself?"

Trixie frowned and took the square back from Myra, resetting the stitch and handing her the needle to complete the pass through the fabric. "Not always, but yes, she was often alone."

"Wasn't she lonely?"

"Sometimes. More in the beginning, a long, long time ago, when she was new. But then, as the years passed and the world grew up around her, it wasn't possible to be alone anymore. People would come there when they needed help, or passage from a world they wanted to leave to a place where they could be safe. It could be what people needed, if they were open to its help."

"So then she wasn't lonely. That's good."

Beatrix laughed. "Oh, honey. It takes more than people to fix that. You can be surrounded by people and still be lonely. And some people . . . some people make lonely seem like the best way to be."

Myra nodded. "Grampa Lou says fences are better than people."

"When it comes to people—plural—I think he's right. People all together can be dangerous. But a person, here and there, that's different. They aren't all the same. Some are terrible, but some—some are wonderful. And they stay that way in your mind, and in your heart, forever, even when they change, or when they hurt you or deny the gifts you give them." Beatrix's eyes glazed over. "Even when you can't recognize them, or when they can't recognize you."

"Granny Trixie? Are you okay?"

"I'm fine, honey." Beatrix swiped her hands over her eyes and reset the smile on her face. "Sometimes grown-ups get a little sad."

"When I get sad in Sunday school, Mrs. Price tells me to think of something happy."

"And what do you think about?"

"Candy canes."

"That sounds like an excellent thing to think about."

Myra handed the square back to Trixie so she could set another stitch. "Can you talk more about the mansion?"

"Of course. It was big, and it sat on a hill above a wide, beautiful river that carved its way through the stone of those hills since before time began. The banks of the river curved around pockets in the rock that widened into hidey-holes and tunnels and rooms bigger than the mansion itself, far beneath the oaks and the waving grasses and wisteria vines, but not many knew those rooms were there."

"What was in the rooms under the ground?" Myra watched Trixie's narrow fingers, their quick motions with the needle and thread seeming as instinctive, and as effortless, as her mother's with a pen as she wrote study notes late into the night. Trixie could pierce the fabric in her lap with an unbroken rhythm, rarely taking her eyes from Myra's face. Myra had to hold the embroidery close to her eyes to see the stitches that broke the line of thread into barely visible dashes and dots.

"The rooms beneath were filled with magic." Trixie knotted the thread and pulled it taut to snap it, handing the fabric back to Myra. "There were warm breezes blowing from fires that can't be seen, fires that burned before any living thing walked on the ground above. And pictures, sometimes, carved into the rock by hands that turned to dust before living memory."

"Did the Lady know about the rooms?" Myra wished she could follow Trixie's stitches with the same level of precision, or that she could move her needle without following it with her eyes, because she loved watching Trixie while she told stories. Trixie's eyes could pull Myra deep below the surface of the real world, tugging her into the magical rooms beneath the house she described. She struggled to focus. She had asked, in the beginning, whether she could wear a thimble on every finger to protect them from the needle. Trixie laughed and told her that learning to avoid pain was less important than learning it would always be there, and that you often caused it yourself, so it was best to learn to live with it.

"The Lady knew about the rooms," Trixie said. "As I told you, there wasn't always a house. But on that wide sweep of water and stone, there was always shelter. And it got to where, over the years, it was hard for people to separate the Lady from the refuge she provided. She was always there. And there were others like her, few and far between, in places where the wide world swept by the current seemed to flow on a different timeline. A person might not notice. But people—plural—people talk, and get ideas. And sometimes, what starts as a haven becomes something frightening, or sinister. And people started to tell stories."

"About the Lady?"

"About the Lady, about the house, about anything that didn't make sense in the world the way they understood it. People tell stories about things they don't understand. And when that thing is a lady, the stories take a lot of different forms. Some become miracles, like a lady in a sparkling lake who hands out magic swords. Or they can become myths, like a lady on an island who can turn men into pigs, or ladies singing from rocks to lure boats to disaster. Or they can become even darker or scarier, like stories about succubi, or trolls, or witches. And the ladies who turn into that kind of story? Well." Beatrix stabbed the lapis fabric as she set her mouth in a grim line. "'Thou shalt not suffer a witch to live.'"

Myra's blue eyes went wide as saucers, her long lashes catching the light in the sewing room and casting spidery shadows on her pale cheeks. "What about the house? Couldn't she hide there?"

"Sometimes. But not forever. Sometimes, being safe meant letting the world reset itself for a while. Letting things settle, so people would focus on other stories instead of inventing tales about the house and who lived there. And that meant the Lady had to leave. Sometimes for a few years, and sometimes for a lifetime. Until stories became memories, and memories faded into the river's mist, and it was safe to return as someone else."

"Did the mansion wait for her?"

"Always. It was a part of her, and she was part of it. And guess what else?"

"What?" Myra leaned forward, breathless.

"She never really left it behind." Beatrix put the quilt square down on the table. "Do you want to see it?"

· 13 ·

PARKHURST, ARIZONA, 2015

"WHAT DOES HE MEAN, IT'S HIS HOUSE? HOW CAN IT BE his room?" Myra paced back and forth, her heart keeping time with her steps pounding across the wide plank floors.

"Hold on. There are some attachments."

"Don't click on any attachments!" Myra shouted. "My whole life is on that computer!"

Gwen rolled her eyes. "Here. I'll check it on my phone, and then it won't be on your computer." She reached into her handbag—a crocodile print in lime green, consistent with her usual level of subtlety—and scrolled her thumb absently over the phone in her hand, then gasped. "Myra. You have to see this."

"Please tell me it's not a penis."

"Jesus, you *have* looked at some attachments, haven't you? No, it's not a penis." Gwen held up her phone, a picture of a bed on the screen. The bed had an oak headboard with sliding panels, a blue counterpane with crushed velvet spread across its surface. "He's got some attention to detail, that's for damn sure. He's not the first one who's tried to re-create a room from the Mansion, though."

Myra couldn't speak. She held out her hand toward the phone, wriggled her fingers in a silent demand. Gwen handed it over.

"Like I said, it's a good imitation. But we've seen better. Remember that couple in Sweden? The ones with the bathroom? Now, that was an imitation. Avocado fixtures and everything, and they still made it classy! You've got whole shops on Etsy that try to reproduce stuff from the Mansion, you know." Gwen frowned. "One of these days, we need to get around to sending some cease and desist letters. Why do you have that look on your face, anyway? It's just an old bed. That kind of headboard was a popular design in the seventies. He could have gotten it anywhere."

"I'm not looking at the bed."

"The bedspread, then? God, crushed velvet's anywhere. You can get it at Walmart. I don't know why anyone would get it anywhere, of course, but there's no accounting for taste—"

"I'm not looking at the bed, Gwen. I'm looking at the credenza." Myra pointed at the upper-right corner of the photo.

"That's kind of a cool piece, isn't it? I like that aqua color. It even makes the bedspread look like it's part of some ocean-toned beachy color scheme instead of a polyester adventure in terrible taste. What's that part over on the right side?"

"It's a record player."

"A vinyl lover! I'm not sure if that makes me more or less creeped out." Gwen looked at Myra's face and frowned again. "I think, from your expression, it makes me more creeped out. How do you know it's a record player?"

"Because I have that same piece of furniture. Well, a smaller version of it. The Mansion has it."

"Really? I don't remember seeing it, but you've got all sorts of stuff in there."

"You haven't seen it. It's in a room that I—a room I redecorated. It isn't there anymore."

"Did you ever post it?"

"No. Never."

"Are you sure?"

"I'm completely sure. No one's ever seen it."

"Well, if it was a miniature, it's possible it was modeled on a full-sized piece of furniture. It's weird, but it's not impossible."

Myra pointed again. "Look at that leg. The one underneath the record player."

"The pink one? What about it? I mean, it doesn't really match the piece."

"That's because the piece has hairpin legs. But one of them was broken, so I replaced it with a leg from another piece I took apart, just as a temporary fix, until I could get another hairpin fitting. The leg came from a desk. A wobbly pink one. I didn't bother to repaint it."

Gwen squinted at the photo again and flicked her thumb across the screen, zooming in. "That's . . . weird."

"No." Myra shook her head slowly, the outward borders of the room going fuzzy at the edges. "It's impossible."

Gwen took the phone back and started scrolling again. "Nothing's impossible for a determined-enough fan. That cease and desist idea is sounding better and better, though. And maybe we ought to talk to someone if we're veering right into Creepsville. Wait. No way." She squinted at the screen again. "That can't possibly be right."

"What?"

"This picture. It can't be real." She held up the screen, and Myra didn't have to look closely at all, because she somehow knew from the top of her blond frizz to the tips of her toes what the photograph would show, and she was right.

Alex Rakes, the essay's author—if you could call it an essay—sent another picture with his submission, and this one was a photo of the Minuscule Mansion itself. Myra had never posted pictures of the full house. There were hints of its contours on the site, as she highlighted and photographed the different rooms, but they were parts of a whole that was always changing in ways she didn't think the world would understand. Gwen had pushed and cajoled her into sharing her pictures and stories, but she couldn't make her share everything, and the whole of the Mansion—its hinges and brass buckles, its little wheels, the platform Grampa had made—were just for her.

Alex's photos showed the outside of the house photographed from some distance beneath it, perched on a wide hill. The wrought iron fence was painted a fetching cream color, and the carving on the front door was somewhat concealed beneath a layer of triumphant crimson. Myra took the phone and turned it over, almost sure she'd be able to see the back of the house, where its brass buckles should be. A house this big, this real, shouldn't hinge open, of course.

By rights, though, it shouldn't exist at all.

· 14 ·

ELLIOTT, ARIZONA, 1985

"TRIXIE, CAN YOU TELL ME A STORY?" MYRA SNUGGLED into the space between the crook of Beatrix's arm and her slight body, which was always the warmest spot in any room.

"It'll be time for bed soon, Myra. If you'll let me tuck you up in bed, I'll tell you a story." Beatrix padded silently around the A-frame's large central room, switching off lamps, turning off the television. "It's been a long, rainy day, and I'm so impressed with the square you quilted. Your little eyes must be so tired!"

Myra nodded. "I wanted to finish my name."

"You did such a great job with that runner stitch. Perfect and even and tiny, like you wrote every letter with a pen. Everyone will always know you made that square."

"Can you show me how to make clothes, like you?"

"Every tool I'm showing you is something you can use to make clothes. We can start cutting out and pinning patterns tomorrow before your mama comes to pick you up. Or we could make clothes for some of those little clothespin dolls. Would you like that?"

Myra shook her head. "I have enough clothespins." They had made a little family—the first looked like Myra, yellow yarn like an uncontrolled halo around her head, a dress fashioned from a handkerchief of Trixie's. Then another, with hair the color of Trixie's, a brown yarn with a few threads of red, but cut short. She used a ballpoint pen to color small dots on the clothespin's round cheeks and chin and under its drawn-on nose, around its gentle smile. The last clothespin was smaller, wearing a little dress like the bigger clothespin. Though Trixie asked if she wanted to keep them in the Mansion, Myra put them to bed in the hatbox where they kept the furniture. The Mansion wasn't a dollhouse, and these weren't dolls. They were practice.

"I want to make an apron for the kitchen, for when we make cookies," Myra said.

"That's a really easy place to start. Good idea."

"And then I want to make a gown for Mom."

Trixie smiled. "That may be a bit of a leap, but it's not bad to have a goal in mind. You just have to focus on that next stitch."

"Every stitch a good thought, every thread a memory."

"That's right, my little acorn. That's what sewing does. It gives us a way to warm and shelter the ones we love, even if we can't be there to do it ourselves. Just like your grampa and his buildings, like your cabin and this house."

"Like the mansion on the river."

"That's right."

"Can you tell a story about the Lady?"

"I don't see why not." Trixie scooped up Myra into a floppy bundle of sleepy four-year-old wrapped in a crocheted afghan and carried her up the stairs to the loft and trundle bed where she spent Diane's late college nights. Myra's eyelids fluttered in the dim lamplight.

"Did the Lady have a family? Like us?"

"Not for a long, long time. But over time, as the years flowed into centuries, and countless souls passed in and out of her care, and the world grew more suspicious—those dark and scary stories I told you about—fewer people came for refuge, and the house felt empty and invisible and cold. The Lady felt herself begin to ebb, like the river slowing at the bottom of the hill."

"Was she dying?"

"She could choose to. She could fade away into the chambers beneath her feet and let her spirit return to the unseen flames under the earth, and her house would fade into the mist in that curve of the river. But if she didn't want to do that—if she wanted the refuge to live on—she needed to find a way to transfer what she knew and let someone else take over the burden she held. Her spirit would have to pass into someone with the energy to carry on. But she needed help."

"When I need help, I ask my mom."

"So did the Lady. She asked the ground beneath her feet, and the ground gave up a place to store all that she knew, a small place to keep it safe until she found another willing to take it."

"Like a locket?"

"Something like a locket. The ground gave her a stone, bluer than the deepest depths of the river flowing by and through the caves below, cracked through with silver like the veins of a beating heart."

"That sounds pretty. But I wish it were pink."

Trixie laughed. "We can't always choose the details of our burden, Myra. But we bear it just the same."

"What did she do with the stone?"

"She kept it in her house."

"The big one, or the little one?"

"You have a lot of questions for someone who should be going to sleep." Trixie tucked the blanket on the folding bed under Myra's chin. "Both. The little one came from the big one, and they were linked, no matter where they were. She always kept the little one with her. Until she could find a new keeper."

"Did she ever find one?"

"She did. She brought one into the world herself, and later—much later—another one was put into her arms. In that way, I suppose you could say she found two. But both times, she failed." Beatrix sighed. "It isn't enough to find a new keeper. There has to be a match. And there needs to be time enough, and love enough, to complete the transfer. The first time, there wasn't enough love. And the second, there wasn't enough time." She kissed the top of Myra's head. "But three is a pretty powerful number."

· 15 ·

ATLANTIC OCEAN
(ABOARD THE *QUEEN MARY*), 1937

THE MORNING LIGHT SPARKLED ON WATER THAT SPREAD to every horizon, the cloudless bowl of sky overhead glaring white. Willa held a black silk parasol overhead, wishing that the faint breeze would do a better job cooling her neck beneath her short waves of russet hair. Her dark blue traveling suit drew the sun's rays like a magnet, and she felt hot enough to combust. But the ocean liner's wide upper deck was the only airy place available, and Willa was stronger near the water. She breathed deeply and let the air from her lungs blend into the salt and heat.

The young man who approached behind her thought that he was being quiet. Willa could feel in his quiet gait that he did not intend to disturb her. He wouldn't speak aloud unless she spoke first, but she could feel the resonance of longing in the air, a wish for conversation. Willa had watched him watching her at dinner the night before, holding a soup spoon full of cream of asparagus for so long that the substance congealed before he could tear his eyes from her face. It wasn't the first time she had been noticed, but it was the first time in an eternity that she could recall feeling that vibration.

She turned away from the ocean and ran her silk glove along the railing, making eye contact with the young man. She watched as his face opened into a wide and welcoming grin. The extra oil in his hair gleamed on sandy-brown curls that weren't quite tamed, and his beard glinted with a hint of fire. Willa smiled at him. "Don't I know you from somewhere?"

"I was lucky enough to be a dining companion at your table last night, yes." The young man's grin held a hint of invitation. He was withholding the full truth, and she could tell that he recognized she knew it.

"Before that," Willa said. "I think I've seen you—"

"In class, perhaps." He shrugged with a nonchalance too practiced to be real. "I have a great appreciation for the arts."

"Ah, yes. That's it. Third row from the back of the gallery seats, if I'm not mistaken. Hard to miss the shine from your hair."

"It's nice to be remembered, though I'm not sure 'shiny hair' is the feature I'd like to be most known for. You, for example, I remember for your painting. You're a very skilled portraitist, particularly given the fact you were painting yourself. I didn't see a mirror, either. Do you have your own face memorized?"

Willa closed her eyes and thought of the bright lights in the open studio, dozens of easels arrayed around a central pillar featuring a subject the artists could choose to paint, or not. She had enrolled in the course at the University of London as a distraction, needing some way to fill her hours as she listened for some signal that it was time to return to Lockhart, and to move back into the house, ostensibly left to her by her deceased aunt who was really—as always—an earlier version of herself. The first time she walked into the class, she was surprised to see the lecture hall seating on one side of the room, and more surprised to see observers who attended. She found out only later that the open studio hours attracted several skilled artists of some repute, and the opportunity to watch them paint was advertised. The young man had attended only twice, but she had noticed him both times, and the second time she realized it was his scent that attracted her notice. He smelled faintly of old timbers, water, and wet stone. Like Lockhart. Like home.

She did have her own face memorized. But she wouldn't tell him that. "Just because you didn't see a mirror doesn't mean I wasn't using one," Willa said.

"Well, your skill was apparent all the same. What did you do with the portrait?"

"I brought it with me. It's with my luggage. I thought it might make the house seem more like mine after being empty for so long."

"Ah, yes, to the Manor born. That place always looked lonely to me. But you looked lonely out here, too, staring out at the ocean by yourself. It's terribly hot out here, don't you think?"

"I couldn't stand another moment indoors."

"That's entirely understandable. I couldn't stand another moment indoors without you."

"I think that perhaps you have forgotten yourself, Mr.—"

"Rakes. Rutherford Alexander Rakes. And my apologies for forgetting things. It should surprise you not at all to hear that you have that effect on people, Miss Laurie."

"Ah, yes. I am Willa Laurie, though I suppose we're past that, seeing

as you've obtained my name without any need for a formal introduc-
tion. How . . . refreshing." The rules of society were particularly rigid in
London—as rigid as they'd been in France, and in Virginia, and in
every other populated place that had formed and grown in the wide
world around her gates. It was exhausting when she had to leave,
spending years or decades away from her refuge in Lockhart. It was
exhausting to be a woman traveling alone, rooting out the places
where that solitude was less remarkable or remarked upon. It meant
never staying anywhere for long, and she had left France in rather a
hurry, feeling disturbances in the unfamiliar ground and anxiety in the
crowd of people around her. Something important—something violent
and desperate—was coming.

And Willa had been long enough away for Aunt Amarantha's death
to become plausible, pinned on age and a reclusive reluctance to see
anyone but her beloved niece in her small pied-à-terre in Paris. The
uncanny resemblance between the women—and their seeming timelessness, and the fact that they were never anywhere together—might
have been more noticeable if the situation lingered overlong. As it was,
Willa said her beloved aunt had gone to take the air in Nice, and went
to meet her there. When Willa returned to Paris alone to close up the
apartment in grief, all seemed natural. And then she was gone.

Willa and Rutherford fell into companionable silence, their hands
next to each other on the metal railing. Willa hadn't just noticed Rutherford Alexander Rakes in her painting class, the way his eyes followed
her hand with its soft brush across the canvas. She noticed him again
the moment they had boarded the ship together, when he stood aside
and motioned for her to precede him up the narrow ramp. She had
sneaked an extra sway into her gait, lengthened her spine in a way that

drew attention to her white and slender neck, her dark hair tapered to a point beneath her bob.

He was correct that she had a forgetful effect on people. She had a strange ability to impose a kind of absentmindedness in those around her. But she was not going to tell Rutherford how rare it was for her to care that she was noticed, or that she had never found herself longing more for someone to remember her. Something in the air between them crackled, like lightning about to strike some miles away.

To anyone observing the two along the rail, their distance from each other would have seemed completely appropriate. But Willa felt Rutherford's presence as closely as if his breath caressed her cheek.

"Has anyone told you that your name sounds like something out of a Brontë novel?" Willa asked.

Rutherford laughed. "Not in so many words. It's a family name, and you can't pick family. Can't account for taste, either. But you can find a nickname. My friends call me Ford."

"Am I your friend?"

"I'd like that very much."

"You don't know anything about me, Ford."

"I don't? Hasn't anyone ever told you that an ocean liner is a floating gossip mill? I know that you're American but you've always lived abroad. I know you attended Oxford and summered in Paris. I know where you're headed."

"Do you know you're conversing with an unmarried woman?"

"Your marital status was the very first inquiry I made."

"I've been the subject of inquiries before, but none quite so determined. Or so bold."

"I've heard fortune favors the bold, and I hoped you might, too. I couldn't let this ship reach port without trying to meet you." Ford moved his hand only an inch in Willa's direction on the railing, which seemed to carry a magnetic charge. "Besides, I had to know more about this beauty and why she was moving into the Witch's Manor."

"Oh, please tell me it's not really called that."

Ford shrugged. "It was when I was growing up. I never paid it any heed."

Willa narrowed her eyes. "Did anyone?"

"You know how kids are." Ford shuffled from side to side. "It's been mostly empty for years, you know. For as long as I can remember. I don't think anyone's lived there since my dad was a child."

"People have sheltered there, I'm sure. And my aunt always had caretakers for the place, at least enough to make sure it didn't fall into complete disrepair."

"Was your aunt the Lady of the House?"

"I don't know what you mean."

"The Lady. When I was growing up, kids called her either the Lady of the House or the Witch, depending on who was talking. Kids I knew only ever talked about it when they were daring each other to do something, like touching the gate while crossing your fingers, or hopping the fence to tap on a window. Silly stuff. I was much older when I heard the house had an owner, and people just called her the Lady. No one ever saw her."

Willa shook her head. "She didn't live there."

"Why not?"

"I don't think she felt welcome there. She became a traveler."

"Like her niece."

"Yes, like me. But she always stayed connected to the house."

"People still saw her in the windows, or so they said." Ford smiled again. "I didn't believe them, of course, and I never saw anyone. It always looked lonely to me, the house. Like it missed having someone who cared about it. Last I saw it, it looked like it was being held up by ivy and wisteria vines."

"There are worse ways to be supported."

"That may be true, but an empty house always makes me sad." Ford reached into an inside pocket of his jacket and pulled his hand out wrapped around something small. "I guess that's because my family specializes in filling them." He reached for Willa's hand and, as he deposited a minute rocking chair in her palm, she felt a spark pass between their fingers. "You can keep that, if you like it."

"It'd take quite a while to fill a mansion with furniture this size."

Ford laughed. "That's just a sample. Some of the manufacturers in Europe give them away. The real salesmen's samples are bigger, of course, but I think they figure a little goodwill through dollhouse furniture still shows off their craftsmanship. I was searching for new cabinet-makers and artisans to make furniture for my family's store."

"Where you presumably sell bigger pieces than this."

"Indeed. We're in an old warehouse on the river. We've built quite a reputation, in fact—customers come from as far away as DC and Boston, even Charleston. We only import and sell the very best."

Willa looked at the rocking chair in her hand. It was a gooseneck rocker, its gentle curves carved out of dark-stained cherry. The seat and back were upholstered in a Florentine tapestry in rich shades of green and burgundy and cream. It was beautiful but also welcoming—the kind of furniture whose beauty didn't intimidate. "I have a place where this can live."

"The real chair, you mean? We'll be getting a shipment in the next few months. I ordered twenty of them."

"I'd love to see one when you do, but I was talking about this one."

Ford narrowed his eyes. "You're petite, I grant you, but—"

"Would it be too forward of me to invite you to my cabin?"

His eyes widened. "Very forward indeed, but in the best possible way."

"Don't get any ideas. I just want to show you something."

"We may be seen."

"Does it matter?"

"Not to me."

"Then come along." Willa led Ford past other well-dressed passengers gathered on the deck in search of any breath of breeze, ignoring their side-cast glances as they walked toward the first-class cabins. Willa's was small and on the interior of the ship, a reflection of some caution with money, but still more than Ford would have expected a recent college graduate to spend. Inside, on the floor, a narrow trunk took up much of the floor space not occupied by the narrow bed. Willa unlatched the brass buckles and, before Ford's curious face, hinged open an entire world.

"Is that—is that the mansion?"

"It is."

Ford knelt in front of the house, reaching out a finger to trace the carving on the front door. "I've seen many dollhouses, but the detail on this one is uncanny. Truly exquisite work. Is it French made?"

"It isn't."

"Swiss, then?"

"No. American."

Ford whistled. "And here I've been searching for craftsmen overseas. You have to put me in touch with whoever made this—I'd love to see their work."

"It was handed down to me. My—aunt. Had it."

"That's amazing. It doesn't seem old at all. It looks better than I remember the old mansion looking, that's for sure. Where will you put the chair?"

"Somewhere cozy. I haven't decided yet."

"I think it would look nice here, in front of the library fireplace." Ford reached toward Willa's hand and retrieved the gooseneck rocker. "There, that's lovely. It needs a friend, though."

"Oh, I don't keep dolls."

"No, I mean another chair. For the other side of the fireplace." He grinned at Willa. "Or where am I going to sit in this mansion of ours?"

"You've embraced a plural noun a bit more quickly than I think I'm prepared to."

"Then I'll have to keep working on it. Have you ever even laid eyes on the place? Do you know how much work it needs?"

"Of course." Willa paused to find a plausible explanation. "In photographs. Enough to know it's manageable."

"The optimism of youth." Ford shifted nearer again, and Willa let his words go uncorrected, let him see her unlined face and not the centuries behind her eyes. People see what they want to see. Ford saw someone who needed protection, and with the headlong abandon of any young man, he'd already jumped into true love with both feet. This wasn't the first time Willa had seen such a thing happen, but it was the first time that she felt an answering tug in her own feet, a physical longing to jump in after him.

Part of that longing, she knew, was exhaustion. Willa faced a task she had confronted so many times before: returning to the refuge she was tethered to, and rebuilding a life as if it were a new thing and not a story she'd woven from the warp and weft of past lives countless times. This time, the life she had assumed for herself belonged to someone young: a niece, an heir to an unmanageable property bequeathed by a deceased aunt. As humanity and society ebbed and flowed around her, she had to establish herself again, and act as if it were the first time.

But there was something beyond the exhaustion. She felt an echo of this young man's energy in her own bones, and realized that letting someone share in her life might also mean letting someone shoulder a portion of the burden that never left her. She let herself wonder—not for the first time—what it might be like to feel protected, and to be less alone. To take refuge in someone else, having offered it so often herself. Someone who felt like home, whose scent evoked the wide sweep of river where she spent the long years of her life alone.

And then, there were other truths to face. An unwed woman in possession of a vast estate was a truth universally accepted to be unacceptable in polite Virginia society. She didn't need society to accept her, but she did need it to leave her alone, not try so hard to invade and bring what was unconventional to heel. That boundary had become harder and harder to maintain.

"It's easier to be optimistic with friends," Willa said. "I haven't had many."

"Well, then, Willa. It's never too late to start."

· 16 ·

LOCKHART, VIRGINIA, 2015

ALEX'S TUXEDO STRETCHED TOO TIGHTLY ACROSS HIS shoulders. He hated formalwear and always tried to find a way around it; even in high school, when he took his best friend's sister to the senior prom, he wore a thrift store suit with a tuxedo shirt tucked underneath, his favorite steel-toed boots peeping out from beneath his trousers. Why hadn't he tried the same strategy tonight? Prom was probably the last dance he attended; now, at thirty-four, he was at least fifteen years past the last time he'd had to worry about one. Now that he stopped to consider it, he couldn't remember why he was wearing a tuxedo in the first place, or standing in this ballroom, its parquet floors gleaming beneath crystal chandeliers that swayed in a slight breeze, their prisms tinkling like chimes. And then there was the music, a Chopin étude storming across the room with no piano in sight, the tune originating in some distant, unseen room. Alex couldn't remember why he came to this dance, or why he was the only one in

attendance, but the music built to a volume that was crashing overhead, stealing his breath—

Alex sat bolt upright in bed, and the ballroom faded away into mist.
His room was dark, the ceiling dappled with faint light cast from
streetlamps on the sidewalk far beneath the mansion, wobbling beams
through leaded glass panes. The air was chill enough to see his breath.
He needed to find a better way to seal away the old house's drafts and
vowed again to spread the windows with cellophane, as he'd been
meaning to for months. There were so many windows. Everything
about the house was too big, and sometimes Alex couldn't blame his
father for preferring the postmodern comfort of his soaring riverside
loft downtown. But the mansion took on a lonely cast when no one
lived there. It felt warmer, more welcoming, when someone was in
residence. Even if that person was Alex, and Alex was very much
alone.

The dream's étude couldn't seem to let him go, playing in his head
long after the rest of the dream faded, and it took a moment to realize
the music was real. He looked toward the mismatched credenza with
its record player, but the turntable was still. The piano was coming
from somewhere else.

The mansion didn't have a piano anymore. There had been one,
belonging to his grandmother, that used to stand in the library. It hadn't
been there since Alex was a small child.

The music transitioned from meticulous Chopin to bright and
cheerful Mozart, and Alex swung his feet over the wide plank floors,
walked to the paneled bedroom door, and turned the brass doorknob.
The door squeaked as if expressing annoyance at the late hour. Alex
walked out into the hallway, trying to trace the music to its source. It

swept from the foyer below, crashing around the elbow of the curved staircase, careening against the walls like a trapped current. He padded down the stairs.

The house was exactly as he left it when he retired to bed with his MacBook and his iPhone and his iPad and his Kindle, every blinking, rectangular link with which he tethered himself to the world and its endless problems, every screen a torch in the darkness of his own loneliness. The carved front door was still locked. The black-and-white ceramic tiles in the entryway were cold, Alex's bare feet leaving condensation outlines of his high arches, his narrow toes.

When the mansion had a piano, the old upright Steinway sat between the arched windows in the library, underneath the oil portrait of Willa Rakes, her dark blue eyes peering out beneath a fringe of russet curls. Her style was difficult to pin down; her smile was full of warm beauty with an undercurrent of mischief. She had vanished from Alex's life so completely, and so long ago, that he could never be sure if the images in his head came from his own memory. His father kept no photos of her. He remembered she played the piano, but couldn't remember how long after her disappearance the piano was removed. He could almost see an impression of the wheels in the thickly woven rug.

The music wasn't coming from the library. It had faded and surged and faded again as he walked through the house, its origin impossible to trace. As he stood in front of Willa, it receded again, a shadow of a sound that made him question whether it came from outside or inside his head, until it stopped completely. He tilted his head to match the angle of his grandmother's. "Did you play Chopin and Mozart? Or only 'Chopsticks'? I honestly can't remember." The portrait gazed back at him, unchanging.

He had almost closed his bedroom door again before he heard a few matched notes of "Chopsticks" following him lightly up the stairs, like a cat he'd never catch.

He wouldn't be able to sleep again. Every night like this—and there had been several since he moved back to Lockhart, against his better judgment, at his father's repeated and increasingly desperate behest to come and help with the business—he would find himself staring at the ceiling, or a screen, or both, until dawn blotted pink across the morning sky. He would rise bleary-eyed, maybe brew some coffee in the silent kitchen and sit on the wide back sweep of veranda, overlooking the slope of yard and oaks to the river below.

He would wonder again if he should move into the bigger bedroom at the rear of the house, with arched windows overlooking the curve of silver water, where the sun rose first each day. But he preferred the irregular geometry of the turret room overlooking the street. Though he had only recently moved back into it for the first time since he was a small child, the room still felt like his. It was the room he slept in until his father sent him away for boarding school when he was five. The fact that he now collapsed into its bed as a world-weary thirty-four-year-old didn't diminish its attraction, and he wouldn't feel as comfortable anywhere else. The room at the rear of the top floor had been empty since Willa disappeared, and no one—not him, and certainly not his father—felt at home in the space. It didn't even hold any furniture, other than an enormous mahogany chifforobe that was far too large and heavy to move.

But as of yesterday, he knew that space—and every other space in the house—had a mirror image, albeit a much smaller one, somewhere across the country. Decorated by a hermit, evidently. In some distant desert. He tried to remember the name of the blog the girl had shown him at the store, and typed miniature mansion into the search box of his MacBook.

The very first result was *The Minuscule Mansion of Myra Malone*. He clicked the name, and his eyes were immediately assaulted with a barrage of pink words, and while the color struck him as something a seven-year-old girl might pick, the font and layout and overall design of the space seemed much more sophisticated. Whimsical, like the boutique toy store down the street from Rakes and Son—a little quirky in a way that made you want to browse awhile, thinking you might come across something unusual that no one else had noticed. Given, of course, that he'd already noticed the namesake Mansion was his actual family home, he couldn't imagine what other unusual things could possibly surprise him.

He clicked on "Frequently Asked Questions."

What is the Minuscule Mansion? The Mansion is a miniature house—some might say a dollhouse, but please don't, it takes slights very personally—in an eclectic architectural style that embraces Victorian and Gothic influences, as well as a few other mishmashed elements thrown in just for the hell of it. I don't know why, and I've never asked, so if you're an architect or someone with interest in architecture, *yes I get your emails and no I don't know why it looks this way.* It's the kind of house that would drive a homeowners' association wild, but since it's tiny and the only house that occupies my attic, the neighbors are pretty quiet about its oddities, and I don't like to pry.

Alex smiled. The real, full-sized mansion was a not-infrequent stop for tour buses in Lockhart, and sometimes their passengers were bold enough to enter the gate and knock on the carved front door, try to get some details about the very mishmash that Myra—Alex felt like he could call her Myra—pointed out. After the first few visits, Alex learned to stop answering the door. And there was no HOA on that wide hill, where the mansion was the only residence for miles, having predated a sweep of riverfront parklands and forests preserved through conservation easements and ordinances. The subdivisions that had sprung up at the bottom of the hill, however, were precisely the kind of cookie-cutter neighborhoods where a turreted house with gingerbread trim, pointed arch windows, stone columns, and a wraparound veranda would set off alarm bells. Possibly from a fire alarm, because some of those cookie-cutter residents would probably like to see it burn down.

The few classmates Alex had from the Lockhart area at boarding school went wide-eyed with the knowledge that Alex lived in "Witch's Manor" or "the Lady's House" or, as some parents called it, "That Monstrosity," but Alex had always attributed the odd mix of styles to the age of the land there, the fact that a house had reportedly been on the site for centuries and had grown along with Lockhart into an amalgamation of whatever seemed most imposing at the time. It wasn't imposing to everyone, of course—not to someone who lived there, or to someone who loved it. It was imposing to outsiders who approached without the right frame of mind. Ordinary people, who wanted adherence and conformity and normality. People who had their own shelters and didn't much care for the kind the Mansion had to offer.

Not that it had regularly sheltered anyone to speak of in quite some time. Alex's father had often left the place vacant, only occasionally renting to tenants for a year or two in exchange for exorbitant rent, a good story, and some promise to provide just enough maintenance to keep the structure from collapsing on its hill. Single tenants stayed longest, but almost never through the term of a lease. Tenants with families didn't stay long at all, often complaining it seemed impossible to get their children out of the house for anything, so transfixed were they by the many rooms and secret passages. The Rakes family's longtime employee, Ellen, intermittently stayed in the house to freshen it, insisting that a few coats of paint or removing a few layers of dust were all the interventions the place needed to feel like home. It seemed more like one when she stayed there, but the house still felt incomplete somehow.

Alex clicked on the next frequently asked question.

Where is the Minuscule Mansion? My granny Trixie used to say the Mansion is everywhere and nowhere, which I think is just a spooky way of saying, "We keep it in the attic so no one cares whether or not we dust." The Mansion doesn't entertain visitors and keeps its own counsel, but it lets me know when it needs something, and it gives me comfort to think about the other hands that have helped it tell stories. It shows me the stories it wants to tell.

Who are you? It's right there in the name, folks, but I didn't pick it—my name, or the name of the site. Gwen, much as she loves me, told me that some people find dollhouses creepy and that it helps to have a name. Otherwise, she insists, it's just a bunch of alarmingly tiny furniture. As much as I've tried to tell her that the Mansion isn't a doll-

house, against my better judgment, I agreed. So, fine. I'm
Myra Malone. I live somewhere in Arizona, I'm somewhere
in my thirties, although I prefer to think of myself as "time-
less," and I have yellow hair that is almost, but not entirely,
less manageable than the frizzy yarn you see on my clothespin doppelgänger. I inherited the Mansion when I was six
years old, and it's given rhythm and meaning to my days
ever since, which I realize as I type makes me sound *every
bit as creepy* as Gwen said. Sorry. I promise I'm very normal.
Please don't come and verify that personally.

Where does the furniture come from? Here and there. Some of
the pieces are original to the Mansion and were handed down
to me by Trixie when I inherited it. Some—very few—are pieces
that have been sent to me by readers like you, and it always
amazes me when something shows up in the mail that looks
like it was meant to be here. It doesn't happen often, but sometimes you'll see a piece in the Mansion that came from the
outside world but fits so seamlessly that you'd never notice.

A good example is the little *Oxford English Dictionary* on the
podium in the library, which actually has about a dozen pages
you can flip through that are legible only with a magnifying
glass. The podium used to hold a tiny Bible, but I much prefer
the *OED*, and it came to me from a reader in Denmark.

Some pieces are Frankenfurniture—stuff I've cobbled together from a bunch of different things to make something

different. And some are entirely handmade by me. Grampa Lou was a woodworker and Trixie was an amazing seamstress, so some items, like the oak wardrobe in the biggest bedroom upstairs, are entirely original. I only bought the hinges and the knobs (true metalwork is a little beyond my skill set, although I can do amazing things with paste and epoxy), but the dresses and the cabinetry are all things I made and painted and sewed myself.

Don't look too closely at the sweaters folded on the top shelf—I went through a brief experimental mini-knitting stage after seeing some things online, and it's a knack I never quite mastered in regular size, let alone in an itty-bitty one. I'll tell you a little secret: only the clothing you see on top is real. If you see layers, I often use paper and paint to mimic the look of a folded sweater or hanging coat if I find myself impatient to photograph a room. If I think I'm going to redecorate soon, I don't always go back to replace those things with real ones, but sometimes I do. It depends on how long I can live with the knowledge that the room is secretly incomplete. And sometimes that's up to the Mansion. It knows its own mind about things.

That sounds familiar. Alex heard a few more plinking notes from the piano that no longer stood in the library and, on a whim, looked through the site's archives on the right side of the page, organized by room. Clicking on "Library" gave him the results he knew he should expect but still could not believe: while the details were somewhat different, there were numerous pieces of furniture arranged in precisely the same spots as their full-sized counterparts downstairs.

He navigated around the room virtually, looking so intently for similarities that he didn't notice the differences at first:

A dark-stained upright piano still graced the wall between two wide windows.

Above it, a portrait. Alex gasped as he recognized Willa Rakes mischievously gazing from a minute gilded frame, just the same as she did downstairs.

Except for the diagonal cut slashing across Willa's face, everything was identical.

Alex continued clicking on archive posts. Each paragraph, every quippy sentence, made Myra more real. At times, it felt like she was sitting in the room next to him, pointing out small features in the rooms he might otherwise have missed. Floral engravings on the handles of silver knives tucked into drawers. The way the light in a kitchen window sparkled against stone water in the farmhouse sink, the blue depths fashioned from swirls of agate, one small dish filled with small flecks of crystal to mimic bubbles. The light in Alex's room began to quiver and change as the sun rose above the horizon, and Alex still sat next to Myra, laughing at her jokes, longing to ask her about Willa's painting, ask her if she knew where Willa was, who they were to each other.

He didn't realize how motionless he was, or how long he had been that way, until he saw his father standing in his open doorway, a deep frown creasing his face. Alex jumped and slammed his laptop closed, recognizing a familiar feeling from boarding school: the feeling of getting caught with something illicit. The look on Rutherford's face confirmed that something was wrong, and evoked a much older feeling—something that harked back to when Alex had been sent away, young and terrified, to boarding school.

"What's going on here?" Rutherford's voice was harsh and suspicious with an undercurrent of fear. He shifted the bag he was holding from one hand to another, the grease spots on the paper showing that he'd stopped to get them both breakfast, as he did from time to time.

"Just—reading, Dad." Alex jumped up from the bed, stiff from hours of curling around his laptop, and stretched. "What are you doing here?"

"I brought breakfast. We're getting a shipment in today, and I wanted you to come and help with the unloading, so I thought a bribe might help." Rutherford reached into the bag and pulled out a glistening croissant, releasing steam into the bedroom, which had gone curiously cold. "When I came through the gate, I heard music and thought you might be up, but everything was dark downstairs."

"I haven't been down yet this morning."

"The music wasn't coming from your room."

"No." Alex yawned. "It wasn't last night, either. Was it piano? Has she at least moved on from 'Chopsticks'?"

Rutherford dropped the bag he was holding, opening his mouth like the bass he'd bring home from his fishing trips. His eyes darkened with fury. Alex remembered the look from his childhood, when his father's fists would clench as tightly as his jaw, every word a staccato hiss from behind his white teeth. Alex felt his feet shuffle backward against his own will, the memory of bewilderment and fear transforming him into a frightened child.

"*She* is gone. There is no *she* in this house. And I will not allow you to play tricks on me or act as if it's funny to say ridiculous things." Rutherford took a step toward his son, stabbing the air between them with an upraised finger as Alex took another step back toward the wide windows above the street. "Where were you playing music? Did you install an intercom, something like that? I was quite clear that you were not to make any changes to this house."

Alex shrugged, bewildered. "Dad, I don't know what you're talking about."

Rutherford, as usual, confused his son's perplexed reaction with nonchalance. "I said I didn't want you to move back in here—we could have kept the place rented and never set foot in here again—but you insisted, and I should have reminded you then what I'll remind you of now. You do not make decisions here. Not about the business, not about the house. And if you're going to play games with me or this real estate albatross around our family's neck, I'll cut you loose."

"Cut me loose? Oh, you mean like sending me to military school, Dad, as a small little kid, all by myself and terrified? Hate to break it to you, but you already played that card, so it doesn't have much punch as a threat these days. Or maybe I'll have to make my own way out in the world? I've done that, too, and I did just fine, not that you've ever asked me a single thing about my life." Alex felt his breath slow into jagged gasps, and his face and hands were freezing, as if he were trying to climb a mountain in a snowstorm. The sudden anger rising in his chest matched what he saw on his father's face, and it seemed to come from outside both of them, pouring into their bodies from the room in which they stood. "Why do you hate this place so much, any-way?" Alex demanded. "Why do you hate *me*? You could just get rid of us both!"

"You think I haven't tried?" Rutherford's face bore the desperation of a hunted man. "You don't know how hard I've tried to rid myself of this place."

"And me." Alex clenched his fists and set his shoulders back, the chill in the air seeping into his bones and clouding his breath in the charged atmosphere sparking between them. *Why is he so angry? Why am I so angry?* Crashing chords of Mendelssohn charged up the staircase, a musical earthquake building beneath the floorboards. *How did we get here from a bag of croissants?*

Rutherford shook his head, a deep breath sighing from his chest as the music died down around them both. "I never tried to get rid of you, Alex. I wanted to protect you."

Alex's right wrist burned with the memory of a poorly set break, the airless and jerking sensation of being dragged away from something he wanted so badly, so badly, but that his father wouldn't let him have. He felt younger than conscious thought would take him—two years old, perhaps—and the image blurred from view in a haze of pain and loss. "If you were trying to protect me from you, Dad, I learned to do that myself. I wouldn't have come back here otherwise."

"I wanted you to come back. But so did . . ." Rutherford trailed off, the hunted look on his face giving way to something like resignation. "I wish you'd find an apartment." He bent over suddenly, his right hand flying to his waist, his left hand thrusting into the air in a preemptive attempt to warn Alex away.

The cold air whipping through the room dissipated so quickly that Alex wondered if he'd imagined it. He leaped toward the cane-back chair in the corner and put it behind his father, stepping away as Rutherford sat down and they both pretended his sudden loss of strength was natural, almost casual.

"I'm fine right here." Alex walked toward the bureau in the corner. "Just sit and rest for a second. Give me five minutes to get dressed, and we'll go check out the shipment."

Rutherford's breathing slowed. The tension and anger receded from his face. He seemed grateful for the change of subject. "With any luck, there'll be a few more of those bamboo settees."

"With any luck, there'll be a fire at the warehouse before we can put any more of those travesties in stock." Alex laughed to see his father's shocked face. "Sorry. I hate them. And the insurance on them would buy a lot of funky thrift store remainders." The joke bounced lightly around the room, through clear air that no longer felt charged, anger melting into mist as suddenly and inexplicably as it had flared.

"Not all of us have your innate sense of sophistication, my boy. And for that my pocketbook, at least, is grateful. We couldn't feed ourselves with what a piece like that would fetch." Rutherford gestured toward the aqua credenza.

Alex shrugged. "When you don't have money, you find new ways to feed yourself, Dad. Just like you have to find new ways to love yourself when you feel unloved."

"You were never unloved."

"Save it for the family therapy sessions we'll never get around to. For now, let's go unload some ugly couches made of money."

· 17 ·

LOCKHART, VIRGINIA, 1937

WHEN THE SHIP LANDED IN NEW YORK CITY AND WILLA and Ford disembarked, what happened next began as simple playacting—a wholly familiar activity for Willa, and one that Ford seemed well versed in, too. He shouldered the trunk containing the miniature mansion himself before handing it off to a porter, quipping that he should take great care—*my wife can't travel without it.* He looked over his shoulder at Willa and raised his eyebrows in an expression that said, *All right?* And Willa nodded, because it felt right. It felt all right. Then they found a hotel, one Ford said he never stayed in, *too fancy for a guy like me, but now, with you . . .*

They checked in as Mr. and Mrs. Rutherford Rakes. And every guest book after that bore Ford's spidery handwriting with the same coupled names. In Philadelphia, a cabinetmaker who had known the family for years boomed his congratulations to the happy couple—*Your father didn't say a word, my wife will be heartsick that she missed it*—and Ford winked conspiratorially and said the word wasn't out yet.

Their subsequent path back to Lockhart had meandered slowly down the Eastern Seaboard. Ford had manufacturers and factories to visit, dotted in towns and workshops throughout the Northeast. He had eventual plans to return south, but none that were immediate, and Willa—once back on American soil—didn't feel the same urgency to move that she had felt beneath her feet in Europe. She knew she would return home eventually. In the meantime, she was content to remain with Ford.

In her past travels, she was pulled mostly to the water, crossing oceans to other shores and rivers, finding ships and other passages abroad. When she was away from Lockhart, she rarely stayed landlocked or on the same continent for long, instead working to outpace the stories that grew around her and eventually drove her to flee long enough for the rumors to die down, until death and distraction closed the mouths that carried them. But a woman traveling alone, in any era, set more mouths in motion. Ford was not the first man she had traveled with. But he was the first man she wanted to continue to travel with, wherever he might go.

At the next factory they visited, the owner came out to meet Ford with a telegram in his hand. *From your father.*

COME HOME IMMEDIATELY STOP

THIS WILL KILL YOUR MOTHER STOP

NOT HOW YOU WERE RAISED STOP

CALL WHEN YOU ARRIVE STOP

Ford ignored it. He ignored the next telegram, too, in Baltimore, on a silver tray in the front office of a man who specialized in adding exotic wood and stone and precious metal into pieces of furniture, interlacing them into the whorls and knots of wood in any desired pattern. Willa talked with him at length, amazed at the seamlessness of his designs, asked if he would accept a commission. An oak tree, with stone as blue as the sea she'd just crossed, set into a round table. They set a price, and Willa said she would send materials when she returned home to Lockhart.

Willa asked that night, as Ford lay beside her and ran his smooth hands up the inside of her leg, how long he was going to wait to face his family.

"As long as the accounts are paid," he said.

The next telegram, in Arlington, called his bluff.

NOT ONE MORE PENNY STOP

COME HOME IMMEDIATELY STOP

"I guess it's time to catch another train." Ford kissed Willa on the forehead. "I promise they aren't monsters."

"They may think I am." Willa clenched her jaw, reprimanding herself again for falling in love with a young man from too close to home, a family with roots in the soil that protected her. His familiarity came with a price she had already decided to pay, but she had let herself forget—for a short while, at least—that the price was not hers alone, and that Ford came from people she would have to meet and interact with. She couldn't have him all to herself. Not yet.

"What, because of the house? Nonsense. My father doesn't believe in fairy tales, and my mother is more likely to want to help redecorate than she is to cast aspersions on your aunt. We'll be fine." Ford kissed the top of her head. "Besides, Mom's been harrying me to settle down since before I knew what settling down even meant. A cousin of hers opened a boarding school down near Asheville right after I went to high school, and even a couple years down there weren't enough to turn me into whatever it was she thought I should be. But once she sees you—once she sees how happy I am—everything will click into place. I just know it."

The first dinner at the family home confirmed each of their suspicions, as different as those suspicions were. It was as if they attended two separate meetings. When they arrived at the Rakeses' austere Federal house, its orderly red bricks stacked with military precision, Willa felt her dread building as they ascended each stone stair to the knocker on the front door, a brass ring gritted in the teeth of an irritated-looking lion. The uniformed girl who opened the door curtsied quietly and gestured them into the parlor where Ford's parents waited, standing on either side of a marble fireplace.

Ford's father, Theodore "Teddy" Aloysius Rakes, stayed stone-faced as Ford introduced Willa. He didn't extend a hand in greeting or open his face into any expression Willa could discern. Once Ford finished his short sentence—*Father, Mother, I'm so pleased to introduce you to my wife, Mrs. Willa Rakes*—Teddy Rakes merely looked at the diminutive woman beside him, his wife, and nodded with the expectation that she would handle this strange social occasion by speaking for both of them.

Ford's mother stepped toward Willa and extended her hand. "I would love to say that we've heard so much about you, my dear, but I'm afraid we weren't given much chance." Mildred Elizabeth Rakes gazed at her son with reproach, then back at Willa. "We gleaned what we could, of course. We're so terribly sorry to hear about the loss of your aunt, and how distressing to lose her abroad. Were you very close?"

Willa cast her eyes to the ground in what she hoped was a convincing show of grief. "Not very. She paid for my education, for which I will always be grateful, but she was a very private woman and not much accustomed to the society of others, I'm afraid."

"And leaving you a foundling, a beautiful young thing like you, all alone in the wilds of France. It's such a shame she made no arrangements for you to be a companion or apply yourself to some other reputable calling. How fortuitous you found your way to England on your own. And then to have met someone so very kind with his heart, like our son." The *k* in *kind* cracked out of Mildred's mouth with a hard edge that seemed meant to lead a different word, like *careless*. So very careless with his heart, was Ford.

Willa smiled as if she heard only the gentle and melodious voice, and not the acid underneath the words. "My aunt left me well provided for." She reached for Ford's hand and he took it, grinning down at her with an expression that made clear where his loyalties lay.

"Of course she did," Mildred said. "Bless your heart."

They left after a meal that Willa found excruciating and Ford expressed went better than he expected, walking with a spring in his step to their car on the street. There was, indeed, a carelessness about him, but his mother's hard-edged assessment had not been fair, in Willa's view. Ford seemed the kind of person who could move through discomfort unperturbed, moving past awkwardness or social judgment with a good humor that could be mistaken for obliviousness, but Willa had come to recognize he picked up on exactly the same niceties and violations and judgments she did—he simply didn't care. There was a kind of shelter in the way he let rules bead up and roll right off his shoulders. He knew what mattered and what didn't, and his confidence made Willa feel secure.

Ford drove them back to the small inn where they would stay until the mansion was ready to occupy, as they both agreed—without having to talk about it—that the house on its wide sweep of river was where they belonged.

"Dad can be a tough nut to crack," Ford said. "But Mom warmed right up to you."

"Your father's a harder sort than a nut. More like a stone. And as to your mother—I think your temperature gauge may be off a bit." Willa leaned back in her seat and sighed. "She's very protective of you."

"Most mothers are."

"I think she doesn't like me at all."

"I think you're wrong. But does it matter?" Ford's fingers crept along the nape of her neck, pulling her head to rest on his shoulder. "I like you a lot."

"I like you, too. What are you going to do if they cut you off?"

"I suppose I'd have to conceive of some other way to support myself." Ford cast a sidelong glance at Willa. "Maybe throw myself on the mercy of a rich older woman."

Willa arched her left eyebrow. "You'd have to be very compelling."

"When we get back to our room, I'll be as compelling as I possibly can, just in case."

He compelled her again and again, releasing her from the tether she felt growing between her and the call of the mansion, the caves underneath. She had never felt any desire for release before. The fact that she could let go at all made her wonder what it might mean to let go forever, to finally let herself live a normal life, and pass the rest of her burden on to someone else. The decision was so great it paralyzed her, and she let herself drift through the current with Ford instead, unmoored by the need to think of anything but their happiness together.

PARKHURST, ARIZONA, 1988

MYRA COULDN'T STOP CRYING ABOUT THE CAKE, THE OLD nightmare rolling into her undisturbed sleep as it always did when the weather got cold. Even as her eighth birthday approached, three years had done nothing to fade her memories of the crash, or to stop it from colliding with her dreams.

It always started the same way, with Myra standing on a stool in Lou and Trixie's kitchen as Trixie guided her small hands on the ends of the rolling pin. They flattened the gumdrops individually, then sculpted them around toothpicks into leaves and blossoms pinned into the surface of the number five, for Myra's fifth birthday.

Myra longed for a garden like the one Trixie coaxed outside Grampa Lou's house, wisteria vines hanging from the eaves of the A-frame in a way that made Diane shake her head, never having seen that vine grow willingly in the Arizona desert before. The rosebushes bloomed pink and magenta and deep crimson with an undertone of blue, velvet depths that swallowed the light from the sun. Cuttings and vegetables from Trixie's garden filled the house with delicious scents regardless of season, and when Myra said she wanted her cake to be like that, too, Trixie said they'd try to make one together.

Their efforts to make a candy flower basket were so successful that Myra begged Trixie to take her back home to the mountains early, wanting to surprise her parents instead of waiting for them to drive down to pick her up. The weather wasn't good, but Myra was so excited that Trixie said they'd try, and maybe they'd manage to stay ahead of the storm.

Before baking the cake, they'd spent the morning the way Myra loved best—working together on the Mansion. Trixie had told her she was old enough to work on the library, and Myra arranged the miniature volumes by color and shape, stringing them like beads across the wooden shelves, interspersing them with the wisteria-painted porcelain every so often. As she worked, Trixie told her she had a special gift for her. *My greatest treasure*, she said, *and treasure is a responsibility, my little acorn, but I'll help you learn.*

Her smile as she removed the necklace from her own neck and fastened its scrolled silver clasp around Myra's was beautiful, imbued with the entrancing warmth that drew Myra like a moth to a flame. But it was also sad, and Trixie's face seemed older and more fragile as she patted the stone on Myra's chest. Myra felt a little sad, too, and lonely, though she couldn't say why—Trixie was still standing in front of her, but her presence seemed diminished. Dimmed, somehow. Still, though, she had always admired the necklace. It was heavier than she expected. She felt very grown up.

The slick rain pounding onto the highway at Lou and Trixie's house crystallized as their elevation climbed, and Trixie—behind the wheel of Lou's choice of car, an enormous sedan with rear-wheel drive—said they should turn back. Myra cried. She was so proud, and they were almost home, and she wanted them to see it. Trixie set her mouth and murmured, *Less ahead of us than there is behind, I suppose*, and pressed on, while Myra held the cake in her lap with great caution. Everything perfect. Everything magical.

The crash woke her as it always did, leaving her gasping in the cold alone, before anyone came to help. She always knew, in that moment, that Trixie was gone, because she felt it. She couldn't turn her head, and her eyes gazed upward into the white sky. She felt herself wanting to go wherever Trixie had gone, to let herself drift up among the spinning snowflakes and the quiet whisper of the wind along the highway.

A second crash sounded from the attic above her head, and Myra sat up, fully awake. She shook her head to clear the snowflakes and slipped her bare feet onto the floor, sprinting out of her bedroom door and up the stairs to the attic.

The Mansion was open, its brass buckles unmoored and the hinges spread wide. This, in and of itself, was not particularly unusual. Murmurs of music or flashes of light would sometimes beckon her upstairs in the wee hours of the morning, revealing a new room or secret passageway in need of decoration, and Myra's parents would find her asleep in the morning, her small form curled on the floor around the corner turret.

This morning, there was no new room. A few small notes emerged from deep inside at the back of the Mansion, where the library was. They were off-key and quiet, like a piano that has fallen out of tune and can't quite accept it.

Myra lowered herself to her knees, her heart in her throat, and peered into the library. The room looked destroyed, as if a small tornado had touched down in the heart of the house and then popped back up into the sky again, looking for other victims elsewhere. The books were scattered around the floor and hallway, some hanging precariously off the edges of upstairs floors, those that opened torn along their spines, paper fluttering in a breeze that was still blowing through the attic, though all the windows were closed. The room was cold enough to see her breath, which caught entirely when she saw the smashed porcelain all over the floor. The portrait above the piano had a wide slash across its face. Throughout the room, anything fragile or breakable was shattered. A corner bookshelf, once filled with porcelain vases and plates and teacups painted with wisteria vines, now looked as if it were coated in sparkling sand. No piece had shards big enough to mend, to glue together in the vain hope that something could be salvaged.

Myra ran one small finger along a shelf, porcelain dust like sugar clinging to her skin while she sobbed. The wisteria china came from Trixie's hatbox, and placing the tiny knickknacks was one of the first things Trixie showed her how to do, the very first time she showed her the Mansion. *Not too many things in one place, or the house can't breathe. But don't put just one thing on a shelf—groups of three and five, so nothing gets too lonely.* Plates, cups, candlesticks—every grouping smashed, leaving Myra herself very lonely indeed. She traced the contours of the bookcase, her fingertips feeling the carving that her tear-filled eyes couldn't see.

She heard a tiny *click* and a *whoosh*, and the bookcase swung open as if springs were behind it, filling the room with music and light.

· 19 ·

PARKHURST, ARIZONA, 2015

"ARE WE GOING TO WRITE HIM BACK?" GWEN SAT CROSS-legged on the floor next to the Mansion, her laptop propped on her long, folded legs, peering at the overflowing inbox of the Mansion's official email account. "Alex, I mean. Mr. Rakes. He of the terrible taste in bedroom furniture." She looked at Myra, saw her disapproving face, and grimaced. "Sorry, not sorry."

"That furniture is original to the house. Well, some of it is. Some of it's just original to the hatbox." Myra walked to the box and reached in, retrieving a pink tufted ottoman with a ruffle around the turned wood legs. She held it up to her face and frowned, as if trying to hear where the ottoman itself might want to be placed.

Gwen plopped her laptop on the floor and stretched her body out in her favorite yoga position—corpse pose, a flat and serene picture of stillness that always mismatched the energy inside her. "Hatbox would be a great name for a furniture store, I think."

"Great. You should open one."

"I meant for you."

"Could you stop coming up with business ideas for me, please? At least until we get through this latest one?"

"Fine. Have it your way. And that brings us back to doe, my deer, my *female* deer. Will you write your suitor back?" Gwen's singsong trilled through the attic and made Myra roll her eyes.

"This isn't *The Sound of Music*, Gwen, and you're no Maria. Also, he's not a suitor."

"Do I need to get the tuxedo doll back out and make more kissy sounds? He's a guy, your age, who's fascinated by the Mansion and the woman who maintains it. Granted, he's fascinated with it because he apparently lives in it, and he might be an off-kilter stalker, but every story starts somewhere!"

"You're a little too anxious to pair me off with a stranger for someone who claims to be my best friend."

Gwen laughed. "I'm not really pairing you off. And I've looked into him, you know. Not everyone's as good at keeping their photos off the internet as you." She sat up and grabbed her laptop again, then flipped the screen around to show a picture. The man on the screen was taller than the older man standing beside him, but the likeness between them was unmistakable. The younger man's hair was sandy brown, and his short beard and mustache were peppered with glints of red. Deep-blue eyes peered out above a sharp nose that held a pair of wireless glasses. He was laughing, holding his hand perched above his dour-faced father's shoulder. Myra peered at the caption. Rutherford Alexander "Alex" Rakes III shares a joke with his father, Rutherford Rakes, on the opening of their new furniture gallery.

Myra had never seen a man who looked less likely to joke than Rutherford Rakes (presumably *the Second*). He looked as if he'd been born frowning and that the years following that event had only served to confirm all his reasons for irritation.

Gwen nodded as if hearing Myra's internal thoughts. "Yes, okay, the dad looks like one of those angry Muppets who always shouted at Kermit the Frog from the box seats, but you have to admit the son's kinda cute."

"Why are we having this conversation right now?"

"Because he's submitted a bid to have lunch with you, Myra."

"He didn't write an essay."

"He didn't have to! Do you have any idea what your followers will do if you post what he *did* write? They'll lose their minds. A real house like the Minuscule Mansion? A real guy who lives in it, and who's your age, and who wants to pay to meet you? Do you have any idea the gold I could spin out of this pile of straw? God, it's like a reality show—" Gwen's face split into the widest grin Myra had ever seen cross her face. "Oh my God, it *is* a reality show. It's a *Today* show interview, at the very least. I need to make some calls."

"And you say I'm the creepy one."

"No. I say the Mansion is a little creepy. You, I like."

"I like you, too." Myra stared at Alex Rakes and his father, standing together in front of a furniture store—of all things—backed up against a flat canal-like expanse of southern river, brick warehouses dotted to the photo's edges. Something about the way Alex's eyes crinkled, the way they didn't have enough room on his face when he smiled, sparked a spreading warmth in Myra's chest, something she hadn't felt since the first time she met Gwen. It had been so long that she could hardly remember what the feeling meant: the filling of an empty place she hadn't known was there. And Alex—she felt like she could call him Alex—seemed to shift subtly in the photo on the screen, almost as if he felt her looking at him.

"I really like the new chandelier, by the way."

"The what?"

"In the library." Gwen pointed into the Mansion toward a sparkling chandelier hanging just above the Lady's portrait, its diminutive crystal prisms spinning rainbows against the walls, the furniture, the hand-painted titles on the shelves. "Another mail delivery?"

"Um—" Myra bit her lip. "Yes. I like it, too."

"Whoever sent it has excellent taste. It looks like it was meant to be there. Not many of the mailed-in pieces do."

Myra resisted the urge that she always had to confess everything to her best friend: that the chandelier wasn't mailed, wasn't sent, hadn't been there earlier that morning. That it had appeared, as if it grew out of the ceiling of its own volition, sometime in the last five minutes. While Myra looked at Alex's picture. Which she now felt herself compelled to do again.

Alex smiled at her from the screen, and the smile said the chandelier was meant to be there.

The smile said Alex was meant to be there, too.

Gwen shut the laptop and looked into Myra's eyes. "Wherever you are, you don't seem to be here anymore. Are you going to keep mooning at that photo, or are you actually going to contact the guy?"

Myra grimaced. "I don't even know how to start."

"It's like falling off a log, Myra. Only the log is a publicist, and you're falling into the warm and welcoming arms of a viral media sensation.

This metaphor is getting away from me. Point is: you have me. And you know what I do particularly well?"

"Push me into doing things I really, really don't want to do?"

"That, and talk to guys who don't know why they should be interested in what I have to say. Until I tell them."

"You're going to email him?"

"No. I'm going to call him. And then he's going to talk to you."

"When?"

Gwen already had her sleek rectangle of a smartphone held to her ear, and held her finger up to her mouth. "Now," she whispered.

"Gwen!"

"Shhhh." Gwen hit the speaker icon.

A polished voice rang through the cold attic air. "Rakes and Son, how may I direct your call?"

Gwen squared her shoulders, turning into the marketing genius version of herself that Myra so rarely saw in person but should have recognized the potential for when they were kids. "Yes, good afternoon. This is Gwen Perkins with the Alcove Agency in Phoenix. I represent Myra Malone, the proprietress of *The Minuscule Mansion of Myra Malone*. I'm calling for Mr. Alex Rakes. Is he available?"

"Mr. Rakes isn't in the shop today, Ms. Perkins. He and the senior Mr. Rakes are supervising a delivery at another warehouse at the moment. Could I put you in touch with another of our sales team to assist with your inquiry?"

"I'm not inquiring about a sale. Mr. Rakes entered my client's contest, and I'm calling to discuss his winning entry."

"Oh, how exciting. What kind of contest?"

"An essay contest."

"Well, doesn't that beat all. I never knew Alex was a writer. How interesting!"

"Quite *shockingly* interesting, in fact. To whom am I speaking?"

"This is Ellen. I've worked with the Rakes family since before Alex was a glimmer in his daddy's eye. Or even his granddaddy's."

"Do you happen to have Alex's cell phone number?"

"You know, I do . . . but I'm not in a position to share it."

"I completely understand." The sincerity of Gwen's face as she moved through this phone call was mesmerizing; Myra couldn't look away. "Oh, I know! Could I give you my cell phone number and ask you to have him call me? Or even text me? I know he'll be terribly excited by this news."

"I don't see why that would be an issue. Is this essay going to be published somewhere? I would love to read it."

"Oh, yes. The precise details are still being ironed out, but I expect we'll be posting a whole saga about it soon!" Gwen crossed the fingers on both her hands and waved them back and forth at Myra with excitement.

Myra felt as if she couldn't breathe. After Gwen got off the phone, she opened the laptop and looked at it again, scrolling through a dossier she'd created with links to articles and social media profiles and anything else she could find about Alex Rakes. "How much have you been snooping into this guy, Gwen?"

"Only the best for my best friend. I had to make sure he was legit and that this wasn't some elaborate hoax."

"How do you know it isn't?"

"It could be, but it's looking less likely. I called in a favor with a client out in Virginia and asked about the house. She grew up near Lockhart and said everyone knows 'the Lady's House.' Said it just like that, too, as if she was holding up extra-spooky finger quotes. It's a real place. And it looks just like yours. Just . . . bigger."

"I still can't understand how that's possible."

"Me either. But you know who might have some idea?" Gwen held up her phone as it pinged with a text message. "Mr. Not-So-Minuscule Mansion Owner himself. A texter, I see. I wouldn't have made a phone call, either."

"What does he say?"

"Well, well, well. *'Can I talk to Myra?'* On a first-name basis already, I see. I'm texting him your direct email. That was easier than I thought." The main routes of contact on the Minuscule Mansion's site went directly to Gwen, not Myra. Myra had an unlisted account and unlisted phone number, and her work for clients of Gwen's company was always facilitated by Gwen or another member of her marketing team. She was not accustomed to give-and-take conversation with anyone other than Gwen or, more rarely, her mother or father. The interactions she had were all one-sided: either she was writing for herself and for an audience whose faces she never saw, or she was chatting to—not with—a miniature house that didn't talk back. At least not with words. Not yet, anyway.

"What am I even supposed to say to this guy?"

"You're the writer, Myra. I'm sure you'll think of something."

· 20 ·

LOCKHART, VIRGINIA, 1937

FORD SLIPPED INTO THE FLOW OF THE HOUSE WITHOUT A ripple, as if he always belonged there. Most of what he added to the mansion he added silently—small pieces he brought home from shipments or his travels that reminded him of Willa and her taste, like the fluted Venetian glass vases shining the same blue as the ocean they'd crossed together. His taste usually matched hers, and the few out-of-place additions were usually not his choice; his parents would sometimes send ostentatious heirlooms from their own house, like the gargantuan chifforobe that took six men to wrestle into the mansion and, ultimately, upstairs to the room with the river overlook—the only chamber with an unbroken wall wide enough to accommodate the piece. The first time Willa opened it, the door almost came off in her hand—it had a broken hinge. The gift suddenly made sense—too expensive for Mildred to countenance getting rid of it, but too imperfect to keep in her own surroundings.

The wardrobe didn't come alone. The men who wrangled it up the stairs were overseen by a slender red-haired girl who looked no older than ten, and who marched up onto the porch to shake Willa's hand before Willa realized she'd even extended it. "My name is Miss Ellen Maria Kennedy, and I'm here to make sure that wardrobe doesn't get damaged. Mrs. Rakes didn't seem particularly concerned about whether it might damage your house, mind you, but I'll keep an eye out for that, too, don't worry. And then we'll see how else I might be able to help out around here."

Willa tilted her head, confused. "Help out—around here?"

Ellen nodded. "Mrs. Rakes said you're new in town and may need a little help with a big place like this." The girl stepped past Willa into the entry, whistling lightly as she gazed up and took in the scale of the house. "And it is big, isn't it?" She turned around and smiled at Willa, then winked. "You're thinking I'm a spy, aren't you? Somebody you didn't ask for just showing up in your house because Mrs. Rakes sent me, and who knows what else she sent me to do? Are you going to offer me some tea, by the way? It'd be nice to talk things over with some tea. I can make it myself. Let me just find the kitchen . . ." She trailed off, walking determinedly through the entry hall and toward the back of the house as if she knew exactly where to go and was used to people following her. And Willa did.

"Did you say that you were going to—"

"Help out around here? Yes, that's the idea. Her idea, anyway, though I thought it would be better to talk it over with you." Ellen reached the kitchen and found, on her first try, which cabinet contained the everyday cups and saucers, and placed two on the scratched kitchen table before filling the kettle with water and putting it on the stove. The air in the mansion seemed to part in order to accommodate her, as if it were eager to make her more comfortable. "So, a little about me. Let's call it an interview. My father is a craftsman—a woodworker who specializes in inlay work, which he supplies to the Rakes family. His workshop's about an hour from here, in a tiny little no-account place, but you'll notice I didn't say, 'My daddy does the inlays.' My mother has finishing school aspirations and a normal school budget, and she always made sure I sounded like a well-bred young lady. But I don't have much interest in teaching."

"You . . . don't look old enough for a classroom." Willa didn't add *where you're not a student.*

"To lead one, you mean? Oh, I'm not. I finished all the schooling anyone could throw at me before I even turned fifteen. But fifteen's too young for university. They let me graduate high school anyway, mostly because they were sick of me, I think. People my own age bore me to tears. That said, no one wants a girl like me at loose ends, least of all myself. So my father asked Mr. Rakes if he might need a shopgirl whose brain somehow happens to be a little older than the rest of her. And here I am."

"This isn't a shop."

"No, it isn't. But I gather Mrs. Rakes is more concerned about matters outside the shop, and wants a little bird to perch in this place. And she thinks she's found one. She hasn't, though." Ellen rummaged through another cabinet and found a tin full of tea that Willa didn't remember having. "That doesn't mean we can't let her think she has."

Willa wasn't sure which of the words careening through her head were the best ones to choose. She opened her mouth, and the word that came out first was "Why?"

Ellen shrugged. "Mrs. Rakes, a lady like the other Mrs. Rakes couldn't be troubled to set foot in a place like the town where I grew up, but she's the kind of person who thinks she can buy someone like me for the right price, and to be honest with you—I just don't like a bully." She smiled. "Besides, I've heard a lot about the Witch's Manor, if you don't mind me saying so. The girls in my town would be green with envy to know I'm even here, but they always said I put on airs."

The teakettle whistled, and Willa crossed to take it off the burner. Ellen beat her to it, pouring it over the tea in the cups and sitting at the kitchen table. Willa joined her, lowering herself into the opposite chair and looking at Ellen intently, listening to hear what the house had to say about her, but there was nothing—she fit, somehow. "If what you're telling me is true, how could I trust you?"

Ellen shrugged again, and the gesture had a kind of grace and non-chalance that seemed older than her fifteen years. "I suppose you don't have to. But this sure seems like a lonely place, for all that you've got a wonderful husband, from everything I've heard. He has to be wonder-ful, because his mother's mad as a wet hen that you've married him, and that just tells me he makes good choices." She leaned forward, conspiratorial. "If battle lines have been drawn, I think I'll have more fun on the scandalous side."

Willa sighed. "I never intended any battles at all. I simply fell in love."

"I may be young, but even I know enough to tell you that's the same thing." Ellen squinted. "How old are you, anyway?"

"That's something they teach you not to ask in finishing school, Miss Kennedy. A lady never admits to her own timelessness." Willa sipped her tea and grimaced; it had been in the cupboard a long time.

"I'm not accustomed to having help with this place. I don't even know the kind of help Mildred thinks I need, or what information she thinks you'll bring back to her about me. What do you propose we do?"

"I could come here, maybe two times a week, when I'm not working at the store. Mr. Rakes has promised me on-the-job training in sales and some other tricks of the trade, and my father says he's not the kind of man who'll try to teach me anything else, if you know what I mean. There are some others who would, I think, so my parents will be glad to know I'm spending regular time with a fine lady."

"And Mildred?"

"I'll make up just enough to pique her interest. I'd say I'd try to win her over for you, but I don't think that's possible."

"I could just say no, couldn't I?"

"Of course you could. I have no desire to spend time where I'm not wanted. But I have to warn you—she's set herself against you, and one way or another, she's going to find a way to keep eyes on you. At least this pair is attached to a person who'll give it to you straight."

Willa thought about Ford, the delicate kiss he'd given her before he whistled down the flagstone path to meet his father at the furniture warehouse to work that day, and the many not-so-delicate kisses he'd cascaded down her body the night before. A blush rose in her cheeks. She could regret many things, but never Ford. Even if he came with complications she should have been wise enough to expect.

"Would you like another cup of tea?" Willa asked. "And maybe—if you're going to come back and drink more—I could ask you to pick up a new tin?"

"I'm partial to Earl Grey, myself." Ellen smiled. "I'll bring some on Thursday."

· 21 ·

Don't Call It a Dollhouse

(From *The Minuscule Mansion of Myra Malone*, 2015)

WHEN I WOKE UP THIS MORNING, THERE WAS A BIG BOX outside my bedroom door that my mother had wrestled up the stairs, and I have to tell you: a big box is almost never a good sign. There are a lot of enthusiastic readers of *The Minuscule Mansion*—hi! Thank you!—but not all of them have a clear understanding of just how small *minuscule* really means, or what the Mansion can actually contain. A few months ago, I opened an absolutely stunning wooden box, hand-painted on the outside with tiny Scottie dogs, and inside was—lord, I hate writing this, but it's true—a Scottie dog. A taxidermied Scottie dog. If you sent it to me (there wasn't a note), I appreciate that Graham Cracker was a very special boy, and that you wanted him to spend eternity "in a place as magical as he was." I'm so, so sorry for your loss, but please send me your address, because Graham Cracker is not Mansion-sized, and I need to send him back to you. Also, I'm allergic to dogs. I'd never had occasion to find this out before, so this is a time of discovery for all of us, evidently.

Graham Cracker may be the biggest prospective resident I've been sent so far, but he's not the only one. Not by a long shot. Which brings me back to this morning's box: it was chock-full of dolls. A plethora of lovely, exquisitely detailed porcelain dolls. We're talking a clown car's worth of dolls, here—every twist of newspaper was hiding another one.

Whoever you are (why is it always the dolls and Scottie dogs that come without notes?), thank you, really, but no. No. This is clearly someone's much-loved personal collection, and I have to think that someone must have died and someone else decided to pack them up and donate them to the weird lady who puts a tiny mansion on the internet, but: the Mansion is not a dollhouse.

The Mansion is not a dollhouse, folks. It's just not.

Gwen and I used to fight about this all the time. To her, when we were kids, the Mansion was just a bigger, fancier, more handcrafted version of a Barbie Dream House. (I've never seen one in person, but I've seen them online, and I think they have a lot to do with Gwen's massive beach house aspirations.) Barbie can keep her flashy Malibu digs, because the Mansion is not for dolls. It's for real, breathing, full-sized people. And there's no room for them—their eyes and their dreams—if its spaces are occupied by little porcelain families, however charming they may be. I agreed to add my clothespin doll, in part, to get Gwen to stop harping at me. But I also agreed to help establish the scale of the rooms for those who don't understand the size I'm working with. Some of you may have missed this. Spoiler alert: a clothespin is a lot smaller than a Scottie dog.

Now, just because I don't put dolls in the Mansion doesn't mean its rooms aren't ready to receive company (that's all of you). That's one reason they're so detailed. I want it to look the way Trixie always made it look—as if someone just stepped out through the door for a moment and will be coming right back. If there's a nursery, the crib has a quilt draped across its side, trailing toward the floor. (Have I gotten emails about incorporating safe-baby, quiltless tableaus into the Mansion? I have. I'm sorry. The room's trapped in the 1940s at the moment, when nurseries were a different sort of place.) There's a glass bottle, open, with its rubber nipple next to it on the little end table next to the rocking chair, because someone just left for the kitchen to retrieve a refill. The hungry baby's with them, too. When they come back, they'll find the room just as they left it, right down to the stuffed bunny in the crib, the open book of children's nature poems on the side table, the floor lamp ready to light a bedtime reading session. The rocking horse in the corner is one I made as a child with Grampa Lou, so it's like having a little bit of myself in the nursery, ready to play.

But not as a doll. Because the nursery, and the Mansion, needs to be ready for anyone who wants to look at it, to see themselves in its rooms, to take refuge in the shelter it provides. A doll, a pet—even a full-sized Scottie dog—would only get in the way.

· 22 ·

LOCKHART, VIRGINIA, 1943

BY THE TIME WILLA STOPPED COUNTING HOW LONG SHE'D gone without sleep, it had been three days. She had never been so conscious of the passage of time and yet so unmoored in its flow, so unable to find an anchor in its current.

The baby would not stop crying. He looked at Willa with reproach, blue eyes squinched into furious half-moons that shielded deep reserves of anger. He was unimpressed by song, rejecting notes and measures drawn from the dawn of time itself. Poetry, stories, and epic tales of wonder left him unmoved. Willa escalated her efforts to full-blown pleas, begging her son to open his pinched face to see the beauty of the world around him, to stop screaming at its imperfections and let a little of it meet his standards. It didn't seem possible that such a small chest, such tiny butterfly lungs, could contain so much noise.

Beneath the weight of centuries, Willa stood unbowed, but eight pounds of rage-filled infant cracked her to her foundation.

"Rutherford," she whispered into her son's red-tinged shell of an ear, a perfect whorl his shrieks couldn't stop her from admiring. "Ruth. Please stop. I know you can hear me." The shortened name seemed apt; though meant for a girl, Willa put great stock in the meanings of words, and Ruth's association with grief and distress matched Willa's growing despair, even if it didn't quite describe her son's inexplicable anger and disdain for everything she did.

Ford wouldn't approve of the nickname, but Ford was mired in the muck and blood of some European battlefield; Willa felt her connection to him snap in the wake of his son's delivery, all her energy consumed. Rutherford Alexander Rakes Jr. was nothing like his father, and though Willa knew on some unconscious level it was, perhaps, unfair to make such a judgment so early in her son's time on earth, she also felt certain his soul had been there longer, waiting for something. He clearly hadn't found it yet, and Willa felt his blame searing through her with every high-pitched wail.

She couldn't call him Ford. Rutherford, yes. Ruth, perhaps. But not Ford.

She wasn't sure she could ever say Ford's name again. Some moments she would find herself looking over her son in minute detail, desperate for some echo of him, the wry and confident young man who approached her on the deck of that ship and whom she allowed, for a time and against her better judgment, to be an anchor, pinning her drift through time, letting her rest. Aside from a few glints of copper in Ruth's hair when she held him in the light—he hated the light almost as much as he hated the dark, though the shades and gradations of his rage were difficult to parse—there was no echo. Little echo of herself, either, save her blue eyes, but in a colder shade—the color of a shimmer at the bottom of a flame. Or so she thought, when he opened them enough for her to see.

She longed for Ford, longed to ask him what to do with this squalling bundle that came from both of them and contained so little of either. He was so certain of everything that he would know what to do here, too, how to handle the unaccustomed sensation of the unfamiliar. A few months ago, Willa would have said there was nothing about the world surrounding her that was unknown, and in a way, she was refreshed by the surprise. Or would be, if she weren't so exhausted.

Her intent had been to rest, to find a point of transition. They had spent their first days together in the mansion, once they had cleaned it and aired it and made sure it was ready for them to move in, and then they had walked together outside its walls, Willa showing Ford the hidden paths along the river's edge, though she did not lead him into the caves concealed there. They would row together on the water sometimes, Ford having announced that the empty dock needed a boat and bringing home oars and a canoe one evening, then handing Willa a parasol and saying he'd always wanted to spend an afternoon on a calm river with a beautiful woman. The river was not always calm—sometimes it raced with a speed and viciousness that Willa could hear from the house far above—but it was smooth when she was on its surface, and the time they spent there, eating small picnics of berries and sandwiches out of a wicker basket, passed entirely too quickly.

They decided to try to have a child without ever discussing it aloud. Willa would find items brought to the house that hadn't been there before, all of them showing how much he longed for one. A cradle was delivered to Rakes and Son in a shipment Ford laughed off as a mistake, but he brought it home and placed it gently near the windows in the turret room upstairs.

Ford would bring sheet music home sometimes, putting nursery rhymes and carols in the piano bench before the Steinway upright. Willa walked into the library one day to see a carved rocking horse sitting in a corner, its bright red saddle shining out from the room's blue walls. And she found books, too—*A Child's Treasury of Nature Poems* was splayed open on Ford's rocking chair one morning, a poem about a jellyfish whose words flashed with rhythmic longing and loss:

> *It opens, and it*
> *Closes and you*
> *Reach for it—*

Willa had known immediately when she was pregnant. She felt heavier, more weighted down in the mansion's unpredictable flow of time. So many books and stories described the feeling as a quickening, but there was nothing quick about it—everything seemed suffused with deliberate slowness. She was cautious on the stairs, the sidewalks, the flagstone path. She expected Ford to notice any moment, and expected any moment to tell him. And then the disturbance she felt beneath her feet in Europe crossed the wide ocean and landed on their doorstep.

She knew what a draft was, of course. It wasn't the first time she had seen young men marching in starched uniforms, polished buttons fastened by the smaller fingers of the women who had to let them go. She had never had to let anyone go before. But the echo of her despair in Ford's eyes made her decide, with sudden resolve, that the only thing that could make their parting harder would be telling him just how much he was leaving behind. She felt the way his fingers interlaced with hers, a new and desperate tightness that would be yet harder to unwind if he knew about the baby. If anyone knew, she would have to admit to herself what was happening: that he was leaving. That she would be alone again. That she wasn't quite sure how to manage solitude anymore.

Her despair brought another strange experience to their house: the experience of feeling complete agreement with Mildred, whose dread eclipsed her own, to the point that Ford's mother even suggested another tour to find new furniture—perhaps in areas where there was not so much danger, where a young man of eligible age wouldn't be missed. Somewhere he could disappear for as long as safety required. Willa felt her heart vibrate with trepidation and hope that Ford would agree to his mother's suggestion.

"There is no such place, Mom. This is too big to escape. Better to choose it, and face it head-on," Ford had said simply, kissing the top of her head in a way that seemed more dismissive than reassuring. And he did, in fact, dismiss Mildred, sending her back to her redbrick Federal house where her husband and their staff could better comfort her. "I want to spend this time with my wife," he said. The look on Mildred's face said Willa would never be forgiven for the choice. The pressure of Ford's fingers said Willa shouldn't care.

And after that, Willa didn't want to share him, not even with the small life she felt growing inside her. She wanted every waking moment of him entirely to herself. She devoured every moment with an insatiable hunger that the baby mirrored and amplified—waves of frantic activity giving way to utter exhaustion, and grief, and determination not to waste a single minute she could spend absorbing memories of Ford, like a spark stored deep in a pile of rags to smolder until a fire could be started again. She wondered, at times, if the baby could hear her—if they shared thoughts the way they shared blood, and if that furious swing from elation to desperation might be infectious. If the baby might know, somehow, that Willa's priorities were elsewhere.

Four years with Ford had passed in the blink of an eye, and she could not guess how many blinks it would take to return him to her side, or if his eyes would close forever. She kept her secret to herself and soaked up the short weeks until he donned his uniform and marched down the flagstone path, away from her.

Then she turned inward, and started to plan what the baby would mean. She tried to reestablish herself in the rhythm of the house without Ford. The only interruptions in the flow of time were Ellen's bi-weekly visits for tea. The Tuesday after Ford's departure, the girl bustled into the house with a fragrant brown paper bag, twisted tightly at the top, which she poured directly into the chipped enamel teapot. "I brought you something new." She poured a sour-smelling liquid over honey inside Willa's teacup and slid it across the table to her. "Raspberry leaf tea. The women in my family swear by it when they're carrying a child." She shook her head at Ellen's sharp gaze. "No use denying it to me, Mrs. Rakes. He's a good man, your Mr. Rakes, but a little slow on the uptake, if you don't mind me saying so. And even if you do, I'll say it anyway. You sure can tell he's an only child. I'm not—but I'm an oldest, and I can always tell when a lady is expecting."

Willa covered her face with her hands. "I didn't tell . . ." She trailed off, absently resting her hand on the handle of her teacup, its contents untouched.

"No. You didn't. Because he's coming back. He's coming back, Mrs. Rakes, and you can tell him then." Ellen reached her hand across the table and set it lightly atop Willa's. "But if you didn't tell him, you surely didn't tell—"

"Mildred. No. No one knows." Willa closed her eyes. "I can't, Ellen. I can't fathom losing him, and his mother here, where he should be, trying to insert herself—" She bit off the words. "I don't know what to do. And you, here because she asked you to be . . ."

"Yes. It's a shame we've had a falling-out."

"What do you mean?"

"I'm not coming here for tea anymore. You expressed terribly offensive feelings about—oh, let's think—Mrs. Rakes herself. Something that confirms everything she's ever thought about you, and will justify the fact that I can't return here to associate with you anymore, as a matter of loyalty."

"But I haven't—"

"No, of course. But Mrs. Rakes is the kind of woman who's most satisfied and relaxed when she's right. She'll have no reason to confront you—she's already expressed to me several times that she's hoping your husband might find some 'better kind of woman' while he's abroad, though what kind of social opportunities she thinks war might afford, I can't imagine. But be that as it may, she won't bother you, and she'll be all too glad to know I won't, either."

Willa felt a momentary stab of loss. "You . . . you don't bother me, Ellen."

Ellen smiled. "I'm glad to hear you feel that way, because I'll keep not bothering you some evenings, when I'm supposed to be bothering eligible young men of good breeding. And there will be doctor visits, of course, and—"

Willa shook her head and then stopped, seeing the alarmed look on Ellen's face. "Of course, and thank you for your concern. I have the medical arrangements settled. You needn't worry."

Ellen looked skeptical, but the difference in the women's stations meant she didn't press further. "Are you saying you don't need my help?"

"I don't need help." The walls of the house felt solid around her, but their strength was underpinned by a feeling Willa vaguely remembered from ages before, when her world felt more open, and welcoming people inside didn't feel like such a risk. Before society became Society, and her age and fatigue didn't make navigating the rules of each new time seem so daunting.

"Do you need anything else, then?" Ellen rose to leave.

"Ford would say I need a friend." Willa pictured his face, the way it lit up when she opened the small house on the ship. *It's never too late to start.* "If he's right, I'll send for you."

She thought he would be wrong. But babies have a way of making their own plans without consulting you. Ruth was small and incomplete, but he knew his own mind, and seemed to know Willa's plans before she fully formed them herself. He was not a refuge. He was a stone wall—one that excluded and did not enclose. She wheeled him back and forth through the wide doors of the mansion, wearing grooves into its floorboards that only she could feel, wondering how the world around her had grown so impossibly full of people if this was the way they came into being.

She had seen children, of course, had at times formed friendships long enough to watch them toddle and stride into adulthood. In past generations, past lives, when visitors were more common and the refuge—and Willa herself—were less closed off, children who visited the house floated through it as if enchanted, and their enchantment was matched by the house, which welcomed their presence and curiosity and laughter. Children had a receptiveness to the house's magic that adults seemed to lack. But as the divide between the mansion and the society around it evolved and deepened, Willa's survival depended on keeping a safe distance from others' curiosity, child and adult alike.

Before Ruth, she never held a baby for longer than a moment or two of discomfort. After Ruth? The discomfort was unending. She had brought him into the world, and he seemed determined to never let her forget what that act meant: she was entirely to blame for everything that came after. Even if, at the moment, it only seemed to mean that he was going to scream until he felt like stopping. And he never felt like stopping.

Willa didn't, either, but her longing for Ford felt deeper than a scream. It was rooted in her own anger at herself, for coming to rely so completely on her link to a man despite all she knew about humanity, and everything her long life had taught her about its transience. Her happiness with him had so suffused her world that his departure cast all that world lacked into stark relief. She had curled around their growing child with grief and believed, in hindsight, that grief and dread and anger had seeped into Ruth's small bones from the very beginning, and those feelings combined with a soul that was older than the body it occupied. They hadn't shared any thoughts, that much was clear. But he had absorbed her wrath at a world that had taken something away. He had no interest in giving back. The world owed him, or so he seemed to think.

"There's a letter from your father, Ruth." Her squalling son gave her a sidelong glance as he drew another deep breath. They both knew the letter was old. Its familiar words covered ground they had both walked together day and night, and Willa read the same sentences aloud over and over again since its brown paper envelope hissed through the letter slot.

Ford could not tell Willa where he was. His language was guarded in a way the man himself never was, and the guardedness widened the miles even more than the ocean between them. He wove curt stories out of threaded details: the colors in the fields through which he marched, the way the breeze felt on his face in the rain. He wrote of loss without specifics and shades of men without names, though Willa felt the pull of other sleepless women with squalling infants, other hearts that jumped with fear at every letter.

He wrote nothing about Ruth. He couldn't, because he still didn't know he had a son at all. As his letters arrived, and as she filled creamy white pages with her spidery handwriting in response, she could not decide if telling him was kind or cruel. Part of her was jealous in a way that was entirely unfamiliar to her: she wanted to be the only tether, the only reason he had to come back. She had expected a little girl, a mirror image of herself, who she thought might make the transfer simple when the time came. Who, when the time came, would surprise and delight Ford when he walked back up the flagstone path. A daughter would be the icing on the cake of his return, another link in the chain of their connection. A girl like her, a new Lady of the House, drawing power from the flames beneath the earth. Someone Willa would know how to teach and how to prepare and, someday, when the time was right, how to leave behind.

When a boy emerged instead, Willa's shocked expression mirrored her son's. Naming him Rutherford was a spell she hoped to cast: something to make him more familiar and restore her to the path she planned to tread. Instead, Ruth rejected her efforts and Willa herself. His palpable dissatisfaction seemed related, in part, to the fact he knew he must rely upon her for now.

Her despair was so complete that, by a few days after his birth, her reluctance to write about Ruth gave way to a deepening suspicion that she shouldn't mention him at all. She lacked a firm grasp on her own feelings and had no desire to figure out a way to allude to the situation in her similarly vague letters to Ford, let alone to state the case outright. Instead, she confined herself to simple stories about the weather and the changing seasons, words she hoped would remind him of the place they once shared, and would keep him alive until he could return. And then? Then they would figure things out together, a word whose value Willa had only recently come to appreciate.

In the meantime, she felt she had no one at all. She used the silent, unfamiliar telephone that Ford had insisted must be added to the mansion, dialing the only number she had ever used—the one for the warehouse where Ford went to work each day. The brisk voice that answered the line made tears spring to her eyes—both because it wasn't Ford, and because it was Ellen.

"Rakes and Son, how may I direct your call?"

"Ellen."

"Mrs. Rakes?" Ellen's voice dropped to a whisper. "Are you all right?"

"Can you come?"

"Now? Is it the baby? Is it—"

"When you can. Please." Willa drew herself up with a confidence she did not feel—afraid to ask for help, and afraid not to.

"Has anyone ever told you you're a hard nut to crack, Mrs. Rakes?"

Willa stared out the window in the kitchen, gripping the phone's receiver, watching the oak trees sway their gentle curves toward the river below. "I've never known how to be any other kind. But he's so angry, Ellen. Nothing I do seems right. I haven't slept in days, and if I don't hear another person talk soon, I think I might—"

"Sounds like you've got a baby there, Mrs. Rakes." Ellen's laughter on the other end of the line was the most beautiful sound Willa could remember hearing in months. "I was supposed to go to the movies tonight, but I'd rather see your new family member anyway. I'll come by after the shops close, and bring a little something to eat, too. But you don't need much talk, I don't think. You need someone to hold that baby while you take a nap." Ellen's voice was the kind that sounded like her smile. "Fortunately, that's something I've practiced quite a lot in my life."

Willa hung up the phone and looked at Ruth in his carriage, where he'd fallen asleep while she spoke—a first. "We're going to have a visitor, Ruth." She sat next to the carriage, stretching out on the hard floor, lengthening her spine from the crabbed position it had assumed, and dropped into an uneasy rest that lasted until Ellen's knock on the wide front door.

It wasn't enough to anchor Willa in the endless flow of anticipation for Ford's return. But it was enough to give Ruth another person in the house, and that reduced the focus of his animosity toward his mother, at least for a time. While her visits were inconsistent, affected by her job at Rakes and Son and her lodging with the family, Ellen appeared on the porch often enough for Willa to feel some small sense of relief, watching her take Ruth for walks and read to him in the library, and always working—with limited success—to bring the toddler into his mother's orbit, and try to convince him to stay there. Sometimes she convinced Willa to join the two of them on excursions out of the house, walking as a trio along the stone path at the public park in town, buying Ruth an ice cream, seeming for moments so wholesome that a photographer snapped their picture once, capturing them and several other families for a Sunday Park feature in the local paper, a light-hearted graphic story meant to cheer those still waiting for their soldiers to return. *Two ladies and a child enjoy the day.* Moments of normality, trying to hide what would never be normal again.

Willa did not know, until she became a mother, that the river of time in which she had spent her long life carried different eddies and currents that could simultaneously shorten each moment and lengthen it interminably, and she would float through the waves while sheltering a child who seemed to despise her.

Come back to me. She would stand in the window overlooking the wide curve of river, the dying light sparkling across its surface as it flowed toward the ocean that separated her from Ford. *Come back to me.* Ford's letters stopped coming, the days kept passing, and time marched on in unison with the soldiers who never marched back.

Until one did, opening the creaking iron gate and stepping along the flagstone path in a disjointed and uneven echo of the steps Ford once marched away from her.

The soldier looked like Ford, the same blue eyes, the same sandy hair tinged with glints of red. His voice was the same. But the eyes lacked connection when Willa gazed at him, sliding away toward unseen shores. The voice lacked resonance, with no tinge of Ford's puckish humor.

It took another spiral in the flow of time for Willa to recognize, and longer for her to accept, that he never came back to her at all.

· 23 ·

PARKHURST, ARIZONA, 2015

"I THOUGHT YOU SAID YOU GAVE HIM MY EMAIL AD-
dress?" Myra tried to sound nonchalant. After Gwen's quick exchange
of text messages with Alex Rakes the day before, Myra resumed her
work on the dining room of the Mansion, trying to focus on capturing
the right sheen for the gravy ladled across the tiny Cornish game hens.
She wouldn't check her email. There was no reason to check her email.
Whatever he was going to write, she would read at her scheduled email
reading time of 3:15 p.m., and not before.

She went downstairs and made tea, forcing herself to linger at the
stove and stare at the silent kettle, determined to disprove that a
watched pot never boils. She poured the water with deliberate slowness over two mugs containing chamomile tea bags, walking one of
the mugs into her mother's bedroom, where she found Diane asleep,
one arm draped over her eyes, as if blocking out the day. She put the
mug on the nightstand and wandered out through the hallway, peering

again at the narrow corridors of boxes she and Gwen were still trying to sort and move out of the cabin, shaking her head. *I won't look I won't look I won't look.*

She lasted twenty minutes.

No mail.

She hadn't slept well, and the longer she stared at her empty inbox, the more Myra convinced herself that there had to be some mistake. Gwen's email must have included a typo, and Alex's message was out in the cold of cyberspace, rejected and alone. She called Gwen in a panic. "Did you remember there's two *n*'s in Vienna?"

"Has it ever occurred to you that an email like viennasausage @minimansion.net might actually increase the risk of those penis email attachments you're so afraid of?" The sound of Gwen's typing increased in speed, which Myra recognized as a sign that she was only half listening. "I got the email right, Myra. He might be busy. Or maybe he's just as afraid of writing you as you are of writing him."

"I use addresses I think people won't guess—that's why you have the admin account. Anyway. I'm not . . . that afraid of writing him."

"Have you done it yet?"

"No."

"I texted you his email address."

"I know."

"It was just as eye-rolly as yours. Only a guy you're meant to meet would use a pun for his email—rakesleaves@closeofbusiness.net? Jesus. He must have bought a domain just to make a sentence. He's perfect for you."

"You make it sound like I'm a big fan of puns."

"You're a big fan of words, and a big fan of clever, especially if it's the kind of clever that's really pretty dumb. So. You haven't heard from him yet. Do you want me to go full therapist, or what? *And how does that make you feel, Myra?*"

"Stop it. I feel fine. Like you said, he's probably busy." Faint music plinked from the interior of the Mansion, and Myra strained to hear, finally recognizing the twin notes of "Chopsticks." The piano in the Mansion's library was a music box that played a Chopin étude, not the few measures of a song a five-year-old might tap, but she could never predict the songs that came from the house. They usually played only in the middle of the night, but it was full morning, and the light was beaming across the attic's dancing dust motes.

"I'm in the middle of some stuff here today, so do you need anything else other than me to tell you to calm down?"

"No. That was mostly it."

"Okay. Calm down. I'll call you later tonight to see if we can hash out some details about the contest winners, including Mr. Bad Pun. I'm sure you'll hear from him soon."

Myra heard a ping from her computer just as the last notes of "Chopsticks" faded away as if she'd imagined them. She opened her inbox and saw a single new message, from rakesleaves.

Has anyone ever told you that a savory sausage–based email address may invite unsavory messages? the email began, and Myra smiled, and time fell away around her as she read. I've started to write this message at least a dozen times, and I've deleted it each time. I have no idea what to say, so I decided to treat this like a freewriting exercise like I used to have to do when I was in college. I was an English major, which I'm sure you'll find absolutely shocking as we correspond. Now that I've read through your blog, I feel like any illusions I had about my own ability to write have been swept away—I wouldn't have thought, a few days ago, that anyone could make me care about a dollhouse in Arizona, or even think of a dollhouse as anything other than absolutely creepy. But here we are: yesterday, at work, I saw someone else looking at the Minuscule Mansion site and talking about "the dollhouse" and I corrected them. I told them it wasn't a dollhouse, just like you do. And I was genuinely resentful! Like they had failed to adequately grasp the Mansion's purpose. Which, to be honest, I still don't entirely know myself. But being a toy isn't it. I know that much.

Myra felt her heartbeat start to quicken. Her computer sparkled with fractured rainbows, and she stopped to trace their source, noticing that the crystal chandelier in the library was rotating slowly in the morning light. She read on.

In the middle of the night last night, I woke up from a bad dream about a dance—I was the only person there—and I heard music from downstairs. I can't believe I'm writing this because it makes me sound crazy, and you haven't met me yet, but I swear I'm just about the most normal person you could ever meet. But then again, you may already think there's something off-key about me because I told you that the Mansion is real and I live inside it. Which, I recognize, is the very opposite of normal. Your publicist seems savvy enough to check on things like this, so I'm hoping by the time you read this you know I'm not making that part up. And I'm not making this up, either. This house hasn't had a piano since I was a little, little kid. But I heard a piano. I went down to find where the music was coming from, and it was coming from the library, where the piano used to be. Where my grandma used to play, back before she disappeared. Her portrait still hangs there. And it looks exactly like yours.

Where did you get the house? Where did you get her portrait? Who cut her—I know it wasn't you, I feel certain and I don't know why. How is any of this happening? I can't sleep at night. I stare at the ceiling in a room that has a smaller version of itself somewhere else, where someone else's hands move the furniture I thought I picked out myself, and I wonder if those same hands move me, too. I wonder if I want them to. I wonder what they look like, and what the person they belong to looks like.

I have so many questions, and I know you have them, too. I don't know where to begin. So I'm beginning with this: hitting send, getting these words in front of you, and hoping you'll know what to do with them. Because the more I think about it, and the more I think about this situation I find myself in—or that we find ourselves in—the more I think you're the only person in the world who might be able to help me make sense of any of this.

· 24 ·

LOCKHART, VIRGINIA, 1948

AFTER THE SUN WENT DOWN, AND THE DYING EMBERS OF its light retreated from the river below the mansion, and Willa could hear the slow and even breathing of her husband through his closed bedroom door, and after Ruth would consent to let her say good night—not kiss him, almost never, but at least let her share some signal that one day was soon to cascade into the next—then, and only then, could she have music.

She tried to play softly, keeping her fingers light on the keys. She started with simple scales and exercises until muscle memory took over, leading her wherever the music wanted to go, whatever measures flowed through her. Many forms ago, the house had been smaller and had served as a tavern for wayward travelers along the river, before rumors of the Lady built to a crescendo that required another generation of retreat. But the travelers' music had enlarged the space, made the refuge seem larger and more complete, and when she returned to it the next time, she installed a piano. It had remained ever since, though its form altered over time, and the music evolved with her skill. She had nothing but time to learn.

When Ford first came to the house, he would sit in the rocking chair by the fireplace in the library, the twin of the miniature version he first gave to her on the ship. He would read the newspaper or review letters and catalogs from furniture companies all over the world, listening to Willa play at the piano. He brought her sheet music as often as he brought her flowers, and loved new songs as much as he loved new books, with which he filled the library. Nights that Willa didn't play, he read to her. They curled together on the rug in front of the fire on cool nights as time flowed past around them.

The man who returned from Europe's battlefields could not bear the sound of music. Any unexpected sound drove him to the ground or, sometimes, sent him careening around the house in rage. The first time, as Willa played an étude that had been a favorite in their years before, his anger was so sudden and so incandescent that he slammed the piano shut across her arched fingers, and her cry did not return him from wherever his mind had gone. When he ran out of the room, Willa found the latch on the swinging bookcase and retreated into the mansion's heart, hiding there until she heard silence and found him unconscious in his rocking chair. In sleep, he looked exactly like the man she loved. She curled on the rug near his feet. *Come back to me.* She thought the words—did not dare to even whisper them—because she hoped some part of him would hear her, and that was the part that would wake up.

The rest of him, she feared. She tried not to let on—not to him, not to Ruth, and certainly not to Mildred, who descended on the house unannounced to "lend assistance"—by sitting in a parlor chair, alternating between cooing over Ruth and criticizing Willa until she became bored enough to summon her driver and return to her house, each time trying to convince Willa to let her take Ruth along and "give her some respite," and each time failing. Eventually, one of Mildred's unplanned stop-bys collided with one of Ellen's, and Mildred hid her anger at what was clearly an established rapport—if too dissimilar to call it a friendship. She gritted her genteel teeth and murmured how wise Willa had been to avail herself of Ellen's services "after such a hard falling-out," but glared at Ellen with the promise of a future confrontation over not telling Mildred about her grandchild, leaving the discovery a surprise after Ford's return.

Willa hid her eyes under cold compresses to conceal sleepless nights, a life tiptoed across eggshells. Ellen's occasional outings with Ruth gave Willa opportunities to try, again and again, to sit with Ford and search out some shadow of the man she once knew. On some days, he would let her sit next to him and hold his hand, the two of them silent, the tea cakes he used to love left untouched. Nothing helped. And those silent moments were brief against the explosive and unexpected backdrops of his terror, his sudden rages, and his waking nightmares.

When Ford and Ruth finally slept, Willa could return to the piano and let the music wash over her. She had to hold herself in check; if she let go completely, the volume would cascade upward through the house and bring the reality of her present circumstances crashing down the stairs to scream at her. She was quietest of all when playing anything he used to love. Songs that mixed the notes into measures of joy and sadness could make her weep, but the weeping made her feel better, the water on her face joining her to the water in the river, in the caves deep beneath her feet. Chopin's Prelude in A Major, op. 28 no. 7, was short, a piece she could play in sleepless snatches of time, the wistfulness of its slow progression through major into minor keys mimicking her own mood. If she left the classical behind and chose something more contemporary, she would play through Scott Joplin's "Solace"—an apt name for the song, played from sheet music that Ford found for her in a bookstore on one of their purchasing trips. The memory was bittersweet, but was at least something that brought her small comfort despite the echo of Ford, who had finally fallen into light and disturbed sleep in the room above her head, where he always slept alone.

She felt someone in the room with her as she played Debussy's "Clair de lune," and turned around to see Ruth standing in the dark of the library, the blue flannel plaid of his pajamas absorbing the light and warmth of the last few flames in the fireplace. Outdoors, the August air hung hot and motionless in the Virginia mist, but the house was as cold as the emptiness in Willa's heart. The fireplace ignited without any conscious effort on her part. The mansion tried to keep her warm.

She held out her hands to her son and tried not to shrink with disappointment as he hung back yet again, looking at her with a skepticism far older than his years.

"Grandmother says I'm to go away to school soon."

Willa sighed. Ruth was only five years old—in body, at least, just a small boy. His spirit felt much older, and he spoke to Willa like a peer, and not a much-liked one. His hostility and impatience and anger seemed drawn from deeper places than a small body could store, and Willa knew he blamed her for the shell of a father who roamed the upstairs rooms, who never had interest in playing catch or taking a walk or doing any of the normal, ordinary things an ordinary boy expected of a father. He had so few people in his world, and two of them—Mildred and Theodore—hated his mother. A third was irretrievably broken. By a simple law of averages, the responsibility for everything bad must be cast at her feet.

When Ford trudged back up the flagstone path, his homecoming had been nothing like the one that Willa longed for. Instead of a ringleted girl, she had a sullen boy, sulking in a linen shirt and short trousers she had sewn herself. She had never told anyone she was pregnant, and only Ellen had guessed, only to be cast out for a time when Willa was determined to handle things alone. She had never gone into the shop or giggled with other women about her impending arrival, or returned to the mansion laden down with packages for a well-dressed infant. When Ruth was born, she had the crib and the rocking chair that Ford had placed in the turreted room. She had stacks of fabric she embroidered to while away the time. She had absolutely no desire to tell anyone else in the world—most of all Ford's parents—that she had a child. She had been determined not to tell anyone at all until she told Ford himself.

But the version of Ford that returned to the mansion didn't greet the news with joy. Joy, in fact, seemed as foreign to him as the shores he'd returned from. He blinked with bewilderment at Willa and at the round-eyed small boy pushing a wheeled cart across the wide front steps. Then he said that he was tired and walked past Willa to the stairs, ascending to a room that had never been his. Willa thought that the silence might end after he rested, but it grew until she thought it might kill her. Before she thought that Ford himself might. There was never anything in between. And when she sent word to his parents—desperate for any sign of the man she married, and hoping they might have some idea as to how to restore him—Mildred's cooing overconcern and invasive, grasping fingers drove Ford into a rage that frightened all of them. And this, too, was clearly Willa's fault.

So time flowed by again, eating up moments with a different kind of hunger than the one that had suffused the time before Ford's departure for war, and instead consuming the years of Ruth's infancy and toddlerhood and milestone moments spent with Mildred and Theodore, safe away from Ford and from Willa herself. And here he was, five years old, and watching her play the piano with the same impatience that imbued their every interaction.

"Mother. I am talking to you. Grandmother says I'm to go away to school soon."

Ford's mother and father had spent long hours in consultations that excluded Willa, discussing the merits of Saint Thomas Academy, a boarding school in the faraway mountains outside Asheville, run with military precision by a distant cousin of Mildred's. Willa remembered the rare descriptions Ford had shared about his short time there. Before he left for war, and became haunted by other things, he had seemed haunted by memories of the school, and the memories were never happy.

Willa reached toward her son. "I'm talking with your grandmother about it, Ruth. And your father, too."

Ruth narrowed his eyes. "You know Father won't discuss it. He doesn't discuss anything, Mother. You know that."

Willa sighed. "I know that. But part of him is still here, Ruth, and I want him to have a say."

"I want to go. And you know I hate that name. My name is Ruther-ford. Grandmother calls me Ruther. No one calls me Ruth."

"You're still so young, darling—"

Another child might stamp his feet or throw a tantrum, but Willa's son could show rage without moving a muscle, as if the world's gravity were shifting slightly around his small form. His voice became quieter. "I'm old enough to leave."

"You're old enough to start school, but that school is very far away indeed."

He smiled, and the expression was uncanny on his face, an exotic bird trying to escape the room. "Grandmother says it's very organized."

"It sounds that way, yes. Would you like that?"

"You know that I would like that."

"It would make Mommy so sad to have you so far from here."

"I wouldn't be sad. The school is full of people, not like here. And we have to come home for holidays. Grandfather says there are lakes full of fish and woods full of deer, and I can learn to fish and shoot and spend as much time as I like outdoors, and the instructors make sure that everyone follows all of the rules, and there are lots and lots of rules. Not like here."

He was so different from Willa. So different from Ford, or the person Ford used to be, before he returned a shadow of his former self. Every sentence that came out of her mouth seemed to strike him with the opposite of her intended meaning; every word was taken as a slight or further proof of her total lack of understanding. And then there was the question of the transfer, her fatigue deeper than the bones beneath her skin, deeper than the caves beneath her feet. It was nearly time, if Ruth was ready, but his resistance to her was so complete—his anger so indivisible from his small form—that she could not find an anchor in his spirit.

Before Ford left, Willa had let herself believe she could begin to rest, and begin to fade away, and leave her burden behind in new hands. In believing that, she had borne a child. And that child had rejected everything that she was or ever could be. Even so, some part of her thought that with more time, with more love, there would be a way to bring Ruth into the warmth of the refuge, a way to convince him to see the beauty of this place he longed to leave and could not, clearly, bear to be tethered to. The effort would take time, and it was time she would not have if he were sent away for school. The idea that she would have another chance—before she lost her will and chose to dissipate completely—seemed so remote as to be impossible. Untold centuries had passed before this chance, and it was slipping past her as surely as the flow of the river.

"Do you really want to go?"

Ruth set his mouth. "I really want to leave. It would make me happy to leave."

She closed her eyes and tried to remember what it felt like when she carried him inside her those long months after Ford went to war. She tried to remember even earlier, when she would entangle her legs with Ford's and listen as he read poetry aloud to her. She tried to remember what she felt. "I want you to be happy, Ruth."

He nodded at her. "Good night, Mother."

The word thudded with a finality that echoed over years. "Good night, my sweet boy."

· 25 ·

PARKHURST, ARIZONA, 2015

DEAR ALEX, MYRA WROTE. THE CURSOR BLINKED AT HER. She deleted.

Hi, Alex. Delete.

Alex, hey. Got your message. This is all SO WEIRD, amirite? Like, where do we even begin? She erased the words with a keystroke so hard the keyboard felt like it might snap. Nothing felt right. Nothing felt normal. Her routines were upended, her dreams disrupted almost every night by sounds above her head.

Beneath her feet, in the cabin's downstairs rooms, Diane remained ensconced among her dwindling piles of boxed merchandise as Gwen continued to ferry parcels out to her overloaded BMW for trips to the post office, where the mystified staff continued to ship box after box to eager eBay buyers awaiting their Valentino and Louis Vuitton and Hermès, tags still on. Myra would hear her mother's elevated tones of protests, but not her words, met and volleyed back by a barrage of Gwen's instructions—*Let that go, no you can't keep that, you know you can't keep any of it.* Gwen's persuasive gifts exceeded Myra's in every respect, including with Myra's own parents. Countless sleepovers and pizza nights and VHS rentals all originated with Gwen—her ideas, her plans, her execution—and Myra's family was swept up into the current. Myra was all too glad to let her handle this latest crisis, too, the way she handled everything. And Myra had never known how to handle her mother. The discovery of her debt had been a surprise, but her wistful explanations had not been. Diane had always seemed to long for a different life, and to blame Myra—however unconsciously—for the life she actually had. She never said the words, but Myra felt them.

It was harder to feel them in the attic, where each step on the stairs echoed another year of distance, another way to deny what their relationship had become.

How to explain any of that to Alex? How to explain anything at all—the cabin, the risk of losing it, the Mansion, herself?

She started again, and instead of finding a beginning for her story, she plunged into the middle. Alex, the library of the Mansion has a crystal chandelier over the fireplace that wasn't there until I saw your photograph online, and I feel like it knew—like the Mansion knew—that I was looking at you. It's always had personality and done things I couldn't explain, and a few things have happened over the years that I've never talked about online because I didn't need any more evidence out in the world that I'm a crazy shut-in who talks to a dollhouse in an attic. I haven't even told Gwen, and I tell her almost everything. But I'm telling you because you're the only person who I think might understand. You're living this weirdness full scale. I can close mine up with hinges and brass buckles and pretend it's not there for a while, even if it does keep calling me back up with music and booms and crashes. I can pretend there's some division between my miniature life and my real one, even if some would say my real one is quite small.

You asked about the portrait. The answer is I don't know who cut her. I can tell you I cried when I saw it. I felt the cut in my own face. I came upstairs one day when I was small and part of the Mansion was smashed. The house was open, even though I'd left it shut, and every breakable thing was crushed. It took me ages to reconstruct everything that was lost, but I did it. In her bedtime stories to me, Trixie used to say everything that transpires in the Mansion has transpired before, and is still happening, and will happen again, because the refuge remembers. It's always been a place that's filled with memories, and there was no question—even when I was very small—that I couldn't let it stay broken. Trixie left it to me because she knew I would protect it. So I rebuilt.

Anyway. The portrait hurt, but at least I could still see her face. Trixie, my step-grandmother, the one I talk about in my posts, always called her the Lady of the House. Trixie is the one who gave me the Minuscule Mansion; it used to be hers, and much of what's inside it came from her. She married my grandfather when I was two, and she died when I was five, and there's not a day that goes by that those three years don't feel just as present in my life—just as defining of who I am as a person—as they did when I was small. She understood me on a level few other people ever have, and I never felt like a small child when I was with her. It might have been because she used to say I was an old soul, and she acted as though she was talking to someone important, which isn't an ordinary tone for a small child to hear. I adored her. I miss her every day.

I don't know why any of this is happening, but I also don't agree with what Gwen wants to do about it. She sees this whole thing as a business opportunity and wants to turn it into a reality show, or something that will drum up interest and money for the site. She's my manager and my publicist, and everything you see on the site—other than the writing itself—was her idea. And as annoyed as I am at her for trying to turn my life, and your life, into some kind of phenomenon that could go viral (a word I hate, by the way), the truth is that she's trying to help me. This whole contest is outside my comfort zone, but as she's pointed out, my comfort zone is about to go away if I don't save it. My house is going to be auctioned. My grandfather built it when he was a young man, and my mother was just old enough to wield a hammer and a nail. I know every inch of this place but somehow let it escape my notice that my mother was filling it with merchandise she couldn't pay for. I can't help but think that all the praise I get for my attention to detail might have been misplaced, when I missed such a big one.

So as I write this, I feel like I need to warn you that you've stumbled into a bigger plot, and probably a bigger mess than you want to get involved in. No matter what the Mansion thinks, there are parts of this story that only I can access, and parts of this world I don't want to share. Which is a very, very long-winded way of saying that you have not won the essay contest, Alex, and I can't let you come here and have lunch with me. I can't let anyone have lunch with me. Maybe, possibly, if I really try, I can let someone else be declared the winner. Someone else, who doesn't have a connection that knocks the wind out of me, could send me some words and some pictures and some furniture, and I can remake a room the way they want, and I can hopefully get enough that way to pay off the bank.

But this situation? The mismatched mirror image of our lives, the portraits, the music? I don't want to let the world into that. You're already here, and I can't exclude you. But I refuse to make it a spectacle, especially when I can't wrap my head around the significance of it. And there has to be some significance to it.

This is simultaneously too big and too little for me to handle. Gwen may be angry at me, but I'll try to make her understand. I hope that you will, too. Part of me thinks you may understand better than most.

I'm sorry for your trouble. Let's not compound it further.

Myra hit send and pushed herself back from her computer before she could second-guess herself. She held her breath, half expecting some reaction from the Mansion, but the house was silent. Part of her was disappointed. Part of her was relieved.

But, of course, the Mansion wasn't ever really quiet. It was listening.

The ping that rang out from the computer happened so quickly that either Alex was the world's quickest reader, or he'd skipped all the way to the end. Which is exactly what Myra herself would have done.

A single sentence blinked on the screen: We don't have to meet. But please don't stop talking to me. About anything you want.

Myra smiled in spite of herself. When she sent her message to him, she meant to shut any further correspondence down—to shut Alex out—because the feelings in her heart were too big, an expansion that was almost painful. Her instinct was to exclude, but a deeper part of her wanted Alex to fight back, the way Gwen always had. And here he was, keeping his toe in the door before she could close it completely.

She hit reply before she could further second-guess herself. That's a broader invitation than I think you realize. Even if it seems pretty small, given the scale I work with. You may think it's all tiny teacups and minia-ture furniture in here, but I inherited stories that are bigger than myself, and I'm used to writing them for a much bigger audience, so shrinking my words down for just you may be a challenge. But if you're in? I'm in. Even if I'm not entirely sure what I'm in for.

Whoosh.

Ping! Tell me about your mom, and these things she's been buying. I didn't know my own mother until recently. More on that later, I promise. What's been going on?

Click. Boots! Amazing boots, and this gown, my lord, I never knew my mother's tastes dipped into such extravagance! The kind of things I'd love to make small, I have to confess—I guess I know where my eye for detail came from, at least in part. But let me tell you how I found out . . .

The chandelier's rainbows chased each other across the attic walls.

· 26 ·

LOCKHART, VIRGINIA, 1948

WILLA HAD NEVER CARED MUCH ABOUT THE CHANGING seasons. When she was in the refuge, the weather around her could be whatever she wished it to be, though it tended to reflect her moods more than any conscious decision to change it. The arbitrary significance accorded to specific days in the societies that grew around her meant little, and in her life before Ford—before she linked herself to a family steeped deeply in the societal expectations she had long avoided—she never decorated.

Then what was left of Ford cast its shadow through the Mansion, and for the first time, Willa couldn't keep Mildred at bay. Her constant presence was meant as a silent reproach, a confirmation that Willa was not equal to the task of Ford's care. Mildred's judgment-tinged intonations echoed through the house and began emerging from Ruth's mouth as soon as the boy could talk. His first visit home from boarding school, from which Mildred insisted on collecting him herself, they walked into the wide front hall and exchanged a glance with each other before gazing at Willa.

"We have a gigantic Christmas tree at Saint Thomas," Ruth said. "I helped decorate it. I stood on a ladder."

"That sounds exciting," Willa said.

"There should be a tree here."

"Oh." Willa glanced around the front hall and felt, for the first time, all of the ways that Mildred—that outsiders—found the mansion inadequate. As she felt judgment, the walls of the house echoed it, looking shabby and showing their age as Willa herself did. "Would a tree make you happy? We can certainly get one."

"I'll have one delivered." Mildred swept her way into the hall and cast her eyes upward toward the ceiling as if measuring the particular arboreal specimen the space would accommodate. "Let's go and see your father, darling boy, so we can make it home for dinner."

Willa looked at her son, already halfway up the stairs toward Ford's room. "Are you not eating here?"

"We thought it would be easier to have Ruther stay with us during his holiday break. You have so much on your plate, my dear, and my son is so sensitive to noises—it's just not fair to a growing boy to expect him to stay so quiet during the holiday season." Mildred's face was a moue of regret that concealed profound satisfaction at a day gone to plan.

"He doesn't have to stay quiet," Willa said. "This is his home. Here, with me, and with his father. Surely you don't expect me to agree—"

"Agree to let your son be cared for by the grandparents who love him dearly, and who will keep him safe and happy so that you can focus on your husband, who is also my son? Whose care we have entrusted to you, against our better judgment, in light of your constant refusal of our assistance? Yes, I expect you to agree. Because for all that your approach to things is—shall we say—unconventional, you aren't a selfish mother, my dear. A five-year-old boy just home from school has needs that will divide your attention, and that, if I may say so, is already somewhat tenuous." Mildred's trilling voice reminded Willa of a mockingbird, effective at mimicking whatever surface emotion she wished to convey while concealing the bitter truth beneath. She tilted her head toward Willa with expectation every bit as pointed as a beak.

Willa was exhausted. She had arisen that morning excited for her son's return and also steeling herself for disappointment. She hadn't expected the latter emotion to dominate so soon. The air around Ruth's small body crackled with his usual impatience, but there was something new—a kind of scorn, a haughtiness that set Willa back on her heels. The unease he brought into the house was so familiar that Willa didn't want to give it credence. It was the feeling that came from outsiders, people who wanted the refuge to conform to their expectations about orderly spaces and predictable rules. The winds blowing deep beneath Willa's feet changed direction.

Her son didn't want to be here, and the shelter above his head didn't want him under its roof. The sensation of threat divided Willa through her heart; threats had always been external. This one came from inside. From her. From the love she and Ford once shared and its product: this angry and suspicious child.

"I want him to stay at home with us, Mildred. Where he belongs." As the words left her chest, Willa felt a powerful pressure from the air that swirled around her, and heard a bellow from upstairs, followed by a furious pattering of small feet down the stairs.

"Father is awake," Ruth said breathlessly. "He doesn't want company."

"He'll feel better soon, sweet. He's just tired today." Willa tried to touch her son's hair, wispy curls of red-tinged russet, but he ducked beneath her hand and stood next to Mildred. Willa sighed. "We'll have a lovely dinner, and he'll be so glad you're home."

Ruth looked at his grandmother with alarm. "You said you would talk to her! You said I didn't have to stay!"

Mildred smiled at him with a warmth that made her attitude toward Willa feel all the more frigid. "Go to the library, my darling, and let me speak with your mother."

"Yes, Ruth, go to the library—I've set out some cake for you in there. German chocolate—Ellen and I baked it together last night, and she said she might drop by for dessert later."

"Is that shopgirl of ours still visiting you? I can't imagine why she hasn't found somewhere more interesting to spend her leisure time. Teddy is entirely too indulgent, but he says she's quite gifted with the customers—"

Willa interrupted Mildred's snobbish monologue as if she couldn't hear her. "And there are Cornish game hens with gravy and little red potatoes for dinner. We'll have a lovely time." Willa tried to infuse her smile with incandescence that would outshine Mildred.

"I hate the library. And I hate it here."

Mildred frowned. "We don't talk to grown-ups that way, young man. Go and wait."

As soon as his stomps faded toward the back of the mansion, Mildred's smile faded. "I really wish that you would be reasonable, Willa. The boy knows his own mind. It isn't fair—"

"He's five years old, Mildred, and he is my son, not yours. I know his mind perfectly well, and that it isn't set yet, because it can't be. He's too young."

"He's older than he looks. He has an old soul, his grandfather says. That's where that strong-willed streak comes from."

Willa drew herself up to her full height and let the space of the house envelop her, imbuing her words with more power than she felt. "I know a bit about old souls, Mildred. And I won't allow you to control his."

"You think that you can?" Mildred laughed. "Oh, my dear, take a little advice from the mother of a son. They're only ever loaned to us until they find their way to other things. Greatness, you may hope. Wealth, if you're lucky. Happiness, if the stars align and fate decides not to snatch it from you. It snatched away my boy, but I'll move heaven and earth to make sure it won't take this one. All the advantages, all the hopes we pinned on Ford, and he threw them all away. I know, wherever his mind now chooses to spend time, that he sees the error of his ways. And that his wishes now are that Ruther takes up his birthright. Letting him have that is really the least you can give him, after everything this world has taken away."

Mildred said *this world* with a tone that carried its real meaning: *with everything you, you interloper, with your feminine wiles and bohemian refusal to bow down to society's expectations, your hidden-away insistence on remaining in this mist-cloaked river bend. Everything you, Willa Rakes, have taken away from* me.

"He can come to your house for lunch on Christmas," Willa said. "And I expect you've already taken his trunk and his holiday school-work to your house because you thought I would agree, but I'm afraid you thought wrong. Please have them brought round when you can. Ford has missed him terribly, for all that you think that Ford's not really here. I've missed him terribly, for all that you don't seem to care. Ruth will stay home."

"This is your home." Willa heard Ruth's whisper hissing from the corner of the room, and she had no idea how long he had been standing there. "It isn't mine. It hates me and I know it, and I hate it, and it knows that, too."

Mildred laughed again. "Ruther, darling, it's just an old house. They have their personalities, like people, but they're only a place to lay your head at the end of the day. And you'll come and spend some time with us soon."

Ruth's expression was hunted, his face closed off in a way that took Willa instantly back to the sleepless days and weeks after his birth, when nothing could soothe him. She had pulled him out of herself and into the refuge with her own two hands, and he had been slapping them away ever since. "Say goodbye to your grandmother, Ruth."

Ruth glared at her and threw his arms around Mildred, burying his face in her narrow chest as a pinched smile crossed her face. "I'll come to you as soon as I'm allowed." He stood back again and nodded, and Willa realized there were tears on his face, and realized at the same time the hostility with which that observation would be met. "I'll come to you as soon as she lets me go."

He ran up the stairs to his room, and the slamming of his door shook through the mansion with an echo that reverberated in Willa's heart.

· 27 ·

LOCKHART, VIRGINIA, 2015

EVERY MORNING, BEFORE ALEX REACHED CONSCIOUS thought—before he staggered downstairs to make a pour-over coffee, or pulled on one of his distressed Ramones or Creedence T-shirts with their curated holes, or even brushed his teeth—he would reach for his phone on the nightstand and tap the little envelope on the screen, looking for a message from Myra.

And every morning for the last several weeks, there had been one.

Sometimes more than one. The red dot next to the small envelope on his screen could hold the promise of one subject line, or half a dozen, depending on how excited Myra was about a project: I made a fiddlehead fern, and I am SO PROUD of this rubber tree, and My mom is sick of tiny plants, so I am BOTHERING YOU INSTEAD.

Myra seemed to write the messages at the same time she wrote new updates for *The Minuscule Mansion*, and the simultaneous drafting made Alex feel a special connection to the posts, as if she were writing them just for him instead of the hundreds of thousands of people who wanted to read about the latest room in the house. Myra's most recent project had been particularly popular, a kind of interior conservatory she'd created in the back of the kitchen, where the best light came from the river.

Or it would, if there were an actual river beneath the miniature version of the house where Alex lived. That corner in the full-sized house was filled with boxes full of dishes and other accoutrements of the more permanent life he kept meaning to build here; he hadn't even moved most of his things in from the portable container he'd had delivered to the mansion's driveway.

But Myra's version of the kitchen corner was filled with minute hand-sculpted plants. His favorite was a croton in a Blue Willow pot, each brightly colored vein painted by hand with a brush the size of a cat's whisker. In every message Myra told him more about the tools she used, and had even sent him pictures of some that she hadn't posted on the site.

CHECK OUT THIS PLANT STAND, she wrote, all-caps shouting at him from a list of subject lines in his inbox, and every so often, he wondered at how—and how quickly—he had become the kind of person who could get swept up in all-caps enthusiasm over a plant stand. And not just any plant stand, but a very small one. It wasn't concert tickets or an all-expenses-paid trip to some exotic locale, but a message—an excited, elated message—from a woman he had never seen, and he clicked on her words with the anticipation of a fan, underpinned with something deeper. Longing. Connection. Joy.

I got a bunch of old-fashioned wooden spools from a craft store that was going out of business and posted a bunch of stuff online. I love these, because they're sturdy but also hollow, so I can thread things through their middle. Is this not the most delightfully tacky thing you've seen in all your life?

Alex clicked through the attached pictures. Myra had carved a scalloped edge into the top of the spool, which was painted white, with green and red bits of holly stenciled—or free handed?—onto its small edges. In the next photo, the spool-table held a bottle brush Christmas tree hung with minute popcorn chains and red cardinals, real enough to look as if they'd eat the popcorn. In the last photo, the Christmas tree was lit from within, its branches made from light. He opened a reply. *That is, indeed, a very cool plant stand, but I see a lot of tacky stuff on any given day—it's kind of my dad's favorite thing to sell, truth be told—and I'm afraid to tell you that, while delightful, it is NOT tacky, just awesome. How did you light the branches?*

Whoosh.

Ping!

It looks like it's a bottle brush, but I actually made it myself with LED wires. Alex heard the breathlessness in Myra's words despite never having heard her voice. *It's strung right up through the middle of the spool, so I can hide the battery pack somewhere else in the room. Every so often I like to do holiday themes in the house—sometimes I'll do a holiday in each room, all at the same time. Christmas, Halloween, Valentine's Day. Christmas is going to be in the bathroom, I've decided. Just to mix things up. I'm going to put this stand right next to the claw-foot tub.*

Doesn't that seem a little dangerous? Whoosh.

Ping! In the best way. No dolls, remember? And I have some hand-

knit green and red towels, too, to hang over the edge of the tub. I made them a while ago, when I was still trying miniature knitting, and they're a little rough but I can call them rustic—

Alex pictured Myra's hands wielding the minute knitting needles, as fine as dental floss, or the magnifying glass she'd told him she needed to use whenever she worked with small pieces of fabric. He could picture its silver handle, flowers and vines wrapped around the untarnished spots where her fingers must have held it.

Alex had never seen Myra's fingers. He had never seen her hands, or her face, or any part of her. He had asked, tentatively, if he could see a photo of her, because he knew she'd seen him. But her refusal was so sudden, and so absolute, that he was afraid to press her further.

But he could feel her touch in every shot of the Mansion's interior, and as he walked through his own shelter, he could imagine hearing her breathing overhead, the walls of the house expanding and contracting in time to her voice, which he knew carried a melody all its own—but one he'd never heard, because they had yet to speak over the phone.

His connection to Myra was entirely written, flurries of words and letters arcing across the width of a continent, but filling a space that seemed much smaller, a space that seemed to belong to the two of them together. The fact of their distance had shrunk in importance; on-screen, and in Alex's dreams, their spaces seemed the same, though the difference in scale imbued a lopsidedness, a lack of symmetry that Alex found charming, as he did all things that were a bit off balance and imperfect.

The mansion itself seemed to sense their connection, waking him at random times of the night to music or sparkling light that should have felt like a ghost story and felt instead like a picture book, where everything was soothing and safe. The feeling followed Alex through his days at Rakes and Son, erecting an invisible wall between the real world with its demanding customers and Alex's interior world, where he composed lengthy messages to Myra about the ebb and flow of his day, trying to match her talent for capturing detail and humor.

> Today a customer asked to alter a credenza. That, in and of itself, isn't all that strange—it happens all the time. They want an island, or a narrow dining table, stuff like that. But this one wanted us to remove the bun feet so the piece sat flat on the floor, and he wanted to replace the cabinet door on the left-hand side with a completely open area, including cutting through the back. And then he wanted us to upholster that whole area, *inside* the piece, with faux shearling. Because, it turns out, he has a pet. Not a cat. Not a dog. An iguana. They want a customized iguana credenza that can sit behind the sofa in their parlor so that Sweetums—that's the iguana—has a place that feels like home, and that home needs to feel like a nineteenth-century bordello, but classy. And we're going to do it! We priced it out, and told the guy, and he got out his wallet as if his Amex had been waiting for this opportunity his whole life. Just when I think I've seen it all, I see a giant credenza lizard.

Mrs. Sherrill returned for her reupholstered bamboo settee and found Alex's hand cold and nonresponsive when she passed him her credit card again; he didn't hear the disappointment under her voice about the scheduled delivery, or the fact he would not bring the piece to her sun-dappled Florida room himself.

Other customers walked to and fro through the reclaimed wood doors and bothered Alex no more than the breeze blowing off the canal outside. He met them with the same welcoming gaze that masked all his prior interactions, but there were feelings behind it now more complex than longing to escape. His drive to describe the people he saw, to capture them for Myra, transformed him into a miniaturist. The florid purple pocket square in a dapper visitor's suit pocket could spin poetry in front of him for hours as he tried to imagine the perfect words to evoke its color: *like a black eye that hasn't healed because he wants to display it.*

Because he never brought much of himself to the store's work—not believing, until recently, that he had much of an interior life to bring—no one noticed any outward difference. No one, that is, except his father. Rutherford watched his son's light steps across the gallery and increased his unannounced visits to the mansion, keeping a random schedule that varied according to his own unspoken whims. Sometimes he would bring food and tell Alex it was time to eat, a task that Alex had increasingly forgotten. Some days, Alex would find Rutherford in the kitchen or the library, after his father let himself in while Alex was at work or sourcing vintage furniture pieces or, most recently, purchasing an ever-more-complicated array of camera equipment with which to photograph the house, the river, the vistas of Lockhart, trying to paint a backdrop for Myra, to give full-sized context to her miniature window on his life.

One morning, he awoke to another message from Myra, a picture of a tiny book appended to its foot. Do you have this book in your library? Mine is silent, seeing as it won't open, but it just occurred to me tonight that you may have it. Alex read the title—*A Child's Treasury of Nature Poems*—and noted the detailed painting on its clothbound cover, a sweep of ocean with the sun setting into the waves. He ran down the staircase and listened, feeling the air in the room part before him like the Red Sea, leading him to a bookcase in the corner.

The only blue book on the shelf was Myra's. He ran back upstairs to his room, photographing the volume, which fell open to a worn page he remembered without any reason he could discern. "A Jelly-Fish," by Marianne Moore, he typed, his fingers falling into the rhythm of the words.

> *You have meant*
> *To catch it,*
> *And it shrivels;*
> *You abandon*
> *Your intent—*
> *It opens, and it*
> *Closes and you*
> *Reach for it—*

This feels familiar, he wrote. This feels like us. Every time we start to get our bearings, the Mansion's one step ahead of us.

When did you get your bearings? Myra responded, almost instantly. I haven't felt like that yet. Thank you for sending the poem—once I finish with the conservatory, I think I may work on some new books for the library. I like it when I can open a new volume for a photograph, so the same words aren't showing all the time.

The words they exchanged were a strange mix of intimate—the kind of conversation old friends might have after a decade's absence, picking up seamlessly wherever the thread dropped in their lives—and superficial, their interactions steered without much input from either of them. The common details competed for attention, their intricate complexity making everything and nothing profound at once.

Talking to you is like being in a snow globe, Myra wrote one morning. I was trying to think of a way to describe it, and that's the best I could come up with. Like we're in our own world together, and everything's a little sparkly, and music is playing somewhere outside. We can see out, but no one else can get in.

And we're both a little shaken up, but in the best possible way, Alex replied. And we don't mind it at all.

A Very Tiny Holiday

(From *The Minuscule Mansion of Myra Malone*, 2015)

MERRY CHRISTMAS, HAPPY HALLOWEEN, AND A VERY RO-mantic Valentine's Day to you all! I've been hard at work putting to-gether some decor for a holiday re-theme of some of the Mansion's rooms. I like to do this every so often—it's easier than a full refresh, because it's mostly accessories and decorations, but still detailed and fun. And I can pick whatever times of year I'd like to celebrate, because every day in the Mansion is all seasons at once. Everything that happens here is happening all the time. So if I want it to be Christmas, Halloween, and Valentine's Day simultaneously, so be it. Until I change my mind.

I focused Halloween in the kitchen, both because I already had all the plants in the mini-conservatory—perfect for draping spiderwebs—and because it gave me an excuse for one of my favorite kinds of projects: packaging! Because Halloween is all about the candy, and as you'll see, I have bowls and dishes of it everywhere, plus cookies. I like to think the Mansion would offer a good selection of both homemade and store-bought treats, but if I had to pick my two favorites in the bunch, I'd gravitate toward the buckeyes in the homemade department, and Necco Wafers in the store-bought category. They're both not particularly complicated or detailed, but there are so many of them that I'm still a little overwhelmed. And the colors of the Neccos—you'll see I have some wrapped in the classic waxed paper cylinders (those are hand-lettered, I'll have you know), and others loose (and stamped!) around the table. Some are on the floor, of course, because it's Halloween, and it's candy, and things get a little loose and exciting.

Or so I've read, at least. I've never done Halloween myself, except this way.

As for Valentine's Day, what better room than the library? Bookcases full of every possible kind of love, in addition to the love of words themselves. What better place for hearts and passion than a roomful of books? I cut out the lace doily hearts from coffee filters, and I think they turned out great. But don't miss the glass heart prisms I've hung from the chandelier, because stringing them onto fishing line was no small feat, no pun intended. I love the color, though—I took a few photos of the way they cast rose-tinted rainbows around the room, but photos don't do it justice. If you could crystallize the feeling of being in love, I bet it would look like a red glass heart. Rich and full of rainbows. Perhaps a bit too easy to break. But beautiful all the same.

And the bathroom—oh, I'm so proud of this bathroom, everyone, I can't even tell you. I decided to do a kitschy Florida Keys kind of look, which is a little outside my normal aesthetic, I'll grant you, but if you're going to have fun decorating, a bathroom is a good, low-stakes place to do it. The Christmas tree and its stand are made of a spool and LED wires, and I'm particularly fond of the lights hung around the picture rail near the ceiling. Every single one of those little huts shading the lights are handmade from pieces of matchsticks and capiz shell, and they took an age, but they were worth it. Yes, I repainted the bead-board in Kiss Me Coral, which clashes delightfully with the red and green in a way I hate-love, and I hope you will, too. And if you're won-dering what got into the bathtub—he's an iguana, and his name is Sweetums. He is a temporary, *temporary*, exception to the no-residents rule, and only because he isn't a doll. He is a plastic figurine, and he came in a set of cake toppers for lizard-obsessed children, and YES, I've also painted his toenails Kiss Me Coral, and I think we can all agree he looks lovely. Don't ask me where he came from, or where I got the idea. I just had a feeling he'd really bring the room together.

Also, no. I'm not sure what's gotten into me, either.

· 29 ·

LOCKHART, VIRGINIA, 2015

WHEN ALEX PADDED DOWNSTAIRS TO THE MANSION'S LI-
brary to replace *A Child's Treasury of Nature Poems* on its shelf, the sharp
light of morning intruded through slender openings in the velvet curtains,
slicing through the room. As Alex crossed to open a set of drapes, he
nearly tripped over his father's polished oxblood shoes. Rutherford himself was nearly invisible in the gloom, sitting in one of the rocking chairs
in front of the fireplace, his eyes screwed shut and his lips pressed together, breathing shallowly. He looked to Alex as if he were either willing
himself, with every fiber of his being, to be somewhere else—or, perhaps,
trying to let as little of his surroundings inside his lungs as possible.

Music in the room chimed lightly from the ceiling, a misting shower
made into sound. It sounded vaguely like Chopin, which was the mansion's most frequent choice, but played at a level that seemed to exclude Alex, as if it were meant only for Rutherford.

"Dad? What's going on?"

Rutherford's eyes snapped open and gazed at Alex with an unfamiliar expression. It took a moment to recognize it as fear, and Alex watched as his father shook his head sharply, trying to dislodge the emotion. "What have you got there?"

"Just a book." Alex crossed the room to return the volume to the bookcase, restoring it to its shelf among shades of greens and browns, the blue of *Nature Poems* glowing like a sapphire on the dark shelf.

"'I wandered lonely as a cloud,'" Rutherford murmured.

"What?"

"That book. Page eighteen, two-thirds of the way down the page. Wordsworth."

"Was this yours?"

"No. Nothing in this place was ever mine."

Alex squinted at his father and then glanced around the library, its paneled walls soaring to a tray ceiling overhead, the track lighting installed in a misbegotten attempt at modernization in the eighties, crisscrossing dark shadows where chandelier medallions used to be. "Dad, this entire place belongs to you."

Rutherford snorted, his face contorting with scorn. "Is that what you think?"

"I think I'm confused. I grew up in this house—well, the first few years. I live here now. You kept it rented in between. I know you've never liked it, but I've never understood why. Didn't your dad—"

"This was not my father's house. This is my mother."

"Your mother's house?"

"Something like that." Rutherford pressed his fingertips against the bridge of his nose, rubbing his eyes.

Alex noticed he had turned the rocking chair to face away from

Willa's portrait. He felt her gaze with warmth, a silent invitation. "Where did Grandma go, Dad?"

"I don't know."

"Is she dead?"

"Possibly. I had nowhere to inquire."

"Willa was your mom, and she was my grandma, and yet I've never seen a single photograph in this house. The only image I've ever seen of her is that painting. You never talk about her. I barely remember her, and what I do remember is so distant it feels like a story someone told me, except no one ever talked about her, because I had no one to ask."

"You still don't. I won't discuss her."

"Do you have any idea how strange it was to get invited to friends' houses, to get picked up for the weekend and head up to these sprawling country estates, and see all these family photos everywhere? People who not only had families, but who wanted you to see them and know what they looked like? I had no frame of reference for it, for that kind of pride. It made no sense to me." Alex sat down in the rocking chair that matched his father's, leaning forward, trying to meet his eye. "Can you help it make sense?"

The laughter that rumbled from Rutherford's chest seemed unnatural, an unhinged peal that burbled from depths outside his body. "I'm the last person left on earth who could. Which is to say I couldn't, not ever. Isn't that right?" Rutherford shouted downward, and Alex shrank back into his chair, feeling as if he had interrupted a conversation between two people who would rather talk to anyone else other than each other. He felt the atmosphere taking on the same sparking electricity he remembered from the morning Rutherford came to his room, a pool of unreserved anger that seemed to emanate not merely from inside him, but from the air around him. The first time it happened, the anger swept Alex up, too, but Rutherford's shouting this time seemed to have nothing to do with him. His father barely seemed to recognize he was still in the room, but Rutherford dragged his gaze up from the floor and looked at Alex, his eyes blazing.

"You shouldn't stay here," Rutherford said.

"I feel like I belong here, Dad."

"That's precisely why you need to leave. I should never have allowed it. Stop *looking* at her!"

Alex realized he was gazing at his grandmother's portrait, drawing comfort from her face as his father's words blew across the room, carried on a breath of hot wind. "Why are you—"

Rutherford jumped up from his chair as if it had ignited beneath him, snatching a fire poker from the wrought iron tool stand next to the fireplace and racing toward the portrait. "Stop *looking* at him!" He slashed the poker's hook down his mother's face, slicing through her russet curls, her blue left eye, the mischievous curve of her lips, catching at last on a stopping point at the base of her white throat. He drew the poker back to slash again, but Alex grabbed his wrist. Rutherford wheeled around, his face an inhuman snarl. He threw the poker toward the fireplace. It collided with a porcelain umbrella stand, shattering it into elephant-painted shards. He shook his wrist from Alex's grasp and strode toward the bookcase, crossing the room with impossibly large steps, pulling the blue volume from its shelf and ripping it open. "I was as lonely as a cloud," he screamed. "I was always as lonely as a cloud, and it wanted that for me!" He ripped the book in two and threw the halves back onto the shelf above, hitting a collection of slim cobalt-blue vases, the hand-blown ridges of their fluted surfaces fracturing.

Alex felt the impact reverberating in his chest, a powerful vibration that nearly knocked him over with muscle memory that didn't belong to him. A sense that this had happened before, more than once. His father's wrath rippled like an echo through the room, through the bones of the house, across the strange and uneven flow of time on that hill above its silver curve of river. The walls of the mansion shuddered around them as if trying to expel a splinter or a shard of glass. Alex thought of the miniature portrait with its diagonal slash, the sparkling remains of crushed glass Myra had described to him. *Everything that transpires in the Mansion has transpired before, and is still happening, and will happen again, because the refuge remembers.*

Alex ran after his father. He was only slightly taller and didn't have much more muscle, but he had the advantage of youth, the advantage of feeling grounded in the space Rutherford seemed hell-bent on destroying. He wrapped his arms around his father and knocked him to the ground, holding him tightly until he stopped screaming, stopped wriggling, until his breathing slowed and became more even. "Hush, now," Alex said, his voice softer than the distant sound of piano, softer than the voice he remembered from his grandmother, though he could not remember how he knew. "Hush. You're safe." The words felt right, despite also feeling upside down in light of the threat that Rutherford himself seemed to pose. "Dad, let me take you home."

Rutherford sat up, his face filled with sadness. "There's a room for you there, you know. I always had room for you, even if you thought I didn't."

"I know. I wouldn't have come back if I didn't know."

"I was selfish to ask you to."

"Dad, you're sick—"

"It was selfish of me." Rutherford rose to his feet, steadying himself on Alex's shoulder. "I should never have let you come."

· 30 ·

LOCKHART, VIRGINIA, 1961

THE SNOW SWIRLED INTO DRIFTS AGAINST THE MANSION'S sharp corners, banking into gentle ripples down to the river, which flowed slowly around the icy fingers encroaching from the banks. The river was as oblivious to the frigid air as it was to shimmering waves of heat, pausing only a moment at its bend below the mansion before moving downstream, searching for more hospitable shores, a place where time didn't feel so slowed by tragedy.

Willa felt the slowness like a betrayal, the sluggishness an almost deliberate contrast to the white-tipped rapids the night Ford disappeared. The storm had raced up from the gulf coast with a fury that thousands of miles had not diminished, dumping buckets of rain that still smelled of the sea, whipping the oak trees with lightning-crackled wind that threatened to uproot them. The hurricane's remains swirled around the mansion with a roar that Ford tried to match, screaming at Willa from his bedroom about the unacceptable loudness of the music she wasn't playing. When she heard his footfalls on the stairs, the air around her shifted in a way she'd come to recognize, and she hid in the room behind the bookcase as Ford raged through the mansion's downstairs rooms. It was two days before Thanksgiving, and Willa was grateful that Ruth hadn't yet returned from school for the holiday.

She sat on the floor in the tiny room, hugging her knees to her chest and resting her head against the turned wood leg of the round oak table. She waited for the storm inside Ford to blow itself out, for him to fall asleep in his chair or somewhere else in the house. And as the pounding rain and thunder died down outside, the noise within the house began to fade until it ceased completely, and she crept out in the morning's small hours to find Ford gone. The carved front door hung open on its hinges, and the wrought iron gate was ajar. The rope on the river dock was curled neatly in a coil, the rowboat gone. The mansion yawned with emptiness that felt like peace. Willa was ashamed of her deep sense of relief—for all that Ford was gone, she longed for him, and she sat on the wide front steps, soaking her dress with the water that cemented dead oak leaves to the planks. She waited, unmoving, for him to return.

She was still sitting there—and couldn't say for how long—as the weather grew colder, and small flakes began to flurry from the sky. She still hadn't moved when Mildred's polished car pulled next to the curb of the sidewalk at the bottom of the hill. Willa blinked at the light reflecting from the black sedan—its presence seemed alien, a visitor from some future time Willa had forgotten she was a part of. Thanksgiving, she remembered. A holiday. Ruth.

Mildred climbed out of the passenger's side, clinging to the door to keep from slipping, and called up to Willa on the porch. "I've already called our tree man to clear things at our place, and then I'll send him here. Do you have power?"

"No," Willa whispered. "I have no power at all."

"Half the city's gone dark, but Teddy said our lights stayed on," Mildred called. "I can't believe how cold it's gotten—snow after a hurricane? And in November? I've never seen anything like it. Did Ford rest at all last night?"

"I hope he's resting now."

"Is he upstairs?"

"No."

Mildred and Ruth reached the porch, and Mildred glanced around the wide front yard. "Some branches down, but I'm surprised the trees are all still here—they must have taproots straight down to Hades. The noise was terrible when it blew through Asheville—Ruther said they all slept in the school gymnasium, can you imagine? The phone lines were all down. I couldn't even reach Teddy to ask him to drive over here. He told me this morning he wouldn't have gone out in it anyway. 'You'd have to be mad to go out,' he said."

"Yes." Willa's voice was deflated. She did not rise as her son approached or even try to embrace him after so many years of rejection. It was as if she didn't see Ruth at all, or Mildred, either. "It was madness."

"At any rate, it's a relief to get back to Lockhart—the major highways are clear, at least. Is there dinner? Have you and Ford eaten yet? I hope you've started a fire, at least." Mildred walked past Willa through the open front door, calling her son's name. Ruth stayed outside and stared at his mother.

"Where is Father?"

Willa looked at her son as if registering, for the first time, that he was there. "He isn't here."

"What do you mean, he isn't here? He's always here." Ruth narrowed his blue eyes, his haughty and dismissive expression reflecting, yet again, that his mother couldn't possibly know what she was talking about. "Where would he go?"

"Down the river."

"Mother, stop. I didn't like your mystery act when I was small, and I like it even less now." Ruth reached into his pocket and pulled out a pack of cigarettes and a flip-top lighter, and began to smoke with a practiced nonchalance that burned Willa's insides with its unfamiliarity. Willa remembered with a start that Mildred had exited the passenger's side of the car at the bottom of the hill, and that Ruth had been driving—that the long months of his absences had stretched inexorably into years spent away at school, punctuated by begrudging holidays in the mansion, where his unhappiness was eclipsed only by his father's wide poles between uneasy silence and screaming fury. His years had passed with hardly a ripple. Ruth was grown.

"Your father took the boat."

Ruth shook his head and exhaled a cloud of smoke. "Don't be ridiculous. The water's too high, and it's freezing. Who in the world would go out on it today?"

"He went last night."

"What?" Ruth tossed his cigarette to the ground and crushed it beneath his shoe, the polished oxblood leather starting to soak in the collecting snow. "Last night? During the hurricane? You can't be serious."

"He's gone, Ruth. The boat is gone. He left last night—"

"What did you do to him?" Ruth's face contorted. "What did you do? Father never left the house—he never would have left at all, and never in weather like that. Unless you did something. What did you do?" His voice, its volume, began to sound like Ford's, and Willa held her hands over her ears and closed her eyes, trying to shut him out.

"What's going on out here?" Mildred stepped back onto the porch. "I can't find Ford anywhere— Ruth, are you crying? What's happened?"

Ruth raised an accusing finger at his mother. "She chased him off. She killed him."

"What?"

"Father! She said he went out on the river! Last night!"

"That can't possibly be—" Mildred dragged her gaze from her grandson to Willa, and clapped her hand over her mouth. "That can't possibly be. Willa, where is Ford?" Mildred dropped into a crouch and gripped Willa's wrists, violently pulling them from her ears, shouting into her face. "Look at me! This instant! What is Ruther talking about? Where is my son?"

Willa shook her head, kept shaking it, tears running down her face, a keening wail emitting from her abdomen from depths below her feet. "Gone." She rocked back and forth on the step and ripped her hands from her mother-in-law's grasp, burying her face into them. "He's been gone for so long that I didn't feel it when he really left. I didn't know. I couldn't feel him anymore. He was already lost."

The sound of Mildred's hand hitting Willa's cheek reverberated off the floorboards. "I will not have this melodrama. We are going to find my son, and if you won't tell us what happened, you can tell the authorities. We will find him and then do what I should have done years ago, and bring him home with us, and you can rot away in this ridiculous behemoth alone, as you should have all along. The rest of us will be better off without you." Mildred glanced over her shoulder to where her grandson still stood, the flakes of snow collecting on his flannel cap. "Take the car to our house, now, and call the police, Ruther. I'll stay here with—her, and wait in case your father comes back. Go now. Bring your grandfather back with you. And be careful of the snow."

Ruth jumped at the sound of his grandmother's voice, then fled down the steep hill toward the car. Mildred stood before Willa on the stairs, as if guarding her from making her escape. Willa didn't move. She breathed deeply and drew strength from the ground; for the first time in decades, the mansion felt like hers again, a revelation that both relieved her and made her incredibly sad.

"You won't get away with this," Mildred hissed.

"He got away from me." Willa sighed. She looked up at Mildred and let the weight of centuries sink her mother-in-law's buoyant suspicions, her determination to wrest control from Willa at last. "I loved him, Mildred. More than words can describe. But he never returned, not really. And you know that as well as I. I would have saved him if I could. But the forces that took him were rooted far from here, and they never gave him back."

"You took him from me. He had everything in front of him—our only heir, the one we knew would carry on what we built. Until you—"

"You told me once our sons are only loaned to us. I'm not the one who collected your debt, though you certainly collected mine." Willa gestured down the hill, at Ruth's skidded footprints through the gathering snow. "I don't get to choose who finds shelter here, or who rejects it. I've tried, and paid dearly for the effort."

"If anything has befallen my son, you haven't yet begun to pay. And when the police get here—when Teddy gets here—"

"They will see what I want them to see, which is the truth, and then

they will go. And you will go, too. You won't return unless invited."
Willa sighed, releasing a little of her grief into the bones of a house that
had begun to recognize her old form, had ceased fighting against her
and the family she tried to create, the links she tried to forge with the
world around a refuge that expected to be chief among her loyalties.
"You are not needed here, Mildred."

"Your son will disagree."

"Yes. And he will leave with you, something else that happened
long ago. But there may come a time he may need me more than he
loves you, and I will still be here." Willa rose to her feet. The snowflakes
cascaded to the ground with force, and the wind picked up speed,
surrounding her with crystalline cold. "I am always here."

Mildred took a step back from the mansion, and then another.
"Every rumor in this town about this place, every ill wind that blows
down from this hill—I never credited anything about any lady of this
house, because no lady would live here. And I was right."

"Perhaps you were. People see what they wish to see."

"I wish to see this place destroyed. And you along with it."

"Yes." Willa smiled, her face suffused with the resignation of someone who had always known this to be true. "You are not the first to say
so. Others have, and now they are gone. You will be gone someday,
too. And this place will still be here."

"You don't know the future."

"But I know the past." The snow curled around Willa's feet, tendrils
of ice rooting her to the spot. Cold wind blew Mildred back another
step, and they were still staring at each other when Theodore and Rutherford arrived with the police, all of whom wandered on the flagstone
path beneath the gathering snow, confused.

All except Ruth, whose blue eyes burned colder than the crystalline ice in the air. "She killed him," he said. "She killed my father."

The voice that came from Willa was older than the mansion, older than the stones beneath their feet. "Your father was lost to the storm. The storm took him before you entered this house, and I have mourned him ever since."

"If he left, as you say, then he was leaving you. And he was right to do it." Ruth and Willa stood in a bubble that excluded the others around them, time slowing to a crawl, the snowflakes suspended in midair. "I know you can send them away." Ruth gestured at his grandparents, the police, the world below the mansion's hill. "I know you can make them all leave and not look further. And I will leave with them. But I want you to know that this is all your fault. What happened to Father, the way he was my whole life, that wasn't the war. That was you. And I will never forgive you."

"You've never forgiven me since you entered this world, Ruth. But I can't apologize for bringing you into it. For all that you hate me, I love you. I loved your father. And you may leave with them, but inside you will always know that you came from here. You came from me. Your arrival came with gifts you've never accepted, but you hold them just the same. The harder you fight against this place, the harder it will fight back, because it holds a piece of you." The snow began to move again, the others on the path blinking with bewilderment. "And so do I."

Mildred wrapped her arms around her grandson, who let himself be ushered away, keeping his eyes trained on Willa, his gaze unbroken. Willa put her hand over her heart and gestured toward her son. And then she walked up the wide front steps, stepped into the mansion, and closed the carved front door.

· 31 ·

PARKHURST, ARIZONA, 2015

MYRA WAS EXHAUSTED AFTER A NIGHT SPENT WORKING on the conservatory and talking—or, more accurately, typing—with Alex on her laptop, which Gwen had set up to receive text messages after growing exhausted with Myra's constant calls for mobile phone advice.

Ping. Sweetums's dad came to pick up his new digs today, and Sweetums came along. On a leash. Thought you'd want to know.

Thank you, so much, for not making me wait for this information, but—

Ping. I can't believe I forgot to mention. The leash was pinkish orange. One might even say coral. Forgive the omission, my lady.

All is forgiven, especially if you tell me you petted him and that he felt like pebbled leather.

I most certainly did not pet him. I almost didn't let him in the store, but I didn't want to have an argument. Aren't iguanas bloodthirsty, or something like that?

I think you're thinking of Komodo dragons.

That must be it. You're remarkably quick with animal facts. Maybe you should consider a menagerie theme one of these days.

Intriguing. Or an aquarium, perhaps.

Only if it has jellyfish.

Their messages volleyed back and forth as Myra sat at her laptop and Alex lay in bed with his phone, trying to imagine her voice. Their words ebbed and flowed as each fell in and out of sleep.

A few hours before the sun rose, Myra finally staggered downstairs from the attic and collapsed into her bed, falling into a deep and dreamless sleep. It was full day when a crash upstairs awoke her.

When she reached the top of the stairs, trudging with more than a little exasperation, the Mansion was open again. "Do I have to weld those buckles shut? Lou never taught me metalworking, but I'm not above finding some online tutorials, you know." She crossed the attic to the house, which was silent—unusual in recent days.

A few feet from the house was the book of poetry, the edges of its ocean scene singed into blackness. When she picked it up, it cracked open—having only been a solid block before. She retrieved a magnifying glass from the desk along the wall, near her computer. *I wandered lonely as a cloud / That floats on high o'er vales and hills . . .*

She wheeled around and stared at the Mansion. "What happened? What's wrong?" The tiny house was quiet. Nothing moved. She could hear Gwen's voice in her head—*Surely you're aware that talking to a dollhouse confirms everything everyone everywhere thinks about people who play with dollhouses?*

"It's not a dollhouse," Myra said aloud. She put the singed book back in the library and walked to her computer. Something is wrong, she typed to Alex. Are you okay? I worry you're not okay. Please write back as soon as you see this.

She tapped her foot on the floorboards, filled with nervous energy, counting the seconds. She glanced around the attic for something to do, some mindless task to complete, but couldn't think of anything— the air felt too heavy to move through, too heavy to breathe. She hadn't realized she was holding her breath until she heard the ping of her inbox and released the air captured in her chest.

I'm okay, Alex wrote. But my dad is—less okay than usual. His bar for "okay" is pretty low on the best days, but today has not been the best day. Something is definitely wrong.

Myra rapidly typed back, their correspondence taking on the contemporaneous speed of a real conversation, a voice she could almost hear in her head. The book you read to me is open, and it didn't open last night. It looks burned, and I found it outside the house. I haven't had time to look really closely to see what else might be broken or missing, but everything is completely motionless and quiet inside, and it hasn't been that way since you and I started talking. What's going on with your dad? I thought you lived alone?

Ping. That's a bigger question than I can type about right now. I'm writing with my thumbs because I'm at the shop. Could we—take a deep breath here, now—actually talk? With our voices? On the phone?

Myra plopped down on the floor and closed her eyes. Alex had never proposed an actual, oral conversation before, and Myra had grown unaccustomed to the sound of her own voice outside the interactions she had with the narrow circle—a dash, really—of people who saw her in person, which was limited to Gwen and her mother. She had known, at some point, that he would suggest an actual conversation.

But she had continued to put the request off in her own mind, telling herself that was a bridge of awkwardness they'd cross when they reached it.

She heard a tiny click and opened her eyes, peering into the heart of the house. The hidden room behind the library bookcase had opened. The chandelier was moving in a slow twirl. "I don't think I asked you," Myra said, rolling her eyes.

Ping. Alex's words were haunting. Your silence is deafening. I didn't mean to scare you. If you'd rather talk this way, I can write you later today. It's just too much for me to type until I get to a regular keyboard. We can wait. NBD.

Soft chords floated up from the hidden room. "I said I didn't ask you."

Ping. You have my number. Ball's in your court. More later. AR

Myra trudged to her desk and pulled open the drawer where she kept her phone. She wasn't entirely sure what kind of plan Gwen had opened for it; she used it mostly for uploading photos and typing notes when she couldn't be troubled to get to her computer.

Gwen picked up on the second ring. "I was going to call you this morning—the conservatory is getting a lot of traffic! At-home gardening is really having a moment right now, you know, and a houseplant's less demanding than a veggie garden. Unless you're me, that is. I killed another cactus this week."

"You overwater them."

"I just want them to love me!"

"Yes. I know."

"But you're not calling about web traffic. I wish you would, of course, because at some point I'm going to talk you into merchandise, which I have no less than a dozen requests for at the moment. Not just toy manufacturers, mind you—your aesthetic appeals to the full-sized world. I've been getting some calls from distributors who won't even talk to me without an NDA, which means it's someone big, and from the digging I've been able to do so far, I think it might be a place that starts with *T* and rhymes with 'Arget.' We've got a hot iron, Myra, and you need to let me start pounding the hell out of it—"

"I didn't call about web traffic, Gwen."

"I know. I know. Okay, what's up?"

"Do I have, like, minutes on my phone? Or something?"

"Oh God, another tech support call? I set up your computer so you wouldn't have to keep asking me, Myra. What do you mean? What kind of minutes?"

"Like, can I use the phone to call someone who isn't you? I'm not sure how this works."

Gwen giggled. "I'm sorry. I shouldn't laugh. Are you actually calling me—using 'minutes'—to ask me if you can use them for someone else? You have an unlimited plan, Myra. You can talk to whoever you want, for as long as you want, at any time of day or night. My God, I sound like a phone commercial. Knock yourself out. You even have video calling! You can strip down to your skivvies and—"

"Gwen!"

"Sorry. Welcome to the twenty-first century. We've been waiting for you. I'm guessing you're going to talk to Alex?"

"Maybe."

"My little one is growing up so fast. I couldn't be prouder."

"Thanks for making me regret calling you."

"Anytime. Let me know how it goes! And call me back, because we need to talk about the contest. Folks are getting anxious for an update and I'm getting anxious, too. We can't let things just linger—"

"Goodbye, Gwen."

"Goodbye, Myra."

Myra's cheeks burned. Part of her had hoped for a technological excuse, though she knew it was a long shot, and felt foolish for even thinking of it. *Your silence is deafening.*

She returned to her keyboard. I promise I'm trying. I have some things I need to do today first. This is all still very new.

She closed her computer and looked toward the Mansion behind her, waiting for some clue or prompting. The house was silent. It knew what she needed to do as much as she did, but it couldn't dial the numbers for her.

She crouched next to the short wooden walls and looked into the library. The portrait was still, the books all restored to their proper shelves, everything as outwardly normal as it ever was—which wasn't very, if she was honest. The room carried the faintest scent of smoke, and she had walked around the attic multiple times, putting her nose close to electrical outlets and lamps and fixtures in a worried attempt to root out any potential danger. But her hunt brought her back to the miniature library and the slightly scorched book of nature poems tucked back onto its shelf.

Myra stared at the portrait. "You're not going to tell me what happened, are you?"

She waited for a response she knew would never come.

"Well, then." She picked up her phone again. "I guess there's only one other person I can ask."

A Box Full of Music

(From *The Minuscule Mansion of Myra Malone*, 2015)

WHEN I WAS A LITTLE GIRL—WHEN I USED TO WORK ON the Mansion with Trixie, but before it became mine—I collected music boxes. My first was one that Grampa gave to me, a squarish, hinged jewelry box that I'm sure Trixie helped him pick out for me, telling him it was high time I had a place for my—I don't know, dead flowers and plastic rings? Whatever I thought was special when I was three years old, which is to say anything that caught my eye.

That first music box couldn't have been very expensive. It was covered with a kind of plasticky coating that looked a little like flowered wallpaper. The clasp was pointed and a little bit floppy, and it would rub green gunk onto my hands if I held it too long—which I did, as it happens, because it was my first jewelry box, and the first thing I owned that made music, and so I slept with it sometimes. And by *sometimes* I mean nightly, until my mom hid it away because I'd filled it with pretty leaves and pieces of snacks I'd forgotten and it was starting to attract ants.

But I digress.

This first music box had a little ballerina inside. She was perched on a flexible spring that made her pop up with a *boing*, like a tiny jack-in-the-box I knew was coming but still surprised me a bit every time. When the box opened, she twirled on her spring, around and around, with a little scrap of tulle around her waist, looking again and again at the little round mirror behind her, and then looking away. When Trixie first started teaching me to sew, I brought the box with me to their house and told her that the ballerina needed a different dress. Which is to say, she needed a *dress*, not an inch-wide scrap of grungy white tulle and a painted-on bodice. No wonder she kept looking away from the mirror.

Trixie said it was a good first project, and she helped me dig through her sewing basket to find a few shiny pieces of fabric that I liked, with swirls of pink and purple on a silky background. It wasn't really sewing—just a little bit of cutting, and then some tucking, and then watching while Trixie worked with a hot-glue gun. But it was so beautiful that I couldn't bear to close the box, which meant she kept spinning. (Oh, I should mention here that I kept the box wound up at all times, and when the melody started to slow—it was a few measures of "Solace," by Scott Joplin, I later learned—I would crank the little handle on the bottom again and again, which must have been lots of fun for my parents.) And every time she spun away from her mirror, I felt so sad that she wasn't able to look at the dress I made her. So, eventually, I held her fast with my finger and thumb so she couldn't move, hoping to give her a longer chance to admire herself and appreciate my craftsmanship.

She snapped off in my hand, and I cried. My mom helped me tuck her into a pillow I was supposed to use for the tooth fairy, with a little pink pocket on the front for holding a tooth. She slept in there every night before I forgot about her, and forgot about the box, and moved on to other obsessions, as I always did.

The moral of this story is *Myra's no good at leaving well enough alone.*

I know this about myself. I know that every time I plan to adjust or update "just a few things" in a room in the Mansion, I'll eventually wind up remaking it completely. I know that when I start writing something, it's a fifty-fifty chance whether I'll wind up letting that story live through the night, or whether I'll creep back to my computer in the wee hours of the morning and delete the words I've poured out. That goes for these words, too, and if you're reading them, I congratulate this story on its survival. It's word-eat-word in here, and only the strongest survive.

I don't know what makes some stories stronger than others; don't ask me. And what goes for words has also gone for other hobbies of mine; I cultivate them to the point of collapse, and then I start all over again. So it was for the music boxes. Grampa's "Solace" ballerina gave way to a host of noisy little boxes, and snow globes, and Christmas ornaments. (Never, ever tell anyone you collect something; you will almost always come to regret it.) Eventually, I got rid of almost all of them, but I had a soft spot for a collection that looked like pianos. At one point, I had four baby grand–shaped music boxes, a couple of pipe organs, one *very* rococo-style harpsichord, and a smattering of uprights. My favorite of these is the Steinway that stands in the Mansion now, and I selected it not because it was the most attractive (it wasn't) or because it fit the best (it didn't), but because the song it played was the one I loved the most.

If you've never heard Chopin's Prelude in A Major—you know what? You have. You've heard it. If you don't believe me, go plug it into a search engine right now. I'll wait.

Are you back?

Immediately recognizable, right?

I used to wind that music box up whenever I had trouble sleeping at night, which was a lot. My parents would find me curled around the outside of the Mansion, where I'd fall asleep listening to that song. It has such a complicated mix of calm and sadness—the kind of song where you notice something different every time it's played, even if it's played by a tiny metal comb scraping across an uneven cylinder (and I'm sorry if I just took the magic of music boxes away from you by explaining how they work, but if you've gone this long without taking one apart, I don't know what to tell you; it's high time you know how the sausage is made).

The other thing I love about it is the way it doesn't matter how I hear it—in a music box, over tinny laptop speakers, or on a radio—because in my head, I still hear it the way I heard it the first time, which was when Trixie played it. I still remember the look on her face during the last Christmas we all spent together, when Grampa held her hand and pulled her outside the house to his long gravel road, where a neighbor's beat-up old truck was waiting with something covered with a tarp in the back.

"I know you missed playing," he said. I didn't even know she played. None of us did. But there was a special kind of magic you could see flowing between them sometimes, and I swear there were things they knew about each other that they never even had to say aloud. Maybe she told him that she missed it, or maybe it was exactly what Grampa said: he knew. He just knew.

He *didn't* know the neighbor who owned the truck had thrown his back out loading up that piano from his own living room, which was where it had spent several out-of-tune years before he mentioned to Grampa that he was planning to throw it out, but wanted to check first if Grampa might have a use for it. So—and this was not an unusual event when it came to Grampa—it took a group of us to unload something really heavy while he huffed and puffed about the amazing deal he'd gotten, and how glad he was to give such a "pretty old lady" a home. He tweaked Trixie on the shoulder when he said it, and she smacked him on the back, and then they just beamed at each other. Watching them was embarrassing sometimes.

But my God, the first time we heard her play. It was like walking out of a house and then walking back in to discover it was actually a church all along. There was a majesty to it—a sacredness. A sadness, too, but one that made every happy feeling richer and deeper. That Chopin étude was the very first thing she played, and even though it was a little out of tune, and she was a little out of practice, we were all entranced.

And then she played "Jingle Bells," and we all sang, and I drank so much eggnog that I threw up a little, but it isn't the holidays without a little vomit from someone, right?

Once Trixie was gone, Grampa covered that piano with the quilt she made. After we lost her, I never saw it again. I don't know what happened to the quilt, either, even though I still remember every stitch I added to it, and still remember watching Trixie's fingers fly with her needle and thread, that same unconscious grace she brought to everything.

That little Steinway brings a piece of her back to me sometimes. When I turn the little key on the bottom and hear that tune, I often do the same thing I used to do with my little ballerina box—I turn it as far as it will go without breaking, and I hold it in my hand, listening to the music until I fall asleep.

It's too small to hold any snacks, fortunately, so we're safe from ants for now.

· 33 ·

LOCKHART, VIRGINIA, 1982

THE FIRST TIME RUTH PUT ALEX INTO WILLA'S ARMS, HE did so begrudgingly—but Alex was not yet one, and Mildred's sudden aneurysm and death had shocked him so completely that he didn't know where else to turn. He couldn't take him back to North Carolina, to Alex's mother—his pride and privilege wouldn't countenance giving back what his grandmother had done so much to secure, the protection of his reputation, a man on the cusp of forty becoming a father under circumstances many—Mildred included—would find unsavory.

But he couldn't keep the infant in his grandfather's house, beneath the roof he shared with his grandfather, suffering a grief that bewildered him and compounded the heartbreak of every wail that came from the child. After another sleepless night that had started to loosen his grip on reality, Rutherford woke to an instinct that hadn't arisen in him in years, and was almost always squelched whenever it occurred. He would go to his mother's house. As certain as he was that returning to the place would raise the same uneasiness it always did, he felt equally certain his mother would know what to do, although he could not say why.

When he pulled up to the sidewalk at the base of the hill, the oak trees were dropping bronze and copper leaves to the ground, and the dry leaves were scraping along the flagstones. His mother was sitting on the steps, waiting for him. He had not called, or maybe he had, in some way. He couldn't be sure.

Alex quieted as Rutherford brought him up the path, gazing around at the changing leaves and wrinkling his nose in the cold and fragrant breeze. Rutherford stopped a few feet away from Willa, already holding the infant away from himself, anxious to relieve himself of this burden that he didn't know what to do with. Mildred had handled all of the baby's care herself. She hadn't even allowed Theodore to hire a nurse or nanny to assist, insisting, *He is ours, and no one gets to share him.* "No one" seemed to include Rutherford himself, who rarely held the child and didn't often seek the opportunity to do so, though he couldn't help feeling a vibrating hum of jealousy when his grandmother cooed and embraced this tiny person who wasn't him. Alex was a sponge for attention, but Rutherford had never learned how to relate to him. Relating to people generally was, as it happened, something of a challenge for him, though he excelled in the surface interactions so essential to brisk sales. He preferred them, in fact.

"Mother." He took a step toward Willa, who did not rise, but blinked at him expectantly.

"So, I am a grandmother." Willa stood up and brushed her hands down the backs of her legs, sweeping the dry leaves that clung to her. "I had not been informed."

Rutherford nodded. "We had it managed."

"I have no doubt Mildred thinks so. But still, not to send a note seems more impolite than cruel. The latter quality never surprised me, but the former seems unthinkable, even for her."

"She's gone."

"Is she really?" Willa frowned and tilted her head, looking for a moment like her portrait that hung in the library that always matched her, though Rutherford was never quite sure when it had been painted or how long it had been part of the house. "Yes, I suppose she is. I hadn't noticed, but now that you mention it, that seems right. Everyone is gone eventually, Ruth. But I'm very sorry for you. I know she meant a lot to you."

"She raised me."

"To my regret, yes. Are you going to introduce me?"

"His name is Rutherford Alexander Rakes the Third."

Willa's laughter bubbled from her mouth so quickly that Rutherford felt the warming heat of his rage, a small coal that burned hot in his youth but still glowed whenever he approached the mansion or thought of his mother.

"It's my family name," Rutherford added, spitting the words at Willa as she laughed.

"I suppose it is now, though your father certainly wouldn't have wished it so. He went by Ford for a reason, Ruth, and to the extent he expressed anything to me at all when he came back here, he did tell me he wished I had picked a different name for you. But in any event, it appears that ship has long since sailed. Hello, little Rutherford the Third."

"He goes by Alex."

"Has he told you so?"

"You know I detest it when you act as if I'm part of a joke I didn't consent to, Mother."

"I do. I also know that you take serious inquiries as insults to your intelligence more often than not. I didn't mean to joke, Ruth. How does he act when you call him that? Does he seem to recognize that name?"

"You're speaking as if he's a terrier. He's a child."

"Names have power, Ruth. You never seemed to appreciate that. But now that I see him closer, I can see that Alex matches well. It suits him. Well done."

Rutherford felt a strange sort of satisfaction at the acknowledgment. Mildred had insisted on calling the baby Ford, after his father, and it was one of the few points of disagreement between them. For all that Mildred had held fond memories of her son, Rutherford himself had very few—Ford was a different man from the one that Mildred raised and the one that Willa married, and that fact had formed the foundation of a deep resentment of which Rutherford rarely spoke. He took another step forward and handed Alex to his mother.

Willa smiled down at Alex, and the air around them took on a color that brightened the fallen leaves. "He has your father's eyes," she said. "I never thought I'd see them again."

"I don't know what to do."

"He's a baby, Ruth. You feed him, and you change him, and you learn to turn off the part of your mind that's shattered by noise, if you can—because the noise is endless. But you'll learn." She stepped toward him and started to hand Alex back, and Rutherford stepped backward.

"You don't understand. I truly do not know what to do. Grandmother did everything, for all of us. Grandfather is shattered. I haven't slept in days. And he—needs things. All the time. I don't know how to manage."

"Where is his mother?"

"Gone."

Willa narrowed her eyes. "That seems to be going around. What are you suggesting?"

"I'm suggesting he stay here, with you." He gestured back toward the car. "I brought some things along—"

"This place has what he needs," Willa said. "Don't look so surprised. I had it for you."

"Some time has passed since then."

"Nearly forty years is not as long as you may think. Will you stay with him?"

Rutherford shook his head violently. "No. I can't. Grandfather needs my help, and the store will need a firm hand. We relied so heavily on her, and everyone will need to know that we'll survive this—"

"What devotion. Have you considered sparing some of that for your son?"

"I don't need a lecture, Mother. I need your help."

"I told you, long ago, that you would return here. And that you would need me when you did. But let's be clear about your expectations: you have driven an infant to my door and expect to leave him, your son, in this place. With me."

"Yes." Rutherford shuffled from one foot to the other, his rage competing with his grief and his embarrassment. "Please."

Willa nodded slowly and hugged Alex to her chest. "He belongs here."

"Until I conceive of a better option, yes."

"You will not send him to that school."

"He's too young. And we have time to discuss."

Mother and son glared at each other across the flagstones, and Rutherford felt a flame transfer between them, and realized that every sense of protection she ever bestowed—or inflicted—upon him had now transferred to this tiny being against her chest.

"Time will not change my mind," Willa said.

"I'll come back." Rutherford was already taking steps backward, returning mentally to the car, the drive back to his grandparents' house, the family business he would return to tomorrow, the inheritance that awaited him soon. "I'll not leave him with you forever, and I'll not leave you without input from me as to his welfare."

"You've never been shy with your opinions, Ruth. Not from the moment you came into this world. And as I've always told you: you are always welcome here."

"Does this place know that?"

"I am this place."

Rutherford nodded. "I'll come back tomorrow."

Willa nuzzled her grandson and murmured into his ear. "And we'll be here, won't we? We will always be here."

Rutherford was as good as his word. Each day, he would work at the store, slowly transitioning his grandfather into retirement, securing another run-down warehouse on the riverfront, converting it into soaring galleries that brought more business, more write-ups in exclusive outlets up and down the East Coast. In the evening, he would go to the mansion, each footfall up the flagstone path becoming harder, like wading through molasses to a place that didn't want him there and that he didn't want to enter. He didn't always hold Alex—didn't quite know how to relate to him, his childish babble and tottering steps across the wide floorboards. He didn't know how to talk to his mother, her deep-blue eyes glowing as she watched his son, a connection that she formed instantly and that he never felt.

He was excluded from their closeness but felt it as a threat, as he felt most things in that house.

Alex was two the day he arrived to find the kitchen empty, the whole first floor devoid of any person but filled with the sound of Chopin playing from the library piano unaided. He searched through the house for Willa and Alex and found them upstairs, in Willa's room that overlooked the river far below.

"This was your grandfather's rocking chair," she murmured, putting the miniature piece of furniture in Alex's chubby hand. "It was the first gift he ever gave to me. And this"—she picked up the piano in the library and wound it, filling the room with tinkling music—"this is part of the mansion's soul, because our souls are filled with music, and the mansion is filled with souls." She kissed Alex's ruddy curls. "Once for love, twice for life, thrice to keep you safe from—"

"What are you doing?" The atmosphere was thick, almost too thick for Rutherford to breathe into his lungs. Willa and Alex both looked up at him, blinking with confusion, as if he were outside a glass dome that enclosed them both.

"What are you *doing*?" Rutherford repeated. "That—that house. I remember that house. I remember—" But he couldn't articulate exactly what he remembered, because the feelings were deeper than words. He recalled the way his hand recoiled when he was small, the first time his mother took him to the attic and showed him the miniature, perfect facsimile of the house where he had spent as little time as possible as soon as he could get away. The house that made him feel as if he were himself a haunted structure, carrying the burden of a place that wanted to claim him, body and soul. The house that felt like a trap, breathing like a living thing, connected to his mother—unified with her. He had always stayed away from the attic and chalked his avoidance up to superstition. It was normal to hate attics. Normal, normal, normal. His family was normal. His mother was not. His mother was not his family, as much as he could excise her.

And he'd left his only son to occupy the void he'd left behind.

Willa's face was sad. "I'm showing Alex what I tried to show you. What I tried to give to you. An inheritance, when he's ready for it. He isn't yet. But soon."

"My son will not inherit anything from you. No obligation, no burden, and certainly no dollhouse. My son will not touch a dollhouse."

"It's not a dollhouse—"

"What are you *doing*, Mother?" He coughed, the thick air swirling through his lungs like smoke. "Grandmother always warned me. She said you were a witch—one of the old ones. She told me not to speak of it, and not to speak of you, and that everyone knew the rumors and that they would taint me. Taint us, all of us, because of what Father did."

"What Father did?"

"Choosing you! Luring him away from his family and his legacy—"

"Ruth, that choice brought you into the world—"

"I didn't choose this! I didn't choose you, the way you pulled me into this place, the way it made me feel to know that it was trying to keep me!"

"None of us chooses our burdens, Ruth." She reached forward and ran her finger gently down Alex's cheek. "But we bear them just the same."

Rutherford reached her so quickly that she couldn't retreat fast enough. He snatched the piano from her hand and threw it to the floor, stomping on it, yanking Alex into his arms so quickly that the child began to cry. Rutherford panicked at the sound, panicked at the feelings—heat and fury boiling in his chest, upheaval that threatened to crack him open and scorch the very air around him.

"You never accepted your gifts," Willa whispered. "You had the very best of me, and all the magic of this place, and you fought it tooth and nail. But it fights back, Ruth. It can eat away at you from the inside if you let it. I tried—"

The voice that emerged from Rutherford was alien even to him. "Leave. Now." The energy pulsated through Willa's bedroom and collided with the walls of the mansion, which pushed back against him and struggled to regain the equilibrium he disturbed. "Leave us. Or I will destroy you. I will burn this place to the ground."

Willa nodded, her expression older than the stones that formed the mansion's foundations. Ruth didn't have the power to expel her from the house, but he had other powers, and she was weaker than she had been before Alex came into her world. Her tentative steps toward transferring the burden had loosened her tether to the refuge, and Ruth was stronger than he knew, and in ways Willa couldn't match. The way he held Alex frightened her.

Alex squirmed in his father's arms, wailing, reaching his arms out to her, and she thought her heart might shatter. But in a deeper place, she was afraid. The shelter of the house felt inadequate to protect her, but the feeling was different from the countless times she'd fled before.

For the first time, the threat was inside the walls. Inside her son. Perhaps if he could finally have the distance he'd demanded all his life—if Willa released him from her presence, and from any shade of the burden Ruth seemed to feel when she was near—perhaps he would change. And Willa would do what she had always done. She would listen for the change in the flow of time, backward and forward, its swirling eddies telling her when it was safe to return. Maybe Ruth would still be there. Maybe Alex would be. Maybe generations would pass by, and the last remnants of the family she tried and failed to build would fade away, and she would be alone again.

The thought gutted her. But she had been alone before.

"I will go, Ruth, but I always return. I am always here. You must know that."

Alex scrambled against his father and escaped, running toward his grandmother, reaching for her hand. Rutherford grabbed his wrist, yanking him back so hard that Alex yelped in pain, pulling him violently back into his arms.

"You're hurting him, Ruth!" Willa reached toward her grandson, trying to calm the air around him.

"A feeling he'll get used to in this family," Rutherford hissed. "Leave this house. Leave this place. Now." His blue eyes blazed with energy. Willa relented, walking ahead of him down the curved staircase, afraid for Alex. She could return for what she needed later, once they were gone; the house would always admit her.

And then she would leave again, until time enough passed to make it safe to return. She did not know, anytime she departed, when the time would come again. But the path would open when it was right.

She felt the opportunity to transfer close again, and her exhaustion was complete; she did not know if she would choose to stay.

Later that night, her packing was quick. The driver of the taxi who collected her in the darkness at the bottom of the hill helped her put her things in the trunk. A small holdall, its gray handle worn to smoothness. A large, brass-buckled box like a trunk, one side uneven and peaked and covered with shingles that looked like stone. Other than that, Willa had only what she wore on her body: a dark blue traveling suit contrasted with silver thread, a pair of polished blue heels the color of the ocean, and a charm around her neck—an acorn, carved from lapis.

She didn't look back as the car drove away. She bent her head over a notepad in her lap, scribbling furiously, and asked the driver to stop briefly on a stately block of brick Federal houses in the finest part of town, where she got out of the car just long enough to walk quietly through one house's wrought iron gate and around a path in the garden to a low door at the rear, leading to the basement. She ripped the paper from the notepad and folded it tightly, sliding it under the door. When she returned to the taxi, she asked to go to the airport.

· 34 ·

LOCKHART, VIRGINIA, 2015

ALEX DIVED FOR HIS PHONE WHEN HE HEARD IT BUZZING, but realized with immediate disappointment that the sound meant an incoming email, not a call from Myra. When he saw her short message—This is all still very new—he shook his head.

She wasn't going to call. He'd told her everything about himself— his father's illness and their complicated relationship, his mother and their lengthy conversations, years spent building what they'd never been able to have. And Myra had told him things, too—not just the stories she shared with everyone else, but deeper truths about herself, her family, her sense of loss. He'd learned more about her than he ever thought she'd share.

It had all happened over a matter of weeks that felt at once like decades of familiarity, while simultaneously feeling like the blink of an eye. But now he feared he'd moved too fast and scared her, and she was never going to call. He couldn't help but think that if she'd come

out of her shell, just a little, the two of them together could start to figure out what was happening. Part of him knew they couldn't move
through this mystery together until they started really talking or, really,
until they met. But another part of him was afraid, because moving to
that next step meant everything that was unreal—everything that was
mysterious and, in its mystery, also magical—would become real. And
worse, they might discover some totally innocuous and boring explanation for the Mansion, the furniture, the music. He couldn't imagine
what that explanation would be; the idea that it was all driven by some
kind of magic—real magic—seemed impossible. But that was also
the explanation Alex wanted, and what he was most afraid of losing.
The magic of an unbreakable link that couldn't be explained.

He'd never had anything like that, not since he was very small. He
didn't know how much he'd been longing for it until he felt its echo in
his correspondence with Myra.

Part of it was the house itself. When Alex had first arrived back in
Lockhart, and his father had reluctantly driven him to the mansion,
Alex had peered up the flagstone path and seen a glow emanating
from the old slate roof, an energy pulsing through the tendrils of wisteria weaving around the rippled windows. Alex hadn't laid eyes on the
house since he left for boarding school when he was five. He couldn't
be sure if it looked the same, but the glow felt like home, and as soon
as he saw it, Alex knew he couldn't tell his father.

Rutherford's letters to him in China had been escalating in urgency,
but in a way that clearly tried to conceal his father's increasing fear.
The attempt to put a brave face on things was the factor that finally
triggered Alex to write his letter of resignation to the director of the
small private school in Beijing where he taught, citing family illness as

his reason for leaving. He told everyone he was returning home—though he did not say, when he resigned, that the place he considered home was a place he hadn't lived since he was five years old. A place his father had all but banished him from, though he'd never understood why.

He'd known his father was sick. His build had always been slight, and his face had always borne a kind of pinched and peaked severity. Alex was an adult before he realized that his father's expression almost certainly meant he was in pain. But that would mean he had been in pain his whole life, as if something was gnawing at him from the inside out. Rutherford had only deigned to finally write the words—*cancer, malignant*—in his final letter before Alex resigned. Before that, Alex felt a kind of creeping dread that did not have a name, and that dread was enough to keep an ocean between them. An ocean felt like a safe distance. Rutherford was the first to impose distance between them when Alex was small, sending him to the horrible school Alex's great-grandmother championed, meant to drum military precision and ruggedness into small, soft children sent away to the North Carolina mountains. The choice frightened Alex then, and bewildered him even now.

He never knew what he'd done wrong. But he felt the wrongness of it every time his father entered the mansion. He would feel comfort as the sun peeked through the windows of his turret room, the music's measures swaying through the house. But if Rutherford's polished wingtips started clipping up the flagstones, he would freeze and cast his eyes around in shame, feeling as if he were about to be caught with something he wasn't supposed to have, though he couldn't imagine what. He thought of his brief relationship with the guidance counselor at his school, her claim that he was too quick to make a connection because he'd never really felt loved. She'd hissed it at the time, because he was breaking up with her to return to Lockhart, to help the father he also feared. *You'll never learn to have a relationship until you figure out your first ones.* The words were strangely vicious, and he thought at the time her demeanor probably wasn't well suited to guiding young minds, but he was on his way out the door. So.

She had a point. His earliest memories of Lockhart were amorphous, a feeling of safety and shelter—so long as his father was away. His memories of his grandmother were shadows, memories of spiced scents and snatches of music, a microclimate of warmth against a soft embrace. She disappeared when he was a toddler, before he could even form sentences clearly enough to articulate his feelings—so much bigger than he was, so full of anguish. Those first five years before he was banished to the school felt cold, long swaths of emptiness punctuated by his father's fits of rage, with small bright spots of feeling protected by the house itself. But never for long.

His mother was absent. She had never lived in the house. He received infrequent gifts—the occasional Advent calendar or Nerf football or action figure. She never signed them "Mom," just "Emily." He remembered rare visits, an uncomfortable day or two punctuated by awkward trips to the zoo. He barely remembered her and grew up thinking she didn't want him, a perception his father had done nothing to diminish. When he was in college in California, as far away from Lockhart as he could get, he gleaned what additional information he could from offhanded conversation with his father, bits of details before Rutherford would raise his voice and demand, *What's this all about, anyway, and why do you want to know? Your family is here.*

Eventually, Alex turned to the nascent internet to find her. Emily

Grace Martin, née Patterson. She was just over twenty years younger than his father. She had, apparently, had the same college aspiration as her son: get as far away from where she grew up as possible. She had married another student, a computer science major who experienced some early success with a software application he'd sold to Microsoft before retiring in his late twenties and having an affair with a girl just out of high school. Their divorce had left Emily with a small cottage in Malibu. She taught second grade in an elementary school nearby.

Alex arrived unannounced on her doorstep one day, determined to confront her. She was overjoyed to see him. Her eyes filled with tears. They talked so much he stayed the night. And as the hours wore on, he pulled the story from her: her North Carolina childhood, her membership in a "Ladies' Leadership" club that bused young women to the ritzy, private residential school for dances and receptions hosted for the students and alumni. Her shock at being noticed by an older man—an alum at the school—with russet hair, his haughty and harsh demeanor dropped entirely around her in a way that made her feel special. She had just turned eighteen, and he drove her back to her house so she wouldn't have to return on the bus. *I visit from time to time*, he said. Soon after, an unexpected pregnancy, and the unannounced visit by Mildred Rakes not long after the baby—Alex—was born.

His mother said Mildred had held Alex and rocked him, had smiled sweetly at his mother in her family's modest house. They all knew who she was, of course—people drove from several states away to shop at Rakes and Son. Emily described Mildred's thin-lipped smile curved around the words she'd said: *Custody battles can be so unpleasant, my dear. Do you know we would have to prove you are unfit? Such a nasty thing to have to discuss in front of a judge and in the papers and to every single person you've ever known.*

Once his mother described the price to him, he understood. The cost of any relationship with Alex at all would be the control of that relationship by the Rakes family; otherwise, it would be thrown into the courts, where money and every conceivable resource would be dedicated to severing that relationship utterly. In the end, of course, the result was nearly as severe. His mother lived hours from Lockhart, an unreliable car's journey away, with unpredictable gas money, and open hostility waiting for her at the end of a long road. Rutherford urged her, when he engaged with her at all, to move on with her life. And eventually she did—earning a scholarship of uncertain origin to a university far away, in California, and meeting her current husband. She never had another child. Her letters to Alex were, they both realized, intercepted.

Alex's time in college gave them an opportunity to rebuild a relationship they'd never really had the chance to build in the first place. Emily's love for teaching, her impassioned descriptions of her students, helped Alex focus his aimlessness into something more concrete: a plan that started as trying to teach, and that became bolder over time, morphing into a determination to see the world that the Rakes family had seemed determined to shield him from. A couple of other students in the English department were signing up for contracts to teach overseas, and the school in Beijing seemed like an interesting place to start. Once he got there, the years passed more quickly than he intended. He and Emily wrote frequently back and forth, and his mother would send him copies of articles from education magazines about student engagement and teaching across language barriers. The student holidays and breaks were his own, spent backpacking from hostel to hostel across Asia and Europe, depending on the amount of time he had. He was often alone, but never lonely.

He wrote to his father much less frequently, and though he received more letters than he sent, Rutherford's correspondence featured the same reserved and unfeeling language as the man himself. Alex had been furious at his father, who didn't even try to deny what he had found when Alex confronted him about his mother, saying only that the family's legacy had depended upon the decisions his grandmother had made, and that Rutherford would not apologize for them. Alex exploded—*It wasn't just your decision to make. What about me?*—and Rutherford had matched his anger with cold fury, defending his dead grandmother to his very much alive son with a dedication that derailed their relationship even further.

But in the end, Alex was the only family Rutherford had, and he knew his father was sick and alone. And though he hadn't been lonely in the beginning, the years abroad had begun to make him feel unmoored. He felt disconnected from the only place that ever felt like home, that still called to him in his dreams, tendrils of wisteria tangling through his thoughts. When he read his father's missive, it was as if he felt the cancer in his own bones. He felt the house where he once lived, and heard its music in his dreams. These sensations seemed both instantly familiar and terrifyingly unreal. Which made them all the more compelling.

And as Alex felt that loneliness again in the stockroom of Rakes and Son, desperate to hear Myra's voice and certain he never would, his phone rang.

"It takes me time to find my way sometimes," Myra whispered. "My world isn't very big, and I'm not very good at letting things grow. There's a reason all the plants in the Mansion are fake, you know. I'd kill any real ones. I don't—I don't really know how to talk to people. And I don't want to hurt you."

"I don't want to hurt you, either." Alex spoke softly, afraid of scaring her off, afraid the reality of his voice would make her hang up the phone.

"Another thing we have in common," she said, and laughed, the most beautiful sound he'd ever heard. "Which is a good thing, because you're much more interesting than a plastic plant, at least so far."

Alex laughed, too, a weight lifting off his chest that he hadn't known was there until it was gone. "That's good to hear. Thanks for not setting the bar too high. And it's good to hear your voice. Where do we go from here?"

"Tell me what happened. Then we can figure out what to do."

"You've embraced a plural noun a bit more quickly than I expected."

"Gwen keeps telling me to step outside my comfort zone, and 'we' sounds easier than 'I,' so here we are."

"Which is where, exactly?"

"A continent apart, but joined at the hip by some very peculiar real estate."

"Right. Just as long as we have our bearings. Let me tell you what happened."

Inside the mansions—both miniature and full-sized—Willa Rakes's smile beamed with light, and the tear across her face began to mend.

ELLIOTT, ARIZONA, 1986

"IF DIANE FINDS OUT YOU'RE LETTING THAT CHILD WORK with a knife, she'll never bring her here again, Lou." Trixie carried a silver tray balanced with cookies and three teacups through the front door of the A-frame, all filled to the brim with pink lemonade. "It's time for you to take a snack break, anyway. It's hot out here."

Lou stood up from the workbench in the front yard, putting down his willow branch that was halfway to becoming a rabbit, and leaning over to pluck the small Swiss Army knife from Myra's fingers. "It's not a chain saw, Trixie, just a little blade. Not much different than those tiny scissors you let her use for sewing. I learned to whittle when I was smaller than she was." He folded the knife and put it in his pocket. "That said—what Diane doesn't know won't hurt her."

"I won't tell Mom, Grampa," Myra said solemnly. "Not till I finish my horse. I want it to be a surprise."

Grampa knelt next to his granddaughter, tracing the short length of pine with his rough fingers. "You've got a good start there, little acorn. Not a whit of bark left. That's why I gave you a pine branch—pine's soft."

Myra frowned. "It's not going to be as good as yours." She pointed at Lou's rabbit, still part of the branch perched on the workbench but looking as if it were ready to leap across the scrub brush of the yard.

"New skills take practice, Myra. But I'm here to help you learn. That's why I picked pine—it's easy to work with because it grows fast, so the wood's always young. Like you."

"It smells good, too." Myra sniffed the peeled edge of the branch. "Like Christmas."

"If your granny says it's okay, you can skip nap time and come with me to the lumberyard in a bit. Best smell in the whole world. Your mom spent lots of time there with me growing up."

"She says she likes books because they smell like sawdust."

"I know. Me, too. And you know, books and lumber and sawdust all come from the same place. Whenever you go to a library, you're really walking into a forest."

"And forests have memories." Trixie sat down next to Myra by the workbench and sipped lemonade from her teacup. "Just like every other living thing." She laughed as Myra leaned against her arm and took a big bite of her snickerdoodle before gulping her lemonade, squinting at the tartness. "Sometimes they need reminders, of course, so they don't do something like drink their lemonade right after a cookie."

"It needs more sugar," Myra said.

"I think you're sweet enough." Trixie put Myra's empty teacup next to her own on the tray and stood up. "If you help me with the door, you can go with Grampa to the lumberyard."

Myra looked at Lou. "Can we wait to go until I finish my horse?"

Lou picked up the bare piece of pine branch and considered. "That's a bigger project than we can finish in just one day. But I'll tell you what: I can work some more on it this weekend, and when your mom brings you back down next week, you can help me paint it however you want. We can make it look like a real merry-go-round horse. Should we pick out some pink paint this afternoon?"

Myra shook her head. "No. It wants to be red."

"Fair enough," Lou said. "I like a horse that knows its own mind."

· 36 ·

LOCKHART, VIRGINIA, 2015

"ONCE UPON A TIME, THERE WAS A HOUSE."

"Are you telling me a bedtime story?" Alex laughed, realizing from the gathering dark in his room that he'd been on the phone with Myra for hours that had passed like seconds. "Never mind. I guess that fits."

"Fits what?" Myra asked.

"It's late here. Or getting late, anyway. Cold, too."

"It's cold here also, but not quite late. I keep forgetting the time difference—I'm a few hours behind you."

Alex stretched across his bed, his back unwinding from its curled posture around his tablet, looking at pictures of the Minuscule Mansion while asking Myra every question he could think of about the house and its contents. "I forget it, too. But the sunrise tends to remind me."

"Do you want me to let you go?"

"Never." Alex could hear her smiling over the phone and longed to picture the face it crossed. He'd still never seen her.

"Good. Anyway, it's a story Trixie used to tell me. Once upon a time, there was a house. It was on a bend in a wide river—"

"This sounds familiar."

"Familiar like you've heard it?"

"No. Familiar in the same way as everything we talk about. Familiar like 'I live there.' That kind of familiar."

"Is the river the same as the one where you work?"

"Yeah. My family bought up a bunch of old warehouses—they started with one and now we have six. They back up to a canal that cuts through downtown, but it's all the same water," Alex said.

"Gwen sent me some information about your house—'Witch's Manor' is a bit much, by the way—but I didn't realize it was on the river."

"Your base for the house doesn't go that far. It has some of the oak trees, but not all of them. And it's flat. My house is on a hill. You wouldn't see the river if you photographed it from the street—you have to see the view from the house itself." Alex paused. "I'd really like you to see the view from the house."

"You could take a picture."

"I will. But it's better in person. You should see it."

Myra breathed in softly. "I don't—leave here much."

"There's a first time for everything. Anyway, I'm sorry I keep interrupting. We left off at 'Once upon a time.' Continue."

"I don't remember much of the story, to be honest. I asked her to tell me about it all the time, but I was so young when—when I lost her. She talked about the house, and I always wanted it to be a mansion, because that was what we played with together—the Mansion as I have it now. And she talked about the Lady."

"The Lady of the House. Yeah, I used to hear about her from time to time—there were enough kids from Lockhart when I went to school that I'd hear the stories."

"What kind of stories?"

"That she was a witch. That she was older than the house, and that you could see her if you were brave enough to jump the fence, cross your eyes and all your fingers and toes, say 'lady-lady-lady' fifty times, some stupid kid stuff like that. 'Bloody Mary in the mirror' stuff. You know how kids are."

Myra gritted her teeth and thought, at first, to let the comment pass. But another, deeper part of her wanted there to be no secrets between them. "I don't know, actually. I was never—I was never really around any other kids. Other than Gwen, when she was staying with her dad. Gwen I could never get rid of. But other kids—"

"Didn't you go to school?"

"No. I was homeschooled."

"Oh. I've never met anyone who was homeschooled before. Was your family—how can I say this without it seeming judgy—you know. Do you come from, like, churchy folks?"

Myra laughed. "No. I don't. I was a complicated kid. I know that may come as a shock."

"Yes, I'm floored to hear that you're complicated at all. That seems totally inconsistent with what I've learned as part of our relationship, which has been completely ordinary so far."

Myra felt her cheeks flushing at the word *relationship*, and her voice softened as her breath quickened. "Right. Well. I also had some—

medical stuff. I wasn't in any shape to go to school at first, and then my parents—my mother—were too worried that my immune system wouldn't be up to it, and that I didn't have the strength for it. And that just kept on being the fear for so long that it just kind of came true. She didn't leave. I didn't leave. I think she always resented me for it, somehow, even though neither of us ever said it."

"What was it like before?"

"We got out more. Not to many places. Trixie and my grandfather—Grampa Lou—would come visit, but most of the time I spent with her was at my grandfather's house, further south. Where it's hotter and drier. Mom was going to school at the time, and she'd drop me off on her way to the valley. Trixie taught me how to sew and how to cook, and Grampa taught me some woodworking—which he kept showing me after. You know. After she died."

Alex was afraid to press further, feeling that too many questions would stop the flow of words. "I don't want to ask. I'm afraid to ask."

"How she died? Don't be. I don't talk about it much. But with you—" Myra paused. "I don't mind telling you."

"It wasn't because she was old."

"No. It was a car accident." Myra's voice caught in her throat. "And it was my fault."

"That can't possibly be true. How old were you?"

"Five. It was my fifth birthday. We were bringing my cake to my parents' house because I was so proud of it, and I couldn't wait for them to come and get me. It was raining when we started driving home, but then it turned to snow. It was December. Nothing anyone should have been driving in, and certainly not in the land yachts my grandfather always bought."

"That's not your fault."

"Let me finish. Trixie wanted to turn around, but I wouldn't let her. I cried and pitched such a fit that even I couldn't tell what had gotten into me. I was just so sure that something important was happening, and there was nothing more important than getting that damn cake up that damn mountain. I was proudest of the roses. They were pink. I made the leaves myself, from rolled-out gumdrops. Trixie showed me how."

"Myra. Oh my God. You were only five. If she kept driving, that was her choice, not yours."

"I know that practically, but inside it's always been my fault."

"That isn't true, but I understand the feeling. I always felt the same way about my mother not being in the picture, even though my family cut her out of my life without me having any say at all. That's why it's been so hard to figure out the relationship—we never had a chance to be mother and son until we'd both moved on to other roles. I don't know why I feel any responsibility for it, but I do, in the abstract."

"I'm not talking about the abstract. I'm talking about reality. If I hadn't insisted, we never would have gotten in that car. My folks were going to come get me later, and we didn't need to drive north. But Trixie had already given me my gift—a beautiful little necklace, an acorn. I still wear it. Trixie always called me her little acorn, and even after she died, Lou would say it, too. It made us both feel like she was still there, somehow. That and the Mansion. He brought it to me when I was six, and it's been here in this attic ever since. I used to help Trixie with it."

"Some kids would call that 'playing.'"

"It wasn't, though. It was something else. The level of detail—well, you've seen the site. It was always like that. We weren't playing with a dollhouse. It was more like curating a museum, or even something like meditation—I remember feeling calm and getting pulled into the world of the house, and hours would pass without me realizing it. It still happens that way even now. It's like—never mind, you're going to think this is crazy."

"I won't." Alex released a breath he hadn't known he was holding. "I promise I won't."

"It talks to me sometimes. Not in words. In something deeper than words. I'll be working on writing or talking to you, and it'll make a noise or something to draw my attention. And late at night— Alex, I've never told this to anyone. I'm afraid to talk about this."

"I'm right here. Don't be afraid."

"I don't talk to anyone, Alex. I've never really known how—every single person in my life is someone who's come into it, not someone I've sought out. And after the accident, after what it did, I was afraid to ever try. And the Mansion . . . it gave me places to explore, widened the world for me in ways I can't explain. And it waits for me. There's a dress—"

"In the Mansion?"

"No. But it's in the attic, and it's a baby dress, really. Trixie made it for me when I was the flower girl for her and Lou. I was only two, Alex, but some nights the dress still fits."

"A flower girl dress?"

"It's like a gown. Like a queen's coronation gown, deep midnight blue with silver thread, the color of the lapis acorn she gave me. It— grows to fit me. Only sometimes, on nights when it's hard for me to tell whether I'm dreaming or awake." Myra paused. "This is where you say, 'Well, it's been a pleasure talking to you, Myra, but look at the time—'"

"I'm not going to say that."

"Why not?"

"Because I don't think you're crazy. I'm in my bed, in my room, looking at furniture you have, too, only smaller. I'm in a house full of piano music where there's no piano, and where the air literally sparkles sometimes. I'm in a house where the temperature can drop forty degrees in the space of a few footsteps. A really fancy dress that grows matches all those details pretty well, don't you think?"

Myra sighed with relief. "I do think, but I'm so glad you do, too."

"Good. What else?"

"How do you know there's anything else?"

"Call it a feeling."

"Let me think . . . oh. Okay. There's the disappearing stuff."

"Disappearing how?"

"Sometimes it's just furniture, and sometimes it's whole rooms, but it's not usually the rooms that came with the house."

"I almost said, 'That doesn't make any sense,' but of course it doesn't. Continue."

"That credenza in your room is a good example. I never put that on the blog at all, and I don't still have it. But when I saw it in your photos, it was the first place my eyes went. No one else ever saw it."

"Are you talking about my mismatched piece? With the record player?"

"Yes. Was it there when you moved in?"

"No. I found it in a little pop-up vintage store here. It wasn't open long—nothing in that spot stays for long. But I got a few funky pieces there."

"Well, I made that one. The turned wood leg came from a sewing table, and I used it until I could make a hairpin leg to match the one on the left. I hadn't gotten around to it before the piece disappeared."

"And you said there were others? Do you remember them?"

"I'd know them if I saw them again."

Alex sat up in his bed and looked around. "I don't think I have anything else in here. But I've never taken an inventory, and I don't think I'd even notice if something walked out the door or walked into it, either. Actually, walking furniture would make perfect sense here. Willa's room is pretty empty, but I should still take some pictures around the house, see if you recognize anything."

"Later. There's more."

"Of course there is."

"Whole rooms come and go."

"What kinds of rooms?"

"All kinds. Sometimes it'll be a lean-to that pops up on the back of the Mansion, almost like a growth, and I know instantly what it's supposed to be. I made a root cellar, braided little ropes of garlic and onions, painted baskets of potatoes, packed for a hard winter. And when I was done, poof. Gone. Sometimes it's been a bathroom, or a butler's pantry, but less often it's something big. I had a ballroom once. It was next to the library. I tried to see how it fit—it made the house bigger inside than it should have been—but it blurred at the edges and I could feel pressure around me, like the air was different."

"Are you saying you didn't like to pry?"

Myra laughed. "Exactly. There are things the house doesn't like me to examine. And there's usually too many interesting things for me to try. The ballroom only had about a third of its floor finished—making the parquet tiles took forever."

"I bet the big crystal chandeliers were a pain, too."

"Are you guessing or telling me?"

"I'm telling you. I went to a dance in that ballroom—it's the one I told you about in my first message to you. I was the only person there."

"Well, it was gone before I even heard from you the first time. The day that Gwen read me your essay— God, I don't know why I keep calling it an essay, it was only a couple of sentences, but I think it must be because they shook things up so much that it doesn't make sense to call it an email. Anyway. By that morning, it had been quite a while since the Mansion gave me any extra rooms or unexpected furniture."

"Maybe it was saving up its energy."

"For what?"

Alex sighed. "For this, Myra. For us. Not a single thing has made sense since that first day, the first time I saw your blog or read any of your writing. Not a single thing except this: talking to you. Hearing your voice. Reading your words and your stories and feeling your presence here, in this house. You're worried about me thinking you're crazy, and I'm worried about you thinking the same thing about me. When I paid that two hundred dollars, I felt my entire life take a giant leap forward, and I think it was bringing me to this moment."

"What moment?"

"The moment I tell you I need to see all of this in person."

Myra felt her reality shift, gravity tilting around her as she tried to steer the conversation back to safer shores. "I mean, Alex, you wouldn't have entered if you didn't want to see the Mansion, but I already told you I'm not ready—it was Gwen's idea and I already said I wanted to remove that as an option."

"I'm not talking about Gwen, and I'm not talking about seeing the Mansion, not really. I'm saying I need to see you—"

"Everyone wants to see the Mansion, all right? That was Gwen's whole point, this whole stupid idea for the contest, that it would somehow fix everything. It won't fix everything. It won't fix—" Myra's voice caught in her throat, a sob that she couldn't bear to let Alex hear. "It won't fix me. I know you want to see the Mansion, Alex. But there are things I can't let you see."

"What are you talking about? I see everything—I'm living the full-scale version of—"

"You are not part of my life."

Alex felt the conversation slipping away from him, the ground tilting beneath his feet. A symphony was crashing up the stairs again. "Myra, I've told you things I've never told anyone. I told you about my dad, about him sending me away and spending my whole life alone." His breathing was ragged, the air taking on the same heaviness he remembered from his fights with his father. "I've let you into places I didn't know I'd locked. Please don't—"

Myra was crying, the temperature in the attic dropping, shadows of snowflakes floating behind her eyelids. "There are things I can't let you see. I'm so sorry. I'm so sorry. But this has already gone too far."

She was gone before he could say goodbye, and the bottom of the world fell out beneath them both.

· 37 ·

WASHINGTON, DC, 1983

THE MAN LOOKED TO BE IN HIS MIDSIXTIES, WITH SALT-and-pepper hair gone a bit weedy and uncontrolled, wearing a comfortable-looking flannel shirt that hadn't seen the business end of an iron since it was ripped out of a plastic-wrapped stack of three. He leaned over the counter with an air of conspiracy, lowering his voice to a level that Willa could barely hear as she stood behind him in line at the airport, waiting to talk to the same ticketing agent. "When you say, 'Everything is canceled,' do you mean everything, or do you mean 'most things, with some exceptions'? And if it's that last one"—at this, the man slid his hand across the counter, concealing a folded banknote—"is there a way to apply for one of those exceptions?"

The ticketing agent set her mouth in a bemused expression, not quite a smile, but not bereft of levity, either. "I'm afraid you'd have to send that application in to whoever controls the weather, and that isn't me. You'd be able to tell the difference, because if it were me, it would feel like Florida outside, and it'd look a lot less like the North Pole."

The man laughed. "Where I come from, this is barely a dusting. But I've been back here enough to know how the South feels about snow. I just didn't expect it to shut down the nation's capital or to come so early in the year. At any rate, I know you'll be dealing with a lot of unhappy people, so take care of you and get yourself something nice today, okay?" The man left the banknote on the counter and turned around to find a place to wait, nearly bumping into Willa behind him, who was lost in thought about where she would go next. She hadn't quite decided yet, and looking at the swirling snow outside, she realized she couldn't go anywhere anyway.

The man looked down at the trunk by Willa's feet. "Looks like you've got a couple loose shingles there."

Willa followed his pointing finger with her eyes, noticing an edge along the house's turret that was peeling up from the roof. She knelt and ran her finger along the edge. "It must have caught somewhere when I was wheeling it in here."

"I bet I can help. Follow me." The man hoisted two enormous suitcases and walked toward a corner of the airport that was not, as of yet, filled with a crush of delayed travelers. When he reached a stopping point, he unsnapped the buckles on one of the cases, which hinged open into a field of miniature rooftops, a city in a suitcase.

"What's all that?" Willa tried not to sound enchanted. The last time a man had surprised her—had inspired the kind of surprise her own miniature house would trigger when she showed it to someone for the first time—it had been with a tiny rocking chair. This case, whatever it was, would hold many.

"Samples," the man responded. "Hold on a sec." He patted his battered jeans and pulled out a wrinkled piece of cardstock printed like a page from an old-fashioned magazine. "Louis Walsh, Supply Sales," the card read.

"What kind of supplies?"

"Building supplies. We have contracts with lots of outfits, small and big, all over the country. Roofing and siding, mostly. That's what this is." He gestured toward the miniature town. "See, most places, they'll show you these folders—I have 'em, too, with big pieces of siding and shingles, so the customer can see things full-sized. But I'm also a little bit of a craftsman myself. I go by Lou, by the way."

"It's very nice to meet you, Lou. Are you saying you made that little town?"

Lou rocked a bit on his feet, looking as if he wished he were wearing suspenders he could snap with pride. "I did, in fact. The colors all match the products I sell, but I had the idea a few years ago to show folks what they might look like on a house, or in a neighborhood. My bosses thought it was silly, but not enough to say no, and damned if I don't get comments every time I show it off. Also—here, let me find a plug." Lou stepped around the pillars arrayed around them until he found an empty outlet. He unwound a plug from a hidden compartment underneath one of the houses, and hit a switch. The houses all lit up from within. Willa tried hard not to clap her hands together with delight. "And that's not all—let me bring something else out here." He reached back into the compartment and brought out a cone-shaped light, holding it high above the roofs of the houses. "This switch right here gives me . . ." *Click!* "Full sunny daylight, or . . ." *Click!* "A cloudy day, or . . ." *Click!* "Twilight, or sunrise, depending on which side of the world you want the sun to be." He looked up at Willa and smiled. "Colors are different in different lights, you know. You don't want someone spending a lot of money on butter-yellow siding only to call you back out unhappy because now they think it looks like pee."

Willa giggled. "And this approach helps?"

"I don't know if it does, but I had fun making it, and it always gets a reaction. Keeps me in their heads, too, you know? I'm not just another guy with folders. I'm the guy with the dollhouse town."

"I could see how that would be hard to forget." Willa reached down to the peeling turret roof. "You said you think you could help with this?"

"Easy as pie. This set gets banged up so much, I travel with extra everything. Now, I don't have slate tile, mind you—that's a little outside the budget for most of my folks, mostly builder-grade clients. But I can find you a good color match until you're able to patch things up. Unless I can talk you into a full tear-off? Asphalt shingles are really durable, you know."

"You're an excellent salesman, but maybe just a patch job."

Lou shrugged. "Suit yourself. Let me pull out some adhesive and see if I can just fix up what you have, and you can stand here and be the sun."

Willa raised her eyebrows. "What's that, now?"

Lou held up the cone-shaped light. "Give me full-on daylight, if you would. The lighting over here is terrible."

Willa took the light and held it aloft while Lou tipped the buckled mansion onto its side, gently poking adhesive up under the roof with a small paintbrush. "Thank you for being so careful," she said.

"A piece of craftsmanship like this?" Lou whistled. "I'd have a hard time even letting someone else touch it, if I were you. I've got a little granddaughter back home. This'd make her lose her mind." He traced the side of the mansion with his finger. "This paint job—I've never seen anything like it. You can almost smell this wisteria. Did you paint this?"

Willa shook her head. "No. I—inherited it. It's always had wisteria." She tilted her head and watched Lou work. "Would you like to see the inside?"

He looked up at her with such excitement that she could picture his face as a young boy. "I would love to."

Willa knelt beside him and unfastened the buckles, swinging the house open. She had put the furniture away in her hatbox when packing earlier in the evening, as the snow started to fall, as the cold bit down around her as it always did in her worst moments. The rooms were empty but expectant, waiting for whatever came next, as they always did. "I have things for the rooms, but they're put away right now."

Lou hardly seemed to hear her. He reached gently into the house, using his rough fingers to walk up the wide staircase in a way that should have been ridiculous but was, instead, rather charming. "It's really astounding," he said. "And this room back here . . ." He peered more deeply into the house, crouched down on his knees. "Could you move the sun for me?"

Willa obliged, shining the light into the mansion's dark corners.

"What room is your favorite?" Lou asked her.

Willa shook her head. "I love every inch of this place."

Lou nodded. "Good answer. I do have to say, though, that this in here"—he gestured at the library—"I'd have a hard time leaving. Reformed literature major, you know. You never quite shake it. Also"—he pointed at the portrait above where the piano used to live—"this portrait . . ."

Before he could look up or tear his eyes away from the diminutive mansion, which had dominated his attention since he laid eyes on it, Willa let herself change. She let a little of the age she held behind her eyes shine through them, let time exude though her skin, making it a bit less elastic. She let a few of the years that had passed her by flow into her hair, threading the russet through with silver. When she smiled down at Lou, she let the wrinkles around her eyes and mouth remain, let the slight loosening from her downcast face pull down her taut jaw. She let herself show a bit more time on her form, matching the slight battering of the mansion at her feet.

Lou looked up at Willa and back at the portrait. "It's a bit of a likeness for you. Someone in your family, I'm guessing?"

Willa smiled. "Something like that."

Lou nodded and creaked to his feet. "Well, it's just a lovely piece of work, the whole thing, Mrs.—"

"Mrs. Ford. Beatrix Ford." She held out her hand and let her old name drop from her fingertips, cascade to the floor, and flow away, as it had so many times before. Amarantha, Perpetua, Semper, Willa, names and lives brought to her in the current and shed back into time to stream away without her. "I'm a widow," she added.

"I'm terribly sorry to hear that. Not least because I'm a widower myself."

"Oh, I'm so sorry."

Lou held up his hands. "Long ago. Cancer, when our daughter was small. She's a good girl—and a wonderful mother—but she came up quieter than I did. Not that she could get a word in edgewise with a salesman for a daddy. Anyway, thank you, Beatrix."

She nodded slowly, clicking off the sun. "Please, call me Trixie."

· 38 ·

PARKHURST, ARIZONA, 2015

SHUT IT DOWN. SHUT THE WHOLE THING DOWN. I can't do this anymore. Myra typed the words so quickly her fingers hardly touched the keys, and then slammed her laptop shut without waiting for the sure-to-be-immediate response from Gwen. She turned off her phone and stuck it back in her desk drawer, closed it, and after a moment of thought, locked the drawer. Then she opened the attic window and threw the key out into the yard.

The Mansion was silent.

"Oh, *now* you have nothing to say? *Now* you're just a stupid wooden box? Fine. Fine. That's what you always should have been, anyway. I spent my goddamn life playing with you and never leaving this house because I was afraid—I was afraid to let anyone see me—and instead you bring the—" For the first time in her life, Myra had difficulty thinking of the right words to describe a situation, lacking sufficient language to articulate the narrative she found herself in. "Instead you bring the world to me, like it or not, ready or not, and—" She was sobbing in earnest now, the only words that came to her mind profane, and those felt right. "And I'm not ready. Worse, he's not ready, even if he thinks he is, because he doesn't know who he'd be looking at." She rubbed her fingers along her uneven jaw, tears squeezing out of her eyes and catching in the scars along her face and neck. "How could you do this to me? How could you betray me like this?" she screamed, and couldn't decide if she was screaming at the Mansion with its smiling portrait on the library wall, the face so like Trixie's that it always comforted her while also filling her with guilt. She didn't know if she was screaming at Alex, or at herself, or at the time that kept passing her by, seconds inexorably ticking toward the loss of this shelter around her but still, somehow, freezing her in place, unable to make any move to stop it.

The house remained silent.

"Not a *single goddamn note* of comfort, huh? Well. You can just . . . stay the way you are for a while, so there. I can't even get into my desk now, so there won't be any photos, and you can just—" She crossed to the house and closed it roughly, buckling it shut. "You can just stay like that. And don't think I'm going to race up here if you call me, because I'm not. I'm not. I'm done."

"Myra. Honey." A gentle voice spoke from the doorway. "Stop talking to the dollhouse and come downstairs to talk to me." Diane leaned against the doorjamb and held out her hand toward her daughter. "It's easier to walk around down there now that you and Gwen helped me sell that stuff. And we need to talk."

"Have you heard from the bank? Was it enough?" Myra remembered, somewhere in the dim back of her mind, that the cabin was still in danger of being sold out from under them. She knew, in a part of her she'd buried, that she hadn't done enough to save it.

Diane kept her hand extended and wiggled her fingers, gesturing for Myra to hold her hand. "Come on, honey. Let's figure some things out."

Myra walked to the attic stairs without a backward glance. Part of her hoped for some soft measures of music to ring out after her, to give her some reassurance that she hadn't broken something irretrievably. Part of her hoped that it wouldn't.

The house remained silent, and Myra descended the stairs with her mother. When they reached the first floor of the house, Myra was surprised to see how empty the rooms had become—the stacks of boxes were gone, but so was much of the furniture. The house felt unused. When she followed Diane into the dining room, she was surprised to see her father at the table, and stopped short in the doorway.

"It's time for us to talk, Myra." Diane approached as if to put a hand on her shoulder, to draw her into the room, but instead stood an uncertain distance away, as if afraid Myra might flee.

Myra looked back and forth between her mother and her father. She couldn't remember the last time they'd been in the same room together—some uncomfortable and silent holiday in recent years, probably, before Myra put a few spoonfuls of something she wouldn't really taste onto a plate she'd take back upstairs to the attic and forget about eating until she felt hunger gnawing her insides. She didn't move from the doorway.

"Myra, you really need to come and sit down. We've waited way too long to have this conversation. That's as much my fault as anyone else's, and I'm here. I need you to be here, too. Come and sit down."

Her father moved his hands up and down in the air, punctuating each beat of his speech—the longest she could remember him making in years—with an awkward patting motion, as if trying to soothe the air in the cabin into something that felt less electric.

The laughter bubbled up from Myra's stomach so quickly that she couldn't catch it with her lips before it emerged, soft giggles giving way to big guffaws. "You have got to be kidding me. You? You, Dad? You're going to sign on for whatever—intervention thingy? Is that what this is? That Mom has in mind? This is ridiculous."

"It *is* ridiculous," Diane murmured. "None of this should be happening."

"Are you talking about the house? Yeah, I'd say the yearslong shopping spree you went on shouldn't have happened—"

"I'm not talking about the shopping spree, Myra! I'm talking about the fact that you entombed yourself in this house when you were far too young to do any such thing, and the fact that we helped you do it, and we never—I'm talking about—Jesus, Dave, are you going to make me do this by myself?"

Myra's father glared at Diane with resentment, and Myra remembered again how relieved she'd been when he finally left, the glowering silence in the house finally lifted, even though it had been replaced by other things Myra should have paid attention to. "I'm here, aren't I?" He pointed at Myra and then at the chair across from him, already pulled out. "You. Young lady. Sit down and listen to us."

"I'm thirty-four, Dad, for God's sake—"

"Well, do us the honor of sitting down with us anyway so we can have an actual damn conversation, because we've got to have one whether you want to or not. This has gone on long enough."

"Fine." Myra crossed the room and plopped down in the chair, crossing her legs and blowing her hair out of her face, feeling seventeen and angry. "Is this about the auction? Because if you're talking about what Gwen came up with—"

"We know what you and Gwen came up with, Myra." Diane sat down next to her daughter and tried to take her hand, which Myra yanked away roughly. "It isn't going to work. You can't buy this house on the courthouse steps with an essay contest. It's just—it's too big. And your father and I have discussed this—we think it's time to let this place go."

Myra's eyes went wide with alarm. "What do you mean, 'let this place go,' Mom? You and Grampa built this place together—"

"They did, and it's where you grew up, and that's a big reason you and your mom stayed here." Dave swallowed hard. "I didn't even try to take you with me when your mom and I—parted ways."

"When you left," Myra corrected.

"Yes. When I left. It made sense for you to stay here then—"

"Because we didn't know we'd never get you out of the house again," Diane finished. "Neither of us ever expected the way this would turn out, and it wasn't until we started talking about the damn foreclosure on the phone that it clicked for us and everything cleared up, like some kind of fog we'd been walking through finally lifted. You have buried yourself here, Myra. You buried *me* here. And I don't know what it was—inertia, or the fact we came so close to losing you, or some weird woo-woo energy—"

"Or all of the above," Dave said. "But even as hard as it was, how terrifying to see your little girl in a hospital you're not sure she'll ever leave, you did leave it, Myra. You were stronger than you ever gave yourself credit for. But you were scared, and we let you be scared, instead of making you go back to school, instead of forcing you to learn to make your way in the world."

"The world hasn't seen me! It hasn't seen this!" She pointed at her face, her crooked jaw, pushed her long sleeve up her left arm to show the network of scars that traced their way up and down her left side. "I found a way to be out there without anyone ever having to see me, and you said that was okay. You bought my computers, Dad. You paid for the correspondence courses, all those years of homeschooling. You paid for the online college degree. Neither one of you said a word against the work I was doing—"

"You're a very gifted writer, Myra, and you always have been. And Gwen—Gwen was a godsend, still is, but even she's reached out to us because she's worried, especially lately. Your work on that site doesn't seem to be leading you more into the world. It's closing you off even more. Gwen said she tried to get you to look into some business interests and you keep shutting her down. That doesn't sound like progress."

"Well *ha ha ha*, guys, the joke's on you—that damn site *has* put me out in the world, whether I wanted to be or not, and it took every single fiber of my being to try to hold it back, and it almost just banged down the doors anyway. So I've shut the whole thing down. It's too much. I'm not doing it anymore."

Dave and Diane looked at each other with confusion. "What about the contest?" Diane said.

"It was a terrible idea, and like you said, there's no way it would pay off the bank anyway. I never should have agreed to it. We're going to give all the money back and figure out something else. Maybe one of those other business deals Gwen keeps trying to talk to me about. Merchandising. I don't know. I'll think of something. I just—don't want to talk to anyone anymore."

Diane shook her head. "Myra, that's exactly the problem. It doesn't matter if you can come up with something else—and I don't think it would happen fast enough anyway. It's that we don't think you should try anything else that involves staying in this attic, in this house, playing with that dollhouse for the rest of your life. You aren't living."

"What the hell would you know about that, Mom? Should I take out a bunch of credit cards and go shopping for a while, like you? Is that living?"

"No." Diane's voice was a whisper. "It most certainly isn't. It's loneliness. Deep, gnawing, hungry loneliness, Myra, and I don't want that for you."

"Neither do I," said Dave. "Your mom and I might not agree on much, but we agree on this. It's time to leave the attic, Myra. And if the only way for that to happen is for this place to go—well, then it's time for this place to go. Grampa would have said the same thing."

"Your dad and I already talked to his brother—remember your uncle John?—and he's got that little guesthouse on his spread up in Wyoming, and he said we'd be welcome to stay there," Diane said. "Or if you'd rather—" She gestured toward Dave.

"Right. If you'd rather, we have a guest room, and Misty and I would love to have you stay with us. And when you're ready, we could look for somewhere you could live on your own, if you want, maybe somewhere near one of us, or near Gwen—"

Myra clapped her hands over her ears and shook her head. Her body and mind felt pulled in too many directions at once, like the potential loss of the house—the scattering of everything she knew—was scattering her, too, and she was powerless to stop it. "Stop. Stop talking. I can't handle this."

"We have decisions to make, honey. We know this is a lot to take in, and we don't want to rush you, but we also don't have a lot of time to figure this out."

"Please don't let the house go."

Dave and Diane looked at each other. "That's not really up to us anymore, honey." Diane reached again for her daughter's hand, and this time Myra let her hold it. "I know this is so hard." Her voice sounded soft and far away, like Myra remembered it sounding in the hospital so many years before. "But we love you, and we're so sorry, and we're going to figure this out."

Myra stood up. "I don't want to figure this out." She started walking back toward the stairs.

"That's not really on the table—"

"Tonight. Let me finish. I don't want to figure this out tonight. I'm exhausted, and I want to go to bed." She turned around at the doorway and looked at her parents, the strange sight of the two of them in the same room filling her with dread. "You two can keep plotting, but for tonight, I'm out."

ELLIOTT, ARIZONA, 1986

THE MORNING OF MYRA'S FIFTH BIRTHDAY, THE SUN DIDN'T even bother to shine from behind a thick layer of soaking clouds. The drizzling rain ran in ribbons down the skylights notched into the A-frame's roof, and the Verde River rushed in a furious swell past the scrub brush in the yard. The day felt heavy, coated with an oppressive grayness that Trixie was determined to counteract. Myra had stayed with them the night before, because her birthday fell on a weekday that also included three of Diane's final exams in Phoenix. The family's plan was to let Myra have a small celebration with Trixie and Lou, and then a bigger party that included all of them on the weekend.

Trixie had not discussed her own plans with anyone. The river outside reminded her too much of another river swollen by a storm, a lifetime before and almost a continent away, but still always present. Water was the same everywhere, flowing with the echoes of lives and tragedies it had carried and passed by countless times. Trixie was determined not to let another chance slip beyond her grasp. Myra was the right age, and their time together had revealed she had the right spirit. With enough guidance, she could assume the role that Trixie needed to pass on. Trixie wanted to give herself the grace of growing old, an opportunity to live a normal life with Lou—one she could enjoy wholly for herself in whatever time she was afforded before it ended. The sense of an ending was a relief. And when it was time, she would take Myra to the refuge herself, and let her fill the full-sized space that waited for her there. The tether of the stone and the structure of the smaller Mansion would maintain her connection until she was ready to fully assume the Lady's role.

Myra's innate curiosity, her warmth, and her kindness gave Trixie hope that the refuge could resume welcoming tired souls who needed its shelter. After so many years of absence and self-protection, the Lady would have a different face; someone who grew rooted in different soil and learned from other hands, rather than only Trixie's. Someone new might be able to extend an invitation that would not be met with suspicion. Trixie felt disturbances building beneath her feet with the same unease she'd felt in Europe a lifetime ago. People would need an escape from whatever was coming, just as they always had. She was confident that Myra—with the right guidance and support—would know what to do in order to provide it.

There would be time to explain everything in the years to come. For the first time in all her long years, Trixie felt the warmth of a family around her. Her first attempts had been so painful. She could still feel the empty hole that tore open inside her when she lost Ford, and how it had become more ragged with every subsequent loss—Ruth's rejection of her, his violent reclaiming of Alex, and his determination to dig all that remained of her out of his life, root and stem. Because he never realized—could never accept—that she was as entwined with him as the refuge itself. There was no way to sever their connection without destroying them all.

Her grief never dissipated, but its rough edges had mended in her time with Lou and his family, and Myra in particular—so much like the little girl Trixie expected to have with Ford. She finally felt the sense of relaxation—of refuge—that she'd expected to find that day her hand touched Ford's on the ship's railing, with their future spread before them, the plans she thought would fall into place.

She hadn't had anyone to ask about how anything was supposed to work. She had spent centuries relying on only herself for counsel, listening to the earth beneath her feet to aid the instincts she'd honed over time. Meeting Lou was the first time in decades she'd felt a connection to another person—not since Ford. And then, the first time Myra toddled toward her, wrapping her small arms around Trixie's legs, she understood. She'd landed here, on the scrub-covered curve of a desert river, because she was meant to.

Soon, she would go and wake up Myra, curled up in the blue quilt on the folding bed upstairs. She'd already mixed up custard for French toast for breakfast. Then they would spend the morning as they often did, working together on the Mansion in the attic upstairs. Trixie grasped the lapis acorn in her hand, feeling its weight between her fingers and hoping she was ready to clasp it onto Myra when the time came. Then they would get started on the birthday cake she'd promised they would bake together. She had a mold to shape it like a number five, and they would decorate it with a flower garden like the one Myra loved outside.

And then she'd show Myra how to plant her own garden, and they would tend it together, for as long as she had left.

· 40 ·

LOCKHART, VIRGINIA, 2015

ALEX AND RUTHERFORD WERE AT THE WAREHOUSE, FLICK-
ing the glistening crumbs of croissant from their sweaters in the cold
December air and discussing where best to display a new shipment of
distressed bamboo cheval mirrors from the same factory that made
the horrible settees. Alex could not imagine a more unimportant topic
of conversation, and his distress at Myra's shutdown the night before
pressed behind his eyes, a pounding ache in his head and his heart
that Rutherford's triumphant crowing was making worse.

"I never would have thought they'd be so successful, but we can get
stuff from this factory for pennies—fractions of pennies, if we increase
our orders—and it's like printing money. I don't know if it's safari
chic or—"

"Bad taste. The phrase you're looking for is 'bad taste,' Dad." Alex
touched the hinge on one mirror, moving it in its stained bamboo
frame, and his hand came away dark with varnish. "It looks like they

threw these into crates without any quality check at all. I hate the set-tees, but at least they're solid. These are crap."

"I'm thinking of a 'Bohemian Bedrooms' section in Warehouse Three. Everything mismatched. These'll go off at $929.99 a pop."

Alex rubbed his eyes, willing the fog to lift. "Fine. Whatever. They're crap and probably covered with lead paint and filled with asbestos in addition to being the ugliest goddamn things I've ever seen, but sure. Have at it." He walked toward the warehouse's rolling garage door.

"Oh, no, where do you think you're going? 'Bohemian Bedrooms' is right up your alley, so stick around for the rest of the unloading and see what other travesties you can't abide. I know you'll make me proud—"

The loudspeaker above them crackled to life. "Alex, there's a call for you on line four."

"He's busy!" Rutherford called up to the intercom. "Just patch it over the speaker!"

Alex glared at Rutherford. "What if it's personal?"

"Then it shouldn't be coming to you here." Rutherford's expression was pointed. "Patch it over, Ellen!"

"Sure, Ruther. And, Alex—congratulations! So exciting! I can't wait to see your essay!" More static crackled as Ellen patched in the call and Rutherford's face wrinkled, perplexed, mouthing, *Essay?* at his son, who shook his head and mouthed, *Later.*

"Alex? This is Gwen Perkins. I'm so sorry to call you in the middle of work—it's bright and early here in Phoenix, but I know your day's well underway. I didn't know what else to do, and I know you and Myra have been talking—a lot—and she won't answer any of my calls. I'm about to drive up there."

"Is she okay?"

"I can't imagine how she wouldn't be, since she never leaves that damn attic, but I won't lie—I hoped this whole crazy coincidence might pull her out of it. She emailed me last night and told me to shut everything down, and I guess she meant the contest, because she sure as hell can't mean *The Minuscule Mansion*—"

"I wish I could tell you what she meant, but she—she shut down pretty abruptly on me last night, and I'm not sure why. She doesn't want me to come there, that's for sure."

Rutherford continued to look back and forth between the speaker hanging from its exposed wooden beam on the ceiling and his son, whose face was pinched with tension.

"I'm sorry, Alex. Really. I'll try to talk to her in person the next time I have a chance to get up the mountain and see her, but I've been slammed here. The Mansion's still not my day job, so it'll have to wait a bit. I do want to try and convince her to salvage this whole essay contest—"

"I don't give a damn about the essay contest, Gwen. I only care if she's okay. I never should have sent what I sent in the first place, but I had to know why this was happening. Maybe I never will." As Alex shouted up to the intercom, the light in the warehouse caught the russet in his hair, and his face took on a resigned sadness that made Rutherford sharply inhale.

"What is this all about?" Rutherford said. "Who is Myra?"

Alex shook his head and put his finger to his lips as if Rutherford were a bothersome child, and did so without making eye contact. He missed the scarlet color on his father's neck and cheeks, the ragged rhythm of his breathing, the usual warning signs of an impending explosion. He was too focused on the speaker. "I'll tell you later, Dad. Gwen, will you call me when you get to her?"

"Of course. I'll use your cell—you didn't answer it this morning."

"He's supposed to be working!" Rutherford bellowed, and Alex turned around, finally noticing the air shimmering around his father's mouth and eyes.

"I'll keep it on me," Alex said. "Thanks, Gwen." As the static stopped crackling and the line went dead, Alex looked at his father, who was breathing heavily in a way that created his own pocket of atmosphere, the air dry and sparking. Several other workers in the warehouse stopped what they were doing, setting down cheval mirrors and sofas and entryway tables, rooted to their spots on the floor, waiting to see what came next.

Rutherford's rages were legendary at Rakes and Son—rarely discussed, but never forgotten by those who had witnessed them. Alex had heard whispers about these episodes from employees at the warehouse. They said that Mildred, his great-grandmother, used to refer to them as "moments"—as in *Ruther is having a moment* or, to terrified and bewildered subordinates, *Mr. Rakes needs a moment.* And she would usher him out, the atmosphere shimmering around him, his exquisitely tailored suit emitting the sharp scent of burning wool. A "moment" could be preceded by a business setback, or a confrontation, or nothing at all. When Alex returned to Lockhart, his first day at Rakes and Son was a daylong corporate orientation—no breaks for the family scion—and the company's administrative director gave him a "New Employee Folder" stuffed with a variety of business best practices, brochures, and a half sheet of paper in a calming green hue headed "Rakes and Son: Words to Avoid." The list included *setback*, *delay*, *clearance*, *complaint*, and *Willa*.

Rutherford spat his words through gritted teeth. "You don't speak to me at my own business, in front of my employees, as if I am an in-convenience. Ever."

Alex's heart began to pound faster, an undercurrent of fear giving way before his own anger. "I didn't treat you as an inconvenience, Dad. You really want to hash this out here? In front of everyone?"

"I want you to tell me now, before either of us moves one inch from this spot, what this business with a 'minuscule mansion' is and what the hell is going on."

"Oh!" an excited voice from the door called, and Alex and Rutherford saw Ellen bustling in, pushing a cart in front of her that was loaded with paper bags. "I'm so glad I didn't miss this! Here's lunch for everyone, by the way. Ruther! Did Alex tell you? There's this very popular website about 'the mini mansion of Mona' something or other, but the point is, it's *wild*—this little dollhouse that folks are just falling all over themselves to read about and decorate and what all. It's darling! And they ran a contest to meet Mona—or Monica? Mallory?—and Alex tossed his hat in the ring, clever dear, and he won! I hadn't looked at it much myself, but I checked it out on my phone this morning, and I think it'd be a great little ad tie-in for us. Some of the rooms look like the furniture could have come from here! It's like Margaret or whatever her name is found itty-bitty versions of things that'd be right at home in Lockhart. Isn't that funny?" Ellen walked toward them with her phone in hand, waving it in Rutherford's face. "I mean, look at this *bedroom*! That itty-bitty lamp. That headboard! Can you imagine?"

Ellen's long survival as an employee at Rakes and Son had been premised, in part, on her seemingly utter obliviousness to Rutherford's moods and a perfect instinct for his needs. Alex wasn't sure how old she was or even how long she had worked for them. She was just Ellen, an institution, as constant and immutable a presence as the heavy wood beams that held up the warehouse's roof. She had an uncanny ability to redirect Rutherford without his noticing.

Rutherford took Ellen's phone from her hand and scrolled through the screen. "What—what is this?" He flipped the phone around and stepped toward Alex, who retreated backward, craning his neck away from the screen his father was trying to shove in his face. "This—place. It's practically identical. Is this some kind of joke? Are you trying to play a prank on me?"

"Dad, you need to calm down—"

"I will not have my son patronize me! Whatever ridiculous plot you have to make me feel foolish—"

"Not everything is about you, Dad! None of this is about you!" The volume of the words that tore from Alex's chest surprised even him. "You don't have to be in the loop on every development in my life! Isn't it enough that I dropped everything to come back here, to be with you? Isn't it enough that I did that even though you banished me when I was still a little kid? And now you want to know what's going on with me? It doesn't work that way!"

"I told you I was trying to protect you! And this is precisely what I was trying to protect you from!" Rutherford pointed at *The Minuscule Mansion of Myra Malone* and lifted the phone overhead as if to dash it to the floor, but Ellen furtively reached for his hand and slipped the phone out of it as effortlessly as a pickpocket and backed quietly away. "This—house! . . . has its hooks into you, its hooks into me, and I will not allow it. I will not countenance it. I'm ridding our family of it—as I always should have—as quickly as I can—" Rutherford's eyes darted back and forth, his agitation sparking off his body as he shifted from

foot to foot. Alex realized his anger was a mask for something deeper—
something like fear.

"It's just a dollhouse, Dad—a silly little website that people escape
into, find a little refuge from the real world."

"They don't know what they're escaping to," Rutherford hissed. "No
one understands. But I do. You have until Friday, Alex. Gather your
things. Find somewhere else." His voice contained a calm that was
unearthly, coming from a place outside himself.

"It's Wednesday." Alex felt his anger rising again. "I don't understand what your problem with that place is."

"Friday, Alex. Take the rest of the day off. Get out."

Alex glanced around at the silent employees, still waiting to see
what would happen. "Any of you have any rooms for rent? Give me a
call. Apparently I'm being evicted." As he walked past Rutherford, he
patted him on the shoulder. "Thanks again for your support, Dad.
Really good to be able to rely on you."

He walked back out to the narrow employee lot along the canal
and climbed into his Mini, driving back to the mansion in a daze. Much
of what was in the place didn't belong to him, or belonged to him only
in the sense that it belonged to the family. But he felt a special link to
the pieces he knew existed in Myra's house. He still had the storage
container in the mansion's driveway, holding the belongings he hadn't
yet transferred into the house, and he was glad he'd have a place to
move things back into—not that he knew when he could unload them
again, and where. He couldn't think of anywhere to go. He couldn't
even seem to find sure footing in his own mind, still reeling from Myra
slamming the virtual door in his face.

When he parked his car and stomped up the flagstone path to the mansion's door, the music inside was loud enough to reverberate off the stones. "Cut it out!" he yelled, slamming the door behind him and pounding up the stairs to his room, feeling like a child about to throw a tantrum.

Instead, as he threw himself across his bed and wrapped the crushed velvet around himself, he did what he should have done from the very beginning and tried to find Myra instead of the house. Or, rather, tried to find some clue to Myra's insistence on shutting him out. Searching for her name brought up hits for *The Minuscule Mansion* itself, as well as numerous write-ups about the site and its growing audience. He found a fan fiction site that set stories in the Mansion—some of which were racier than Alex would have expected a site about miniatures to inspire. The few interviews he could find about the site were written Q and As, an archived "Ask me anything" session that sounded nothing like Myra and everything like a publicist, or probably Gwen. A few other blurbs and fawning blog entries from fans even mentioned conversations with Gwen, but not Myra. He noted several uses of the word *recluse* and *hermit*, with one site calling her "the J. D. Salinger of miniatures."

Everything in Myra's voice was confined to *The Minuscule Mansion*, just as Myra confined herself. Alex fell back into the archives for a bit, trying to find a thread of connection.

He got more specific, thinking after some time that a search related to a car accident in 1986 might yield results. The archive for a small local paper returned a few short stories, the sad tale of a grievously injured girl found in a crushed car halfway down a mountainside, the vehicle almost too concealed by snow to find; It is too early, as of this writing, to know whether the child will succumb to her injuries from this fatal accident. The car's driver, Beatrix Walsh, was found dead at the scene. The story included a horrific picture of the car—a twisted mass on a snow-covered slope, crushed beyond recognition. It seemed impossible that anyone could survive, and yet Myra had, trapped nearly unconscious in the cold until someone noticed the tracks veering off the highway and followed them over the guardrail.

Another story talked of a fundraiser at the local elementary school for the little girl who survived the accident but who was decidedly not out of the woods—who might remain confined in those woods forever, in fact. Alex read about the anticipated need for corrective surgeries and subsequent in-home nursing care. She had only entered kindergarten that August, and the December crash had taken her out of it. She had never returned to a classroom. Slow and sad notes of Chopin echoed through the house as he read the descriptions of the serious burns she sustained, the broken jaw, the crushed rib cage. Though hopes for her survival remain strong, she will be forever marked by the experience.

There are things I can't let you see, Myra had told him, and Alex suddenly realized that she meant herself.

"Jesus, Myra," he said aloud. "Do you honestly think I would care about that? I don't care what you look like!" He shouted toward the ceiling. "How can I convince her not to shut me out?"

He walked downstairs to the library, hoping for inspiration, when he remembered the book he read to her from. It was still on the bookcase where his father had thrown it, surrounded by broken glass and porcelain, and Alex carefully swept the glass off the high shelf where it rested, trying not to cut himself as he stretched to reach it, hoping not to need the ladder.

Then he heard a click, and the bookcase swung open.

The room behind it was small, but he'd never seen it before. He couldn't see any light switch or lamp, but the room seemed illuminated from within, with no source he could explain. In the center of the room was a small round table elaborately carved out of dark wood, inlaid with blue and silver that Alex recognized, as he got closer, formed the roots of a tree, its interlaced branches stretching out and down the table's fluted edges. In the center of the table was a small silver box, open and empty. As Alex crossed to look more closely, movement caught the corner of his eye, dragging his attention to a round portrait on the wall of the room.

The woman was slight, but Alex realized she was also on her knees, making her seem smaller. She was in three-quarter profile, looking more to her side than out of the frame, and half of her face was concealed by an unruly mass of blond curls. She wore a high-collared dress, elaborate swirled lace running tendrils up her neck from a fitted bodice in midnight blue. The light played on the surface of the dress, moving like waves and eddies, layer upon layer of silk stretched to the portrait's edges, looking as if it would pour out of the gilded frame like water. The woman's smile echoed Willa's, gently curved, as if concealing secrets older than the face it crossed. Her arms were against her chest. As Alex came closer, he saw that one hand was cradling the other, which was curled and darkened, arrayed just below something hanging from a silver chain around her neck. Something blue and round. An egg?

An acorn.

Alex stared at Myra, almost too distracted by her face to notice the portrait's background, the peaked ceiling, the exposed beams, and toward the outside—just before the world of the portrait tumbled off the edge of its frame—a miniature turret.

He ran out of the room and raced back to the staircase, taking the steps two at a time, to his bedroom and computer. He typed as quickly as he could, snatches of sentences unformed, hoping she would understand: You must let me see you. I've already seen you. And I understand. I think I found her—found Willa—and in finding her I think I found you. I should have told you everything before. I love you. I think I loved you before we ever talked.

As the light died around him, he purchased a plane ticket to Phoenix. The first available flight was at five the next morning, leaving from Washington, DC. He started packing.

· 41 ·

Signing Off

(From *The Minuscule Mansion of Myra Malone*, 2015)

ONCE UPON A TIME, THERE WAS A HOUSE.

Every single story Trixie ever told me started with those words, and she told me a lot of them. It's a nice way to start a fairy tale, and I like it most for its openness, because you're not quite sure—when you start listening—what direction the tale may take you. What kind of a house? you may wonder. After all, a house can be anything. It can be a beautiful cottage covered with climbing roses, sheltering a young princess and three kindly fairies who are hiding her from a vengeful sorceress. A house can be made of gingerbread and candy, concealing a blood-thirsty witch just waiting for a chance to eat a tasty pair of plump children. A house can be haunted and surrounded by skeletal trees whose branches scrape against the windows, convincing you that any moment may be your last before you're dragged off to whatever realms come after this one.

It's a rich narrative device, is my point here. A house may stay put, but a story about one can take you anywhere. Trixie's stories, though, always took me to the same place: the refuge, a house on a wide sweep of river that provided shelter to those who needed it most, and that was happiest when it was needed most. But there was an ebb and flow to being needed, and the refuge that the house provided was tied to the spirit of its protector, whom Trixie always called the Lady of the House. An empty house is a lonely place, and needs a keeper in order to be welcoming to anyone. The problem, as Trixie always explained it to me, is that being tied to a place like that can make people start to think of you as something that you're not.

For these past many months, ever since Gwen convinced me that the Minuscule Mansion was a place I needed to share with the world—that my words about it were something someone else might want to read—I've been playacting as the Minuscule Mansion's Lady, in a way, without ever realizing it. I've been hosting you in this place where I've spent most of my life, and for you, there is no Minuscule Mansion without Myra Malone. But you're thinking of me as something I'm not. I'm not a person with answers. I don't know how you should decorate your house, or what the perfect shade is for your entry door, or whether it's a good idea to mix Queen Anne with postmodern. I don't even know how to walk outside my own front door, or have a conversation with another human being face-to-face. I don't know anything.

I do know that the house I grew up in isn't going to be my house anymore. I know that this wacky idea Gwen had to open up the doors—little and big—to people who would pay for the privilege isn't going to work. I know that very soon someone will hand over a check to snap up the cabin my grandfather built, not because it's a refuge or because it's haunted by a confused woman who doesn't know, as she writes this, where she might go next, because she's a private person (and yes, I realize some may call her a recluse). They'll hand over a check because this place is built in, as Gwen puts it, prime mountain vacation territory, and they won't care what that act takes away from someone else. From me. The ghost in the attic.

I'm rambling and I know it, and this is a very long and roundabout way of saying that this is my last entry for *The Minuscule Mansion of Myra Malone*. I've already told Gwen to process refunds for those of you who have entered the contest, and I'm sorry for all of your time and trouble. I never could have predicted, when all of this started, where this tale was going to take me, or take us.

But that's the problem when you fall in love with a story that starts with a mansion. A house is a very unpredictable place to start.

· 42 ·

PARKHURST, ARIZONA, 2015

I SHOULDN'T HAVE LOOKED I SHOULDN'T HAVE LOOKED I knew he wouldn't listen. The words crashed and tumbled through Myra's head, too quick for her to corral them. Thoughts of Alex began to collide with *Where am I going to go? How am I going to go? How is this happening?*

The Mansion was active when she came back up the stairs, abandoning her plan to return to her room and try to sleep, which she knew would be impossible. Instead she stomped back up into the place she belonged and found the Mansion, predictably, wide-open, with music emanating from the secret room behind the library bookcase. Myra felt hot, like the glimmer of a fever was building up in her chest, the acorn charm around her neck warm against her skin. A flutter from the corner of the attic caught her eye and she found the dress—Trixie's dress—moving as if an invisible breeze, a current only she could see, was playing through the dry air. She went back to the Mansion and peered inside, noticing that the portrait in the library was intact, smiling at her.

"What should I do?" Myra whispered.

The portrait didn't answer. Myra sat back on her heels, hearing the crunch of gravel in the distance as her father's car headed back down the driveway, leaving again. As if it didn't bother him in the slightest to let the cabin go. But of course, he already had, long before. And Diane had, too, it appeared, retreating in a different way that foreclosed any other choice. Myra heard the squeaking hinges of her door closing on the first floor, where she would be unconscious almost immediately after taking her nightly pill. They'd both left Myra behind, feeling again like the little girl in the snowdrift.

"What now?" she murmured to the portrait again. "Oh, Trixie, you always knew what to do. You and Grampa both. I wish you were here." Myra heard a small thump at her feet. The clothespin doll, its yellow yarn hair spread around its round head like a halo, was outside the Mansion. Outside the boundaries of its assigned world.

Myra looked outside the window, seeing the taillights of her father's car shine off the rusted bumper of her mother's car.

She tiptoed down the stairs before she formed a conscious thought of doing it, grabbing her mother's keys off their nail by the front door. She raced across the yard in her soft slippers and slid into the driver's seat.

She had resisted mightily when Diane insisted on her getting a driver's license as a teenager, but her mother had signed her up for the necessary correspondence course anyway, had sat in the passenger seat and taught her to drive herself, and then made her take the driving test—a scarf concealing as much of her face as she could manage—

while Diane sat in the back seat. *What if I need to go to the hospital? What if you do? You need to be able to drive.*

The test was the last time Myra drove a car, and she felt every day of those eighteen years as she struggled to remember the complicated list of steps to get it started. But it did, roaring to life in a way that Myra found both terrifying and a little exciting, and she eased it down the gravel driveway toward the highway. Toward the edge of the rim and down the mountain, an hour away, to the river birch that arched above Trixie and Lou's matched headstones.

Myra hadn't set foot in the cemetery since Lou's funeral, a few days after her twenty-first birthday, which her father—in a joke more solemn than funny—shared with Grampa and Trixie by bringing six bottles of beer to their graves. The bottles—slipped into every pocket of his too-big and rarely worn suit—clinked as the three of them, Myra with her parents, walked to the plot. After the burial, Dave handed Myra and Diane each a bottle, opened them quickly with a bottle opener on his key chain, and delivered a quick toast—*Salud*—while raising his bottle. Myra looked at her father with confusion, and he whispered, *It's what Grampa would have wanted*, and she knew that he was right. The beer, dark and thick, tasted as bitter as her grief, and she couldn't bear to drink much of it. They left two bottles—one for Lou, one for Trixie—in front of their headstones, and Diane stuck silk flowers in a third, placing it between them.

The bottles and the flowers were, of course, nowhere in evidence when Myra parked the car and retraced her steps to the river birch. Her breath came ragged in clouds of steam, the only warm thing in the gathering dusk. If it hadn't been for the tree, she wouldn't have been able to find them; tendrils of tangled ivy curled in evergreen shelter above them both. She wished, as she creaked to sit on the ground in the cold, that her parents had put a bench or somewhere to sit at the site, but of course, she hadn't ever returned and doubted they had, either. The graves looked untended—not forgotten, but dormant.

Lou had selected Trixie's grave because of the river birch. Diane told her, years later, that he had wanted to find an oak tree—that Trixie had spoken so poetically about the oaks where she was from, the shelter of their spreading branches, the glowing colors of their leaves—but her skill at making almost anything grow in the dry Arizona soil perished along with her on the mountainside, and the birch was the best he could find. Its shedding bark, dropping to the ground in gentle curves, was a mixture of beauty and sadness. Myra would have agreed with the choice, if she'd been asked. But she was unconscious in the hospital at the time, barely clinging to life, still caught in a snowdrift in her mind.

She hadn't noticed, when they came to bury Lou, that he'd had an oak tree carved in Trixie's headstone, sprouting from an acorn. The carving was complex and ornate, a sharp contrast to Lou's simple granite block. She wrapped her hand around the blue seed hanging from her neck, drawing strength from its warmth.

"I don't know why I thought you could help." Despite the soft layer of curled bark and leaves she sat on, Myra felt the cold weaving up from the ground through the seat of her pants, and it felt like a comfort—slowing her blood, soothing the pain in her head. "But I felt like I needed to see you. I don't know why I didn't come before."

The wind picked up, tousling her yellow hair the way Lou used to, and she could taste melting ice—a hint of snow about to fall. She felt tugged away, the devotion that tethered her to the small house in the

attic stretched tight in a way that was uncomfortable. The light continued to fade and the wind strengthened again, pushing her to her feet
as she longed to feel some glimmer of recognition, some reaction from
the two people she had treasured so much and been so treasured by.
Treasure is a responsibility, my little acorn, but I'll help you learn.

"You didn't help," Myra said. "I wasn't ready. Whatever you gave me,
Trixie, I wasn't ready, and I've spent my whole life trying to learn without you." Tears ran down her face, freezing in the wind. "I didn't know
how lonely I was until it seemed like it might stop. But that would mean
letting him in, letting him see me."

There was no sound but the wind.

"It's me, isn't it? I'm the Lady. You left it with me before you meant
to, and further away than you planned." She laughed ruefully as the
truth sank into her bones, the acorn around her neck pulling with a
weight that was comforting in its familiarity but took on a new significance, a sadness she didn't know how to absorb. "I feel like I should
ask what happens now, but it's already been happening for a long time
without me knowing it. And I guess I've been a refuge—I didn't mean
it, but Gwen told me so many times. People who watched what I did
with the Mansion, who needed an escape. But what about me?"

The plaintive pitch of her voice caught on the wind and waved
among the branches of the river birch. "You said she was so often
alone, the Lady. Before Alex, I don't think I would have minded, Trixie,
but now—feeling what it meant to let that go—I don't know if I can do
this. I don't know if I can bear the weight of it."

Trixie's soft voice played through her head, from a place deeper
than memory. *We can't always choose the details of our burden. But we
bear it just the same.*

Myra returned to the car, propelled by a sense of urgency she couldn't articulate. The miles up the mountain should have passed more slowly than the ones taken downhill, but she pushed harder on the accelerator, the distance consumed hungrily and fast, fear finding a toehold in the pit of her stomach and glowing like a coal, brighter and hotter, until she spun into the gravel driveway and saw the light flickering in the attic windows, and screamed.

· 43 ·

LOCKHART, VIRGINIA, 2015

AS HE PACKED, ALEX FELT THE PHONE IN HIS POCKET buzzing. When he saw his father's name on the phone's screen, he pushed the button to ignore the call. And the next one, and the one after that. He packed light, stuffing socks and underwear. *Do they wear sweaters in Arizona? She always talks about the cold, but isn't it all desert and cacti? Throw a few in there in case—*

He packed every electronic device he owned, not just because he always kept them but because a story burned in his fingertips, prompting an urge to write for the first time in years, to record the seedling of his grandmother's narrative before it could slip further away through time. He added a heavy duffel bag to his rolling suitcase, feeling a need to take some things with him that Myra also had in smaller scale. He folded up the crushed velvet bedspread, wrapping it around the brass elbow lamp. Ran downstairs and retrieved *A Child's Treasury of Nature Poems* from the library, a few shards of wisteria-painted porcelain. He looked at Willa's picture and recognized the tear across her face had mended without a trace of his father's slash through its canvas.

You have until Friday. Alex wasn't sure when he'd be back—if he'd be back at all—and he didn't know what his father would do with the things he loved here, how quickly he would rent the house out, or sell it, or otherwise exclude him from this place that felt like home. Before he could consider further, he lifted Willa's portrait off the wall and took it out to the portable storage pod in the driveway, tucked it safely against the wall, and covered it with a heavy moving blanket. As he looked around to his boxes of stored possessions, he saw he had more room, and returned to the house to retrieve more objects, whatever caught his eye. He rolled the carved table and its silver stand out of the hidden room, through the front hall, and down the front steps, nestling it in the container among boxes of old books. The aqua credenza in his room—cobbled together as it was—also came apart, and a few moments with the multi-tool in his pocket gave him a chance to divide it into pieces he could carry down the staircase and stash with the other items. The mattress was too wide and heavy to handle himself, but the headboard was lightweight, its sliding panels just veneer, and he managed to wrestle it out of the house, too. The records he loved—Chopin and Joplin and Debussy, vinyl circles full of remembered melodies—he piled into a box that joined the books outside.

He went upstairs for a final pass around his room, and he paused in the hallway, his arms empty. The glass doorknob on Willa's door sparkled in the afternoon light. He hadn't spent much time in that echoing, mostly empty room with its sweeping view of the river. The door swung open soundlessly, showing the same bare floors, the same oversized chifforobe against the back wall. While Alex appreciated the craftsmanship of its gleaming mahogany, it was far too large for the scale of the room in which it sat, and seemed uncomfortably out of place.

He realized he'd never even opened it, and crossed the room to grasp one of its tarnished handles. The door stuck fast for a moment before releasing with a crash. One of its hinges was broken. The dusty interior held only two items, neither of them clothes: a child's rocking horse with a red-painted saddle, and an oak cradle perched on two solid half-moons of wood. Alex felt a spark of recognition and wrapped his arms around both pieces, tugging them out of the chifforobe and leaving the broken door ajar. He carried them both downstairs and added them to the boxes and parcels he'd already stored.

When the tight bands around his chest began to relax, and he felt as if he'd removed pieces of himself beyond the purview of his father's rage, he stopped and closed the storage container, replacing its thick padlocks. He called the storage company for a pickup. Their regular business with Rakes and Son brought them as quickly as they'd come the first time, a truck showing up at the bottom of the hill within an hour. He watched the compartment stacked neatly on its truck and driven away, and then climbed into his car as the twilight started to deepen.

· 44 ·

LOCKHART, VIRGINIA, 2015

RUTH SAW THE DARKNESS FROM THE MANSION'S RIPPLED windows as others might see a glow. The mansion always looked that way to him, with light and dark reversed, the way a photo negative upended your expectations for how an image should appear. He paused on the flagstone walkway and glanced toward the driveway, noticing Alex's storage container was gone, and so was Alex's car. He hoped—he knew—that Alex himself was gone, too, but the ground beneath his feet told him exactly what his son would find wherever he was heading, wherever that damned dollhouse was, whomever it belonged to now. Because it always belonged to her.

I am always here. You must know that.

When he'd banished his mother, driving her away from the place after tearing his own son out of her arms, she'd spoken those words with such calm, such certainty, that Ruth had heard them as a curse.

And it was true. He'd always known it, even when he swallowed the knowledge. Even when he suppressed every memory he had of her.

When he returned with Alex to the house that long-ago night—after taking him to the family doctor, a man whose long association with the Rakes family prevented too many questions about the boy's broken wrist—Willa was gone, but he could still feel her presence breathing through its rooms. Alex cried and fell asleep in the library, beneath the smiling portrait, and Ruth didn't sleep at all. He packed the boy's things the next morning and announced they would be moving into the Federal-style house that once belonged to Mildred and Teddy, where Rutherford really lived. Where he was Rutherford or Ruther, and where he was not Ruth, the name his mother insisted on calling him, the name he heard whispering from depths underground whenever he returned to the mansion and its oak trees and its flagstone path. Where he stood now. Staring at the place again. The place where he started and finished.

He'd put the mansion on the market that next morning, when Alex woke up and protested at the packing, at the leaving, at the driving across town to the gloomy Federal house. *I want to go home*, he cried, over and over again, and Ruth—Rutherford, damn it all, or Ruther—told Alex it wasn't home, but couldn't convince him otherwise.

No one would purchase the place. The agent he trusted to list and show it resigned after a single tour, coming to Rakes and Sons and sliding the engraved business check back across Rutherford's imposing desk. "Not for all the money in the world," he'd said, and turned on his heel and left—not just the office, and not just the building, but Lockhart itself.

The mansion knew that Rutherford wanted it gone and it fought him back, just as Willa said it would. He couldn't sell it, and he could get no peace at night in the Rakeses' Federal house, listening to Alex's keening wails about the mansion and his grandmother. One morning, after only a few weeks, he reversed the move he'd made with his son such a short time before, and returned to the mansion. When Alex got out of the car, the wind in the trees calmed, and the whispers beneath the stones stopped, and the place became peaceful. It was a cautious peace—Rutherford could not be there alone, or not for long, without the same old sense of push and pull that drove him mad. It was just enough to get him through the short years he had left before Alex was old enough to enter Saint Thomas Academy. As soon as the boy turned five, Rutherford sent Ellen to deliver Alex to the school. He put the Federal house on the market and moved into a glassy condominium downtown, overlooking a more exclusive stretch of the river. As for the mansion, he would have been content to let it collapse into ruin, but it steadfastly refused to do so. At night, he felt it gnawing at the edges of his consciousness, and dreaded the thought of finding another agent to try to place tenants in the house.

The morning he received an offer on his grandparents' old house, Ellen leaned against the doorframe of his office, her arms folded. "I suppose I'll need to find another place, then, won't I?"

Rutherford shook his head, as if escaping a dream. He had forgotten the apartment in the basement, the fact that Ellen had never left. She had knit herself so seamlessly into his family that he had assumed, without asking, that she would occupy the separate suite in his new apartment, loyal as ever. But the mansion was a better option—in need of a caretaker, and one who wouldn't bother him. And Ellen never bothered him at all. She smiled broadly when he suggested staying in the house for a while. "For a time, perhaps, Ruther. But that place is not for me, not really. It's for someone else."

"Don't remind me," Rutherford said as the two talked past each other. And Ellen stayed longer than either of them planned, moving out only a few weeks before Alex moved in.

It should have been enough. The business had done well, Alex had done well enough—albeit across the world and filled to the brim with the anger of a young man who blamed his father for everything—and Rutherford felt a sort of stasis, but for the gnawing pain that started when his mother disappeared and that grew like a hungry animal in his gut as the years passed, until he became so tired of telling Ellen to stop talking about visiting a doctor that he finally went to visit one. The diagnosis was no surprise. Its dark prediction was exactly what he expected.

He'd thought that she was gone, but she never was, not really. Not from the portrait, not from the mansion, not from him—exactly as she'd said. They were inextricably entwined, as tangled as the branches of the overgrown oak trees soaring above his head. Knowing she had always been right ignited the coal of wrath that always burned inside him, and it felt good to release it as he walked through the mansion's front door.

The house was waiting for him, of course. It knew that he was coming. He had felt it tugging somewhere beneath his sternum before he even left the warehouse, as he walked around one last time, admiring what his family had built. He felt its pull as a kind of pain, like an aching tooth he couldn't stop touching with his tongue, as he walked into the back office and retrieved Ellen's enormous handbag from the drawer where he knew she always kept it. He pulled her wallet out to look at the only photograph of his mother he knew to still exist, a wrinkled newspaper clipping of a woman of uncertain age next to a younger woman, laughing as she handed an ice cream cone to a small child.

He'd found the clipping, and a weathered note tucked into the same slot behind it, many years before. He had discovered both items by accident. Ellen had scared him by getting dangerously ill one day with what turned out to be food poisoning, and he insisted on taking her to the emergency room himself, filling out the intake paperwork as she lay half unconscious in a hospital bed. He fumbled through her things to find her identification and insurance information and noticed the yellowed paper of the clipping and the note, the sides of both papers worn down to feathered edges. When he discovered them, his fingers did the same thing they did now—the same thing they'd done every time he snuck in to look at them again, retrieving Ellen's wallet, staring at a moment from his own past. He traced the older woman's face with his fingers, and then lifted them to his own, feeling the way the angles of his own features mirrored hers. He pulled the note from its slot, looking at his mother's handwriting.

Watch over him. Watch over this place. I don't know when I'll be back, but I'm never really gone. WILLA

Rutherford tugged his favorite Waterford pen from the jacket pocket where he always kept it. The pen had been a gift from Mildred when he graduated from Saint Thomas Academy. *For my Ruther, my rudder in the storm. Grandmother*

He wrote beneath his mother's words on the faded paper of the note, adding his own handwriting, ruing how much his letters looked like hers.

You can stop watching now. RUTH

Everything that transpired in that place had transpired before, and would do so again. The refuge remembers.

He would burn its memory to ashes.

· 45 ·

I-95 NORTH, VIRGINIA, 2015

ALEX HAD BEEN DRIVING FOR LESS THAN AN HOUR WHEN his phone began insisting again for his attention. He forgot he had it connected to his car wirelessly, and when he tried to swipe it off in annoyance, he instead heard Ellen's voice ring out over the speakers.

"Alex! Is your father with you?"

"No, I'm not even in Lockhart. Why?"

"I can't find him anywhere. He was so angry after you left—we got him into the back office and I convinced him to sit for a spell while I went to make a cup of tea, and then we got slammed with a busload of customers from that active living community in Arlington—you know, the one where all the houses look like Tudor estates—"

"Ellen, does this story end in some kind of point?"

"He was gone when I got back. He wasn't in his office, he wasn't in the stockroom, we can't find him in the warehouse, and he isn't answering his phone."

"Well, fine. What do you expect me to do? He kicked me out. Let him cool off wherever he's hiding and then figure it out when he comes back. It's not like he cares about what I think."

"Rutherford Alexander Rakes the Third, if you think I'm going to let you talk about your father as if he doesn't care about you, you've got another think coming. That man has his demons, that's for sure, and your whole damn family is the most haunted group of snobs I've ever known in all my days, but I've watched out for Ruther since he was born. I watched out for him because his mother asked me to, and I've worked for all of you as long as I have because I love you all, God help me, and I'm telling you that something is wrong."

Alex took a deep breath and pulled his car over to the shoulder. "Ellen, we don't deserve you. He sure as hell doesn't. What do you want me to do?"

"Come back. Please. It isn't like him to just disappear."

"I'm supposed to catch a flight out of DC tomorrow. I have someone I need to see."

"If it's that Michelle girl, Alex, and she's not the kind of person who would understand a family emergency, she doesn't deserve you, either. Please. He's sicker than he told you, and he gets upset so easily. I never should have let him look at that site, but he made me show him and he just got more furious, said he had to make it stop before it was too late—"

Alex skidded back onto the freeway, the twin shafts of his high beams illuminating a cloud of dust as he accelerated toward an emergency road across the wide median and merged into the slow flow of traffic heading south, the opposite direction. "Meet me at the mansion," he shouted at Ellen, letting the line go quiet as she hung up. He pressed the pedal of his car into the floor, not caring if he passed a speed trap, not caring about speed at all, leapfrogging around other vehicles as he tried to get back to Lockhart.

He approached the bridge across the river and saw the red glow emanating from the distant hill.

When he reached the suburb beneath the mansion, the neighborhood was emptied of its residents, all of them out and on the street below the iron gate. He honked his horn, trying to find a pathway through, and then abandoned his car in the middle of the road, stepping out among faces horrified, gleeful, relieved, merely curious—and as he reached the gate, a woman to its left screamed and pointed.

He saw a flaming figure on the roof, leaning casually against the slate tiles on the turret, and Alex raced up the flagstone path, calling his father's name and hearing only laughter, mad and unhinged, carried on ashen breezes from the burning house.

"Dad! Hold on!" He bounded up the burning steps before anyone could catch him, reached for the iron doorknob, and was blown backward by the flames, cradling his left hand. "Dad!" he screamed, looking around wildly for any help, a ladder, a fire truck, someone who could reach his father. He stood back from the mansion's walls, far enough to see the flames leaping in his turret bedroom, through the wide leaded windows of the entry, licking up the edges of the chimney. He looked for his father, and the smoke cleared around him, still leaning against the turret, doubled over with laughter.

"I told her." Rutherford's voice was almost unrecognizable and yet eerily matter-of-fact, the winds around him carrying his words to his son like a blow horn, a message from a past Alex didn't share. "I told her I would burn it to the ground." He walked across the top of the house and patted the turret's sloping roof as if comforting it, or comforting himself, and Alex saw the flames erupting from his fingertips, curving around the sharp angles of his elbows and shoulders, his dour and pointed face, his polished shoes. He felt a sudden rush of air, as if the mansion were inhaling.

And then the roof collapsed.

· 46 ·

PARKHURST, ARIZONA, 2015

This teapot wants to be part of the room, but there's no
room to belong to.

The cursor blinked at Myra, and she blinked away tears, and put
her fingers back on the keyboard.

The sun came up this morning even though I asked it not
to. It's shining on a world completely changed, and I don't
know where to begin.

The smell of smoke filled her head, filled the attic, which
remained—miraculously—intact, its rafters only singed. If nothing
else, the fact that Diane had emptied out the house made it easier and
faster for Myra to race into the kitchen and rip the fire extinguisher
from its rack on the wall, its placement prominent because Myra still

had nightmares about fire, and her parents filled the house with tools to show her she was safe. She ran up the stairs and then up the narrower attic passageway, erupting through the door to see the Minuscule Mansion engulfed, its flames licking the beams above it. She sprayed at the base of the fire, as she'd been taught, and screamed for her mother to wake up and get out of the house, to call the fire department, to help—she didn't know how—as the thing she loved most in the world burned before her eyes. The flames seemed hungry only for the Mansion, feeding itself with every tiny detail it could reach before finally, sated, it let itself be calmed by the white foam Myra wielded.

By the time the fire truck arrived, there was nothing left to extinguish.

The Minuscule Mansion was a smoking hulk. The cabin itself was fine but was, of course, not Myra's anymore—not her family's, or at least not for much longer, with foreclosure looming. Myra had so little she needed to pack, so little she needed to move, and she focused mostly on the need to restore the furniture to the hatbox, to disconnect the Mansion from its elaborate base—her grampa's handiwork—and to fold the whole little world away, fastening its brass buckles for whatever was next. And where that was, she hadn't yet decided.

Now she had even less to decide. The brass buckles were tarnished and melted into useless hunks, the platform blackened and unrecognizable. Not a single book remained in the library. Myra didn't truly break down until she saw the dark rectangle where the Lady's face once smiled, and her tears had not stopped since. Her mother had tried a few times to comfort her, tiptoeing up the stairs with chamomile tea and apple smiles, as if Myra were still a child. She had suggested they both leave to head to Wyoming a few days early, moving into the guesthouse on Myra's uncle's property that waited for their new life, whatever it might be. There was nothing now to pack, nothing to take to whatever waited for her next. But Myra still couldn't bring herself to leave.

She didn't know why she had gotten out her laptop, or why she decided to write. Her words had always been her anchor, and as she felt the lapis acorn around her neck and heard Trixie's soft voice in her head, words seemed like a tether to something greater than herself.

> Gwen would want me to write something about how grateful I've been for all the love and attention you've given to this world. And I am grateful for that now, but I also owe you honesty. I didn't know that I was making this place for anyone other than myself. I didn't know that so many of you had come to rely on it as a refuge from the world outside the screen you used to peer into the Mansion, or that you valued its details and its stories as much as I did. I didn't know what Trixie gave to me, what Grampa gave to me, all those many years ago—the power of it, or the burden of it. I only knew that I was meant to keep it safe.
>
> And I failed.

She stopped typing and rubbed her tears off roughly, taking a deep breath.

> I don't know what comes after this. The Mansion is gone— as gone as Trixie and Lou, as gone as this cabin I've grown up in will be. I've never been so alone.

She stopped typing again and heard taps like an echo of her fingers, and looked around the attic in confusion. There was no noise from what was left of the Mansion, its ashes catching the beams of light from the windows of a late afternoon on a cold December day. It wasn't coming from her keyboard, silent without her fingers.

She traced the noise to the corner where the dress hung, its taffeta singed along some edges, but still intact on its hanger, as small as a dress for a doll. Underneath, sitting on the floor, was the hatbox.

The tapping was coming from inside. Myra never knew what the hatbox would contain when she opened it—pieces of furniture waiting to be cobbled together, tools that suggested some new project, whole rooms looking for a home—but this time, as she lifted off the dusty-rose lid, the only things inside were three clothespin dolls. Her yellow-yarned doppelgänger, the man with his red and brown yarn and ballpoint stubble, and the smaller clothespin with its long, dark yarn in pigtails.

Myra held the clothespins in her hands.

There's no room for you to belong to.

She put them back into the hatbox and wept.

· 47 ·

SOMEWHERE OVER TEXAS, 2015

BY THE TIME THE FLIGHT ATTENDANT SET THE LITTLE bottle on Alex's tray table, he realized she'd asked him three times if he wanted anything to eat or drink, and he hadn't said a word. He looked up at her with confusion when he saw the tiny wine, and she smiled back at him.

"Please don't take this the wrong way," she whispered. "We aren't supposed to do this. But hardly anyone is here, and you look like you need it."

Alex nodded slowly, hardly registering the pain in his gauzed hand, feeling as if the whole of his brain were insulated by the same winding ribbon of cotton softness. He was numb. "My father died," he said.

"I'm so sorry for your loss."

"Don't be?" Alex heard the uptick at the end of his voice, the hanging note of a question he hadn't meant to ask. "He was—it's complicated. He was sick. I think for a long time, much longer than I knew. I think it made him see the world in a way no one else did. It made him fight demons that weren't demons at all." He rubbed his eyes with his fists, trying to dislodge the fog in his head. "I'm sorry; I know I'm not making much sense. I didn't get much sleep."

"Don't apologize. When did he pass?"

"Yesterday."

"Oh, how awful. Are you on your way to the funeral?"

"Funeral?" Alex rubbed his eyes again. "I guess there should be a funeral. I mean, there will be a funeral. But no. I'm going somewhere else."

The woman looked confused, but patted his hand. "Well. I've been there. You're not going to know what end is up for a while, and that's okay. I hope you find some refuge for your thoughts."

"Thank you." Alex pulled the printout he'd folded into his wallet from a kiosk in the airport business center, not wanting to rely on searching on his phone for the Alcove Agency when he arrived in Phoenix. Gwen Perkins looked exactly like she sounded: polished and competent, and she was his only possible link to finding Myra. "A refuge is exactly what I'm looking for."

The little that remained of the mansion on the hill in Lockhart was still smoking when Alex left for Arizona. When the roof collapsed, the flames from within the structure seemed emboldened by the lack of any further barriers, and they ascended to heights that made the milling crowds below gasp in wonder, as if they were watching a fireworks show instead of destruction. When he saw his father disappear, Alex expected to feel grief, but was surprised instead to feel a wave of calm wash over his head with the heat from the growing flames. He barely registered the arrival of the fire trucks and ambulances or the efforts of the paramedics to draw him gently toward medical treatment for his burned hand, to urge him to get checked out at a hospital, which he refused.

He kept his eyes trained on the fire as if he expected to see his father walk through the flaming front door, his slight form glowing like an ember, but it never happened, and Alex knew it never would. Leaving the scene was less of a conscious decision than it was an act of muscle memory, guiding him through the astonished throngs of onlookers, into the driver's seat of his car, up the silent highway to the same airport he'd attempted to drive to earlier. As if nothing had changed, and as if everything had. When he reached the airport in Washington, DC, he thought to call Ellen, who had been staring with horror among the countless others at the base of the hill before he left.

Ellen started talking as soon as she picked up. "They're still searching the house." Alex expected crying, but heard only brisk efficiency. "Thanks for letting me know they shouldn't be looking for you in there, at least."

"Ellen, my dad—"

"I saw. Everyone saw. The roof collapse, I mean. Not the rest of it."

"Not the rest of what?" Alex was still trying to make sense of what he'd seen his father do, how he'd seen him do it.

"I told you, Alex. You're part of the most haunted family I've known in all my days. And I've worked for you a long time." She exhaled in a way that brought her face immediately to Alex's mind, its immaculate cloud of firmly sprayed short curls in a shade of bottle red she refreshed every two weeks, chewing a pen between her full lips painted to match the hair, tapping her red-polished nails. "I'm just glad he's not suffering anymore."

"Me, too." Alex felt out of his depth. Ellen had known him since he was a small child—and was, now that he considered, the most competent person he knew. "I don't know what I'm supposed to do now."

"Well, they're all going to ask questions, Alex. Something like this'll always cause some questions. But you have something they don't have."

"What's that?"

"The Rakes family name, Rakes family money, and Rakes family lawyers." She exhaled again. "And me. And, in a way, your father. He didn't leave any theories to chance. He left a note."

"What? Where?"

"In my purse. Where he knew I'd find it. On a note from your grandmother that I always kept with me."

"What did it say?"

Ellen's voice caught. It was the only time Alex had ever heard anything from her that sounded like tears. "That I could stop watching out for him now."

Alex felt tears spring into his eyes. "I'm so sorry."

"I'm sorry, too. For both of us. But you have bigger things to do, Alex."

"You're right. I have to go, Ellen. I got a later flight than I meant to take, but I still have to go and find her."

The line was silent for a moment, and Alex wondered if he'd lost his signal before she spoke again. "Yes, you do, I think. Your family deserves another love story after the one they lost. I hope to God you find one."

"What do you mean, another love story?"

"Your dad never talked about your grandma and grandpa, but I still remember them. I was only a teenager when Ford brought her back to Lockhart, not long after your great-granddad hired me to work here. I did a better job looking pretty than I did selling furniture back then, unlike now, when I do both exquisitely well."

"Ellen. This is an indelicate question, but—how old *are* you?"

"A lady never admits to her own timelessness, Alex, but I'll confess I did have help, I think. That house—it seeps into you somehow, or it did me. I don't know how to explain to you that I'm ninety-three years young, my dear, even though I feel almost as sprightly as I did when I first walked up that mansion's front steps. My mind was too old for my body back then, and now I think it may be a little too young for it. I don't know how to tell you that I know what you're feeling. But I do."

"I never knew them." Alex felt a sense of loss he couldn't explain. "What were they like?"

"I've never seen a pair of people so in love as Ford and Willa Rakes. It was like watching a big, swoony romance picture, but it was real. But the way he was when he came back here after the war—oh, honey. I've never seen such heartbreak. Nothing was ever the same."

"I don't know if I'm heading into a love story, Ellen. She shut me down."

"Big feelings are scary." Ellen's cigarette lighter clicked. "And it sounds like that girl's kept her world pretty tiny. But some things are bigger than all of us. Leave the details here to me and come back when you're ready. Find what you're both looking for. Good luck."

The line went silent again, and Alex realized Ellen had hung up. He looked again at the printed address in his hand, next to Gwen's professional headshot. "Please help me find her," he whispered. "I don't know where else to go."

After hours of stale and recirculated air on the plane across the country, the air that hit Alex's face when he disembarked in Phoenix was cool and dry, less full—less haunted feeling—than the vapor-filled air of Virginia. He gathered his luggage in a trance and realized he hadn't rented a car, and wouldn't know where he was heading if he had. Instead, he pulled out his phone and dialed Gwen's number.

"Alcove, this is Gwen."

"Gwen. It's Alex."

"Alex! I've been trying to call you. I thought you were going to keep your phone on you. I'm giving up on getting Myra to answer me, and I'm just heading up there. I'll give you a call when I find out what's going on."

"Can I come?"

"What do you mean, can you come? Come where?"

"Can I come with you? To see her?"

Gwen paused. "I'm too worried. I don't think I can wait for you to catch a plane across the country."

"I already did. I'm standing in Sky Harbor as we speak. I don't have a clue where I'm going or what I'm doing, but I figure if anyone knows what direction I should head, it'll be you."

"Damn it, Myra. When I see her, I'm going to kill her."

Alex frowned. "I don't understand. For what?"

Gwen laughed. "I let her talk me out of returning any of the television pitch calls. There you are, standing in an airport, the big, over-the-top romantic gesture that'd grab a million eyeballs, and there's not a single camera to capture it." She sighed. "Such a lost opportunity."

"Every story Myra's ever told me about you is clicking into place for me now. How do I get to you? Should I come to your office?"

"Oh, no. This is too big to pass up. I'll drive over and collect you myself, and then we'll head north."

"Before we do, I need you to help me stop somewhere else to clear something up, if you have all the details. And you strike me as someone who always has all the details."

"You couldn't be more right. What particular detail are you looking for, Mr. Rakes?"

"This auction. Myra's cabin. The bank. How much to fix it?"

"Fix it, as in pay it off? Over a hundred grand. Diane has expensive taste and didn't have a lot of oversight, it turns out. We cleared some of it by selling some of the stuff, but not nearly enough. The auction hasn't happened yet. It's supposed to be next week. I hadn't had the heart to tell Myra yet how short we are."

Alex nodded. "Let me make a few calls while you're on your way here and see what I can do."

"What do you mean, what you can do? Are you the kind of person who can do something about that kind of debt?"

"I didn't used to be, but I think I may be now." Alex sighed deeply. "My father is dead, and my house is gone. The world—it's a different place than it was yesterday. I feel like I can barely stand up, actually. And the only person I can talk to about everything that's happened—about this enormous weight, this burden I feel—I don't know if she'll talk to me."

"She'll talk to you, Alex. I don't know how to explain it. But I think she's been waiting to talk to you her whole life."

PARKHURST, ARIZONA, 2015

MYRA WASN'T SURE HOW LONG SHE'D BEEN SITTING ON the attic floor when she heard the crunch of tires on the gravel driveway. The sound made her jump, and when she looked out the window, she saw her mother walk out the cabin's door and toward Gwen's car. She hadn't planned on seeing Gwen before she left for Wyoming, even though Gwen had suggested, more than once, that Myra try living with her in Phoenix. Instead, she saw Gwen emerge from the passenger's side of an unfamiliar car, walk around the front to open the driver's side, and cajole whoever was inside to get out.

Alex was taller than she expected from his photographs. He looked up at the window and she stepped back, her hands flying to her face. She heard the knocking on the door and stayed frozen, standing in place, unable to breathe, until she heard her mother's heavy footsteps on the stairs, followed by Gwen's fleet-footed ones. Gwen burst into the attic and gasped. "Diane, when you said it was gone, I didn't know you meant—" She shook her head violently, looking for a moment like the seven-year-old child she'd been when she and Myra met. "Not the Mansion. Not this house, too."

"Too?" Myra asked. "Not this house, *too*? What else could possibly have happened to you today that there's a 'too' in there? And what— what in the world are you doing here? With him? Today?"

"I needed her to find you." Alex's voice had a rich resonance that hadn't come through on the phone, that held a different power as it filled the attic. "I couldn't think of any other way."

Gwen put her hand on Myra's shoulder. "I love you more than anyone, Myra Malone, and you may never forgive me for this. But some things are bigger than all of us, and I decided it was worth being yelled at to show you that." She stepped back and gestured toward Alex. "I don't think I need to introduce him, and I think that'd take time you don't have, anyway, with everything you need to discuss." She looked behind Myra at the remains of the Mansion and shook her head. "You've got more in common than you ever knew, and I'm going to leave you two to figure out why."

Gwen closed the attic door behind her and walked back down the stairs with Diane.

"I'm so sorry, Myra." Alex stepped forward toward her, and she took a step backward.

Her eyes filled with tears. "I know I'm not what you expected."

Alex stepped forward and reached for her hands. She saw that his left hand was wrapped with a thick mitten of gauze. "No, that's not what I meant. You're better. You're more than I expected, Myra. I'm so sorry for what you've lost." He let go of her hands and approached the Mansion, crouching in front of its blackened form. "I've lost it, too."

The force of his words hit her in the solar plexus, their meaning immediately clear. "The mansion? It's—"

"It's exactly like this. Except—"

Myra closed her eyes and saw flames behind their lids, felt the heat pressed tight around her, her skin licked by the heat. She heard bitter laughter on an ashen wind. "Ruth." She opened her eyes and gazed at Alex. "Your father. Oh my God. Alex. I'm so sorry."

Alex shook his head. "He was dying. I came back to Lockhart because he was dying, and I was the only family he had left. Part of me had never forgiven him for sending me away, but part of me understands now what he was trying to protect me from."

"He was trying to protect you from me."

"From his mother. From my grandmother. From Trixie. From you."

Myra felt the weight of centuries around her neck, a tether to the flow of time in which she was an anchor, a refuge for those who needed it. She hadn't been ready when Trixie passed the burden, had spent her life growing into it without even knowing she was doing it. The acorn Trixie had looped over her small head was a key for a caretaker, and Myra had dedicated her life to a job she never knew she had. To a place that relied on her. And now it was gone.

"He didn't want to bear it," Myra said. "He came into the world not understanding what it was, and he didn't know how to do anything but fight. He came into the world fighting, and not wanting it."

"But he tried to choose for me, too. If he'd told me, maybe I would have understood—"

"Would you have believed him?"

"No. Not then." Alex rose to his feet and stood in front of her. "I believe it now."

"There's nothing left to believe in anymore. What she gave to me is gone."

"That isn't actually true. The refuge isn't gone."

"What are you talking about? Look at it!" Myra gestured toward the smoking hulk that used to be the Mansion.

"Because you're the refuge, Myra. That mansion—that room in the turret where I spent my time, staring at the ceiling—it only felt like home because of Willa, or what I remembered of her. And then it felt like home because of you. It was where I wrote to you, where I talked to you, where I heard your voice. I spent my whole life, from the time I was a small child, unsheltered. I spent my whole life feeling unloved and forgotten. And then I met you, and now it doesn't matter where I lay my head at night—under a slate roof or a tar paper shack or a wide bowl of shining stars. It doesn't matter to me." He put his face to her cheek, the crooked line of her jaw, and kissed her forehead. "You're the only shelter I need."

Myra's arms flew around his waist, and he gathered her close to his chest. His lips touched hers among dust motes and ashes dancing through the attic light, their own glittered constellation of stars, a planet all their own. Beneath the weight of centuries, Myra stood unbowed, but Alex's love cracked her to her foundation.

She felt ready to rebuild.

"I hope you mean it when you say I'm the only shelter you need, because I don't have any other to offer you," she said. "This place isn't mine anymore."

"That's true," Gwen said from the attic door, which she'd opened again soundlessly, Diane standing behind her.

"I didn't know you were capable of being quiet. How long have you been standing there?" Myra asked.

"Long enough to see the good stuff. Anyway. I'm afraid to say this place is off the market earlier than I expected. It's been paid off."

"I thought we had until the auction to fix it? I thought if we paid it off before next week, no one else could buy it?" Myra's voice cracked, but her longing and desperation gave way to the truth she never wanted to face. She set her lips in a thin line and sighed. "I know it wasn't realistic, Gwen, but I hoped. I thought I could make it work. But I couldn't have. I know. I hope whoever bought it will love it and live here, and not use it for some weird investment property, or knock the place down and build some kind of ugly Swiss-looking ski chalet, or something like that."

"That thought hadn't occurred to me," Alex said, looking at Gwen. "Are there even Swiss ski chalet architects around here?"

"I'm sure we could find some, if the price was right. But it isn't yours, remember. You'll have to ask the owner."

Alex laughed. "No, I think I'm fine."

Myra looked back and forth between Alex and Gwen. "What's going on?"

"I like it just this way, which is a good thing, because they told me when I paid off the loan that it wouldn't be mine. It would belong to the owner."

"And the owner isn't me, either." Diane stepped forward and pressed a key into Myra's hand. "It's you, honey."

Myra opened her mouth, searching for words. "How—how is any of this possible?"

"An awful lot is possible when you use words like 'money is no object' and 'everything as is,' it turns out," Gwen said. "I've never had a chance to use them before, but I've got to tell you, it was lots of fun."

"And about the 'as is' part." Alex leaned forward and kissed Myra again, quickly, the promise of more behind it. "I told them that was fine. In fact, I told them I was counting on it."

· 49 ·

PARKHURST, ARIZONA, 2015

IT TOOK THEM A WHILE TO DECIDE WHERE THEY WOULD live, the first experience either of them had ever had in making a decision together with another person. The choice was big and complicated, and so it seemed all the more appropriate to share its burden. Once they were in the same room together, they became two halves of a whole. They knew without further discussion that all steps from that moment forward would be taken together, and that decision made it easier to bear everything that came after—which is not the same as saying those things were easy.

At first, Alex moved in with Myra. Having secured the cabin for her, it felt natural to stay there in the beginning, where she felt safest, as they took the small steps she needed to take next: learning to leave its walls, taking long and winding walks through the mountains together before tackling more advanced tasks. Going for drives. Going to stores. Taking short day trips. *This is all very new*, Myra kept saying, and Alex reminded her that new things took practice, and he was there to help her learn.

Eventually—after almost a year together—they went to a court-house and took their vows in front of a justice of the peace.

In Virginia, investigations and proceedings played themselves out rapidly, with Ellen handling details and paperwork and retainers so competently that Alex didn't doubt that things would resolve exactly as she said they would. As she had already explained to him, one ben-efit to being the scion of a respected, blue-blooded family was easy and rapid access to respected, blue-blooded lawyers. Multiple men in tailored suits and polished shoes had served the Rakes family for gen-erations and were all too glad to assist Alex with the estate and busi-ness details. And multiple witnesses had seen Rutherford Rakes on the roof prior to the mansion's collapse, laughing at the fire.

There were some raised eyebrows at Alex's timing in removing items from the house, and the fight he had with his father on the floor of the warehouse, but every employee confirmed Rutherford's fits of temper, his unpredictable wrath. And Ellen had turned over Rutherford's note, his handwriting clear, his expensive chosen ink as recognizable as a fingerprint to everyone who worked there.

In the end, attorneys for the Rakes family had generations of expe-rience in lowering raised eyebrows, and Alex soon received another set of legal documents bearing his name—the deed for the land on which the mansion once stood, and ownership of Rakes and Son. From Arizona, he had the remains of the old house razed to the ground and asked Ellen to continue to help until he could come back. She laughed. "I feel as if I should say that I'm too old, and in numbers, that's certainly true. But that house didn't care about numbers. It stayed standing as long as you needed it. And I will, too. After all, I've been doing it all your life." And she was right.

Alex himself continued to focus on his top priority: Myra.

Every morning, they would wake together in Myra's old canopy bed and take a walk in the clear morning air, and every evening, they would sit together and read by the cabin's fireplace, but neither of them made any moves to acquire furniture or make the cabin feel like a more permanent home. It was completely theirs; Diana had already moved to Wyoming as she planned, kissing her daughter on the head and telling her it was time to try to see what the wide world they'd both left behind had been up to while they were gone. She called Myra every day, but the physical space between them felt like breathing room, expanding the tight tension between them. Every morning, Myra woke up to a text with a photograph of some detail in Diana's new home—a newborn calf on a nearby farm, a chipped teacup in a consignment store, a potholder she'd crocheted. This wants to be tiny, the text always said. When you're ready.

Myra and Alex each waited for the other to say aloud what they both knew, and it was Myra, finally, who spoke one morning on a hike, pausing beneath a beam of sunlight slicing through the ponderosa pines. "I think I'd like to go there now."

Alex held his breath. "Are you talking about Lockhart?"

"Yes. I'd like to see where you grew up."

"You know I didn't grow up there."

"Not all of you, maybe. But the part of you that mattered most, I think, was always there." Myra smiled. "And in a way, so was I."

Alex took Myra's hand and swung it gently as they continued to walk along the trail, their feet crushing dried pine needles and releasing their spicy fragrance into the air around them. "If you think you're ready to go, we can go."

"What about the cabin?"

"We'll always have the cabin. It's too important to let go, I think."

"It'll feel so empty with no one here."

"I have an idea about that." Alex stopped and looked to the left of the trail, a gentle slope that gave way to a precipitous decline, and what seemed like half the state of Arizona spread beneath their feet. "My mom still misses the mountains where she grew up, and Parkhurst looks a lot like that area. She's been talking about coming to visit, and maybe even retiring. I think she'd like this place, and she could stay here for a while, or longer, if that's all right."

Myra nodded. It seemed all right. It seemed right. She didn't need to say anything at all.

A few weeks later, when Myra and Alex arrived in Lockhart, their journey followed a series of firsts—Myra's first airport, first airplane, first flight across the country and seeing the way it rippled and shimmered like a quilt so far beneath them. The heaviness of Virginia's summer air surprised her, feeling more like a solid substance than something you could breathe.

But the first time Alex drove her to the base of the hill, unlocked the iron gate, and led her up the flagstone path, the sensation of newness fled. Myra had always been here. Her steps echoed in spaces far below her line of sight, but she could feel her spirit anchoring itself beneath the ground, in the caves she knew she'd visit soon. She felt as rooted to the place as the oak trees towering above her, their branches still singed from the fire but healing rapidly.

She felt complete. She reached for Alex's hand, and they walked on the path together, around the empty space where the mansion once stood, and to the crest of the hill that overlooked the river below.

"It reminds me of Grampa's place," she said. "His part of the Verde curved like this."

"I'm sorry he's not here to see it."

"He's here. They're all here." She held the acorn in her hand and watched the water flow past, the same as it always had, the same way it always would. Water was the same everywhere. "And we'll be here, too."

· 50 ·

LOCKHART, VIRGINIA, 2019

"ONCE UPON A TIME, THERE WAS A HOUSE." MYRA MOVED slowly around the room, switching off lamps and switching on a nightlight, a smooth hump of porcelain in the shape of a moon. The nightlight illuminated the walls of the room, the ceiling painted midnight blue, studded with small lights that looked like twinkling stars. Tree branches twined up the walls, hung with leaves in red and gold and orange, giving shelter to a menagerie of birds and squirrels hunting for abundant acorns. Myra tucked a blue afghan around a collection of clothespin dolls that were laid into an oak cradle.

"Can it be a castle?" said a small voice from the bed.

"Sure, it can be a castle. It can be anything you need it to be." The world outside the iron fence, the latched gates, moved at a different pace than the world inside their house's walls. The sloped eaves reached nearly to the ground, entwined with ivy and wisteria. As soon as they finished building their cabin—drawing influences from a mishmash of styles, in the spirit of the mansion that once stood in its place—they planted the vines around its boundaries. The salesman at the local plant nursery had shaken his head and warned them that both plants would take over any space where they were planted. *They'll hide anything you plant them near,* he said, and Alex laughed and said that was exactly what they were hoping for.

They gave no window into the world they built together, but *The Minuscule Mansion of Myra Malone* lived on in new forms, on new platforms. Gwen's deal with the place that started with *T* and rhymed with 'Arget' resulted in a line of meticulous furniture for dolls and worlds at different scales—inches ranging from six to eighteen, but snapped up by all ages. Myra had begun to try her hand at designing full-sized pieces, cobbled together from the unusual and vintage finds that Alex was so attracted to. They opened a small boutique in the storefront that once held the thrift store, the nightclub, the series of failed businesses that had all given way to the one that was there now—the one it had been waiting for. The store was called Hatbox.

Every morning, Alex and Myra would rise together in the house— its form containing everything they loved most in the world, from the Parkhurst cabin to Lou's A-frame to the stones of the mansion itself, pulled from the foundation and repurposed. They would walk together to their daughter's room, waking her for breakfast and a trip together in Alex's small car to the galleries on the river. Their little girl raced between the pieces of furniture, picked colors for Myra's projects at Hatbox, and learned from her parents the same way Myra had learned from Trixie and Lou.

And every evening, Myra would tell her stories about the refuge that sheltered them all. "I want the house to be a pink castle, covered with roses," she would say, almost every time. She would stretch out beneath her pink quilt and close her eyes, imagining gilded rooms and sparkling treasure. "And I'll be the queen."

Myra laughed. "Of course you will be. And can I come to visit you there?"

"Of course you can, Mommy. And Daddy can visit, too. And the baby, when she's here."

"We don't know if the baby is a she yet."

"It's a she." She lowered her voice to a whisper. "I know things, you know." She reached out and gently patted the brown mane of the rocking horse next to her bed, its red saddle catching in the light.

Myra nodded. "You know many things. Maybe not everything."

"But soon."

"Soon, Everly." Myra cradled her daughter's face in her hands and kissed her forehead, the lapis acorn dangling between them. "But not quite yet."

· Acknowledgments ·

Acknowledgments seems like such an inadequate word for the thanks I owe to the many, many people who made this book possible. In my head, it looks like a thumbs-up emoji: "I acknowledge you." My gratitude is so much deeper than that. I want a better word. *Overwhelmingments. ForeverIndebtedments.* I'll keep working on it. In the meantime, just know that this section of my book could fill several additional volumes and still not encompass all the people who helped make this novel a reality. But I'll try the best I can.

I can't begin any acknowledgments without acknowledging that my family is where I begin and end and none of this would be possible without them. My husband, Andy, and my children, Payson and Jamie, have been unfailing in their support of my writing. This was not my first book; my first book is sitting on a shelf in a handmade binding that my husband researched how to make, and he bound it with our children's help. Our daughter illustrated and wrote "NUMBER 1 BESTSELLRE" on its cover. My kids consider it "their book," but the secret is that all of them are. Every word.

And actually, that wasn't my first book either; my *very* first book was *The Dragon Who Couldn't Fly*, which I wrote when I was eight and which my mother, Jená, also bound into a cover, which she did with all my early writing. She and my father, Dennis, still keep those books in their word-filled house, where they write their own amazing novels, and always believed in mine. My brothers—Drew, Paul, and Dennis— also encouraged me at every turn, and Paul read countless early drafts of this book and others. My brother Ted was a writer, too, and I think often of the words we all missed from him. I couldn't write—would never have written—without the help and support of my family. I love you all so much. Thank you, always.

There are not enough thank-yous on earth for my phenomenal agent, Maria Whelan, and the whole team at Inkwell. Maria believed in this book so strongly (and convinced me not to change it when I was losing hope). She talked about my characters as if she knew them, and she continues to cheer me on no matter how many wild ideas I throw in her direction. There are a lot of them. She keeps reading them. I'm so happy to work with her.

I have been exceptionally fortunate to work with an awesome and experienced team of publishing professionals at Berkley. My editor, Cindy Hwang, honed in on what this book was meant to be during our very first conversation, and I could not be happier with where her insights took me. Angela Kim fielded my million questions graciously and patiently. Rita Frangie took the near treatise I wrote about this book's themes and translated it into an absolutely stunning cover that made me cry the first time I saw it. Thank you, as well, to the rest of the team at Berkley, including Fareeda Bullert, Chelsea Pascoe, Christine Legon, Alison Cnockaert, and Kristin del Rosario. Last, but certainly not least, Jennifer Lynes, the production editor, kept this incredibly complex process—with all its deadlines and responsibilities—running smoothly right up until this mishmash of pages and red lines became the book you're holding now. Thank you all so much.

Like so many other authors I know, I have been lucky enough to find a warm and supportive community of fellow writers online, and many of these have become lifelong friends. Thank you for sharing your wild talents, your humor and your wisdom, your ups and downs, and your friendship. I still feel most days like I somehow snuck into a seat at the cool kids' table and might be asked at any moment to leave, but you've all been too wonderful to do so thus far, and I'm eternally grateful. Below are just a few of these talented writers. Keep an eye out for their names and their work, and read it. You'll be glad you did.

To my original WriteSquad: Joel Brigham, Kyra Whitton, Christy Swift, Kelly Ohlert, Rachael (and Brett!) Peery, Shannon Balloon, Kelly Kates, Falon Ballard, and Laurel Hostetter. I couldn't ask for a more supportive group of idea-bouncer-offers, problem-solvers, readers, and friends. It's still strange to think we never would have found each other if not for Pitch Wars and Twitter, and I'm so grateful that happened.

To Jenn Knott, Kyrie Gray, Julia McCloy, Amanda Lehr, Natalia Kaye, Joseph Thomas, Laura Lewis, Jim Keunzer, Rachel Siemens, Phil Siemens, Leslie Ylinen, Hayley DeRoche, and Jennie Egerdie: thank you for always being there to read weird pieces, for sharing yours, and for always keeping me laughing.

To the Women's Fiction Writers Association and its many support-ive and insightful writers, especially my group in Raleigh, North Carolina, who so kindly took me in when I started this adventure. I'm particularly grateful to WFWA for introducing me to Rebecca Hodge—without whose mentorship this book literally would not exist—as well as Debra Whiting Alexander, Robin Facer, Lisa Roe, and many others.

To Melissa Bowers, Amy Barnes, Melissa Llanes Brownlee, Myna Chang, Stephanie King, Alexandra Otto, Eric Scot Tryon, Patricia Bidar, Kelle Clarke, Regan Puckett, Johanna Bond, Gillian O'Shaughnessy, Tommy Dean, Abbie Barker, Timothy Boudreau, Kristina Saccone, El Rhodes, Sarah Hills, Caroline Bock, and Eliot Li: thank you for your encouragement and peerless precision with words.

And to the many other writers, colleagues, and dear friends who read this book, listened to me in the height of my excitement and the depths of my despair, urged me to keep going, gave me advice, and have just been all-around terrific folks to know—including but not limited to Rebecca Royals, Sarah Wright, Margaret Fallon, Deb Love, Katherine Revelle, Lyn Liao Butler, Rachel Mans McKenny, Emily Flake, Katie Gutierrez, Susan Elia MacNeal, Jill Witty, Shannon Curtain, Caitlin Kunkel, Fiona Taylor, Brooke Preston, Lindsay Hameroff, Sheila Athens, and so many others who have cheered me on. Thank you so much.

I grew up in the kind of huge, loving, extended family that held regular reunions, and those reunions were big enough to require planning committees. So I can't list all of my wonderful aunts, uncles, cousins, and second cousins once removed here, but just know that they've all put up with me for a very long time and are still doing it, and I love them for it. I do want to single out my grandfather Jim, and my grandmother Nina, for having the kind of eternal love story that a book like this can only hope to approach. We lost Nana when this book was on submission. I still think of her all the time. I hope she knows she's in these pages.

I married into a small family of wonderful people who forgave my boisterousness and always encouraged my creativity, and I'm so grateful. Thank you to Amy, Melinda, Tom, Charles, and Ronni for your love and support.

If you're not on this list, please know you're still on this list. The time you took to read this book means the world to me, and so do you. Thank you.

The

MINUSCULE

MANSION

of

MYRA

MALONE

Audrey Burges

· Questions for Discussion ·

1. In many ways, *The Minuscule Mansion of Myra Malone* is about the places and people we always carry with us. What's a place—a room, a destination, a home—that you've never really left behind? What details of that place stick with you? Why?

2. Friendship is as big a theme in this book as love. Who is your Gwen? Who is your Ellen? What moments in your life have they gotten you through, and how?

3. Myra has dedicated her life to an activity that most people would consider a hobby. What's something you're passionate about that the rest of the world may not understand? If you could make it your day job, would you? Why or why not?

4. Alex and Myra fall in love with each other's words first, long before either of them lays eyes on the other. Have you ever started a relationship sight unseen? What happened? Are there words that still resonate with you from the experience?

5. Many of the lessons Myra learns from Trixie and Lou don't dawn on her until much later, when she's grown. What are some things you learned as a child that didn't seem significant until you were an adult?

6. If you could shrink anything you loved down to a size that you could keep it with you always, would you do it? What would it be, and why?

7. A major theme of the book centers on the idea of characters becoming the person they need to be—in Willa's case, quite literally, and in Myra's, Alex's, and Diane's cases, more figuratively. What parts of the story allow them to do this, in your view? Have you ever transformed yourself? What, or who, helped you?

8. This book features several love stories. Which one was your favorite? Your least favorite? Why?

9. The book opens with a blog entry from Myra—"Once upon a time, there was a house"—that invites the reader to imagine

their own perfect space. What would yours be and where would it be located?

10. Did you ever have a Trixie in your life? Who was it, and what did they mean to you?

11. What themes, scenes, or elements of this story stayed with you the most? Why?

12. If you could have a conversation with any of the characters in the novel, with whom would it be, and where would you have it?

Keep reading for an excerpt from

A HOUSE LIKE
AN ACCORDION

The next novel by Audrey Burges.

Coming to Berkley in 2024!

THE HOUSE ON THE WAVES
August 2016

I WAS BRUSHING MY TEETH WHEN MY HAND DISAPPEARED.

I was thirty-nine and naked, holding myself in a one-legged star pose on the marble floor of my bathroom, looking for balance. My focal point was in the mirror—my pink toothbrush—which was, I suddenly realized, suspended in midair, as if hanging from a length of wire hung from the bathroom's vaulted ceiling. I could feel it buzzing in the hand I couldn't see.

I thought it must be a trick of the light. Our house was full of windows, glass and sun bouncing reflections of the ocean into every living space, as cold as the Pacific sprawled beneath us. But no: I put down the toothbrush and held my hand in front of me, and saw that it didn't obscure my face in the mirror, high cheekbones and widow's peak like my mother's. I grasped at my invisible fingers with my right hand and felt them, still solid, but nearly transparent. There was a softness to the skin I couldn't see, as if I could push a bit harder and press right through.

I heard the house begin to wake around me. Ellory rolling her mat out on her floor, ready to force herself through the yoga she'd declared last spring she would do every single day because her routines—senior year AP classes, driving too fast down our winding road along the beach, sniping at her younger sister—were "stressing her out." A summer's worth of classes at the community college nearby hadn't ended her workouts. Mindy, fourteen and complaining already about the pace of high school, not yet a week underway, hitting her snooze alarm for the third time. And Max, bumping into the same corner of the platform bed with the same bruised shin on his staggering path to the kitchen, where the coffee I'd made was waiting.

Max would leave me alone in the bathroom until I was finished, but our mornings had an ebb and flow of predictability, and my disappearing limb was a disruption. I planted myself on the floor, a stump in the current, and flexed my fingers. I couldn't wear my rings at night. The encircling metal felt too constricting and claustrophobic as I tried and failed to sleep. They glinted on the ring keeper perched on the bathroom counter, and I tiptoed over to retrieve them, closing my eyes to slide them over my translucent knuckles. The sharp center diamond—Max's selection, wide and sharp and always in the way—caught a beam of sun from the skylight, casting rainbows around the room and on the memory of my freckled hand. I willed it to reappear.

I jumped at the knock on the door. "Keryth?" Max's voice was tentative, still wounded from our fight the night before. "You in there?"

"Where else would I be?" My voice was harsher than I meant. I evened out my breathing and started again. "I'll be out in a minute."

"Can I get you anything? You want some coffee?"

A peace offering. *I don't want coffee, I want you to leave me alone. All of you, for maybe five minutes, just leave me alone.* I was being unfair, and I knew I was being unfair, which only made the voice inside me more vicious. The fight had been over the doctor—Max's words, glancing lightly like a stone thrown across water, wondering if it might be worth getting some blood work done. Because surely there must be some explanation for these mood swings, some levels and numbers and precise indicia that could be calibrated, the way Max calibrated everything.

I looked at the vein on my forearm, snaking from the crook of my elbow and fading into nothingness. I thought of the unfriendly nurse who always complained about my treacherous blood, the way it hid from her needle, refusing to yield itself up for tests. *Your veins are practically invisible!*

The laugh that barked out of me was involuntary.

"I'll get myself some coffee in a minute." I took the rings off my finger and slipped them back over the porcelain finger on the counter, which was cold and unyielding, but tangible. My robe, oversized and ratty, terry cloth stained with the spit-up of babies long since grown up, was hanging from the hook on the door. I put it on and tied it, sliding my hands—present and missing—into the wide pockets, hoping I looked casual as I loped, slouch-shouldered, to my closet. Beneath the shelves of purses I didn't carry and shoes I didn't wear, I had a dovetailed drawer filled with gloves the California weather never called for. Kid leather, mostly, in every color, with tiny covered buttons down the sides. Elegant, finger-lengthening gloves like I used to see in ads for expensive cars and perfume, back when such things seemed wildly out of reach.

I selected a Kelly green pair and shoved my hand and my non-hand into them, breathing a sigh of relief at symmetry restored. I let my robe fall to the floor and dressed the rest of my body, which was still corporeal, for all that Max said I would fade away if I didn't eat. My long-sleeved shirts were mostly flannel, and August blazed over my head, but I was starved for other options. I put a white tank top underneath a green plaid shirt I left unbuttoned, flapping over jeans I needed to replace with a smaller pair, but hadn't yet. Finally garbed but feeling garbled, I strode out of the closet and bedroom and walked, as casually as I could, into the kitchen.

"Are you cold, Mom?" Mindy, long legs folded underneath her on the window seat next to the kitchen table, cocked her head to one side. "The AC is on too high, Dad."

"It's set to 78." Max turned from the coffeepot and furrowed his brow at my outfit. "Harold," he called to the ceiling, "run a diagnostic on the HVAC, okay?"

"Well, sure, happy to. But I gotta say, kiddo, look who's worried about the thermostat now." The voice that rang out overhead was reedy and puckish, exactly as my father-in-law would have sounded if he were alive. Or so I guessed. I'd never met him—only the artificial version of him that Max had spent his life perfecting.

"Yes, Harold, thanks." Max barely looked up from his coffee.

"Have you thought about putting on a sweater?"

"That's enough, Harold," Max and I said in unison.

Ellory ran into the room in her customary rush, heading toward the coffeepot to retrieve the only substance I could convince her to put into her body before leaving for school each morning. "Mom? Are you feeling okay? Why are you wearing gloves?"

I shrugged and delivered the lie I'd already thought of. "I sliced my hands up pretty good gardening yesterday. These'll help the ointment work."

Max shook his head. "It was the blackberries, wasn't it?"

"No." I felt a rush of defensiveness creep into my voice. Max hated the blackberry canes I'd planted in our yard—he considered them weeds, and hated their thorny encroachment on his otherwise manicured garden, not that he manicured it himself. "It was the roses."

Max nodded. "The ones with thorns smell the best, but it's hard not to like the thornless ones better."

"I was just pruning them back and giving them some fish guts, ungrateful bastards."

"Nature, red in tooth and claw." Max stepped toward me and stopped, his eyes seeking permission, and I nodded. He kissed the top of my head. "What have you got going on today?"

Trying to figure out where the hell my hand went. "Some research, maybe."

"What kind?"

Hand restoration. Hand-disappeared-what-do-I-do. Marty McFly syndrome, you know, when his parents never got together and he started to disappear—

Oh my God.

Two thoughts of equal volume, equal urgency, careened through my head at the same time.

One: my father must be alive. The thought filled me with a peculiar mix of relief and fury, remembering the look on his face as he stepped out of my life and into oblivion as I screamed on the banks of a long-abandoned pond. *How many years?* I pretended not to know. Very nearly fifteen, now, and as vivid as the first moment.

Two: wherever he was, however he was drawing breath, Papa must also have been drawing *me*. Somewhere, somehow, he was sketching the bones and tendons of my hand as he remembered it. Just the left hand—the one I used to brace the page I drew upon as Papa peered over my head, staring down at my drawings.

He was drawing from life. The way he always taught me not to. And if he didn't stop, I would be as trapped as the Steller's jay I still carried with me in the sketchbook I always kept by my side.

Christy Davis / From the Heart Images

AUDREY BURGES writes novels, humor, short fiction, and essays in Richmond, Virginia. Her presence is tolerated by her two rambunctious children and very patient husband, all of whom have become practiced at making supportive faces when she shouts, "Listen to this sentence!" She is a frequent contributor to numerous humor outlets, including *McSwee-ney's*, and her stories and essays have appeared in *Hobart Pulp*, *Pithead Chapel*, *Cease, Cows*, and lengthy diatribes in the Notes app on her phone. Audrey was born and raised in Arizona by her linguist parents, which is a lot like being raised by wolves, but with better grammar. She moved to Virginia as an adult but still carries mountains and canyons in her heart, and sometimes, when she closes her eyes, she can still smell ponderosa pines in the sun.

CONNECT ONLINE

AudreyBurges.com

❶ ABurgesWrites

◎ AudreyBurges

🐦 Audrey_Burges

Ready to find
your next great read?

Let us help.

Visit prh.com/nextread